Three Acres And Liberty

Bolton Hall

Contents

THREE ACRES AND LIBERTY

BY

Bolton Hall

FOREWORD

We are not tied to a desk or to a bench; we stay there only because we think we are tied.

In Montana I had a horse, which was hobbled every night to keep him from wandering; that is, straps joined by a short chain were put around his forefeet, so that he could only hop. The hobbles were taken off in the morning, but he would still hop until he saw his mate trotting off.

This book is intended to show how any one can trot off if he will.

It is not a textbook; there are plenty of good textbooks, which are referred to herein. Intensive cultivation cannot be comprised in any one book.

It shows what is needed for a city man or woman to support a family on the proceeds of a little bit of land; it shows how in truth, as the old Book prophesied, the earth brings forth abundantly after its kind to satisfy the desire of every living thing. It is not necessary to bury oneself in the country, nor, with the new facilities of transportation, need we, unless we wish to, pay the extravagant rents and enormous cost of living in the city. A little bit of land near the town or the city can be rented or bought on easy terms; and merchandising will bring one to the city often enough. Neither is hard labor needed; but it is to work alone that the earth yields her increase, and if, although unskilled, we would succeed in gardening, we must attend constantly and intelligently to the home acres.

Every chapter of this book has been revised by a specialist, and the authors wish to express their appreciation of the aid given them, particularly by Mr. E. H. Moore, Arboriculturist in the Brooklyn Department of Parks; Mr. Collingwood of the Rural New Yorker and Mr. George T. Powell; and to thank Mrs. Mabel Osgood Wright, and also Mr. Joseph Morwitz, for many valuable suggestions; also all those from whom we have quoted directly or in substance.

We have endeavored in the text to give full acknowledgment to all, but in some cases it has been impossible to credit to the originator every paragraph or thought, since these have been selected and placed as needed, believing that all true teachers and gardeners are more anxious to have their message sent than to be seen delivering it.

In truth, teaching is but another department of gardening.

Practical points and criticisms from practical men and women, especially from those experiences in trying to get to the land, will be welcomed by the authors. Address in care of the publishers.

The Report of the Country Life Commission, with Special Message from the President of the United States, is especially important as showing the connection of Intensive Cultivation with Thrift for war time.

It tells us that:

"The handicaps (on getting out of town) that we now have specially in mind may be stated under four heads: Speculative holding of lands; monopolistic control of streams; wastage and monopolistic control of forests; restraint of trade.

"Certain landowners procure large areas of agricultural land in the most available location, sometimes by questionable methods, and hold it for speculative purposes. This not only withdraws the land itself from settlement, but in many cases prevents the development of an agricultural community. The smaller landowners are isolated and unable to establish their necessary institutions or to reach the market. The holding of large areas by one party tends to develop a system of tenantry and absentee farming. The whole development may be in the direction of social and economic ineffectiveness.

"A similar problem arises in the utilization of swamp lands. According to the reports of the Geological Survey, there are more than 75,000,000 acres of swamp land in this country, the greater part of which are capable of reclamation at probably a nominal cost as compared to their value. It is important to the development of the best type of country life that the reclamation proceed under conditions insuring subdivision into small farms and settlement by men who would both own them and till them.

"Some of these lands are near the centers of population. They become a menace to health, and they often prevent the development of good social conditions in very large areas. As a rule they are extremely fertile. They are capable of sustaining an agricultural population numbering many millions, and the conditions under which these millions must live are a matter of national concern. The Federal Government should act to the fullest extent of its constitutional powers in the reclamation of these lands under proper safeguards against speculative holding and landlordism.

"The rivers are valuable to the farmers as drainage lines, as irrigation supply, as carriers and equalizers of transportation rates, as a readily available power resource, and for raising food fish. The wise development of these and other uses is important to both agricultural and other interests; their protection from monopoly is one of the first responsibilities of government. The streams belong to the people; under a proper system of development their resources would remain an estate of all the people, and become available as needed.

"River transportation is not usually antagonistic to railway interests. Population and production are increasing rapidly, with corresponding increase in the demands made on transportation facilities. It may be reasonably expected that the river will eventually carry a large part of the freight that does not require prompt delivery, while the railway will carry that requiring expedition. This is already foreseen by leading railway men; and its importance to the farmer is such that he should encourage and aid, by every means in his power, the large use of the rivers. The country will produce enough business to tax both streams and railroads to their utmost.

"In many regions the streams afford facilities for power, which, since the inauguration of electrical transmission, is available for local rail lines and offers the best solution of local transportation problems. In many parts of the country local and interurban lines are providing transportation to farm areas, thereby increasing facilities for moving crops and adding to the profit and convenience of farm life. However, there seems to be a very general lack of appreciation of the possibilities of this water-power resource as governing transportation costs.

"The streams may be also used as small water power on thousands of farms. This is particularly true of small streams. Much of the labor about the house and barn can be performed by transmission of power from small water wheels running on the farms themselves or in the neighborhood. This power could be used for electric lighting and for small manufacture. It is more important that small power be developed on the farms of the United States than that we harness Niagara.

"Unfortunately, the tendency of the present laws is to encourage the acquisition of these resources on easy terms, or on their own terms, by the first applicants, and the power of the streams is rapidly being acquired under conditions that lead to the concentration of ownership in the hands of the monopolies. This constitutes a real and immediate danger, not to the country-life interests alone, but to the entire nation, and it is time that the whole people become aroused to it.

"The forests have been exploited for private gain not only until the timber has been seriously reduced, but until streams have been ruined for navigation, power, irrigation, and common water supplies, and whole regions have been exposed to floods and disastrous soil erosion. Probably there has never occurred a more reckless destruction of property that of right should belong to all the people.

"The wood-lot property of the country needs to be saved and increased. Wood-lot yield is one of the most important crops of the farms, and is of great value to the public in con trolling streams, saving the run-off, checking winds, and adding to the attractiveness of the region. [Taken up in a special chapter of this book.]

"In many regions where poor and hilly lands prevail, the town or county could well afford to purchase forest land, expecting thereby to add to the value of the property and to make the forests a source of revenue. Such communal forests in Europe yield revenue to the cities and towns by which they are owned and managed."

These revenues would furnish good roads even in the poorest and most sparsely settled districts.

There are a number of other reasons why people do not like to live outside of cities--or do not succeed in farm work. There is the difficulty of finding help. This, how. ever, rejoices the heart of the modern sociologist. Consider--we first teach our children independence and train them for everything but farm help or household services. Then we degrade the "help" below a mill "hand" so that people will not even sit at table with them at an hotel. Next we fix a theory of conduct for them that keeps them constantly under orders and pay them wages that make it hardly possible for them to rise above the station to which we have appointed them.

Finally, when we move away from the haunts of men out to Sandtown-by-the-Puddle we blame them that they do not rush to join us. Most of them would be happier in penal servitude than in the country. The work is as hard and requires as much skill as a mechanic's work, besides personal qualities that are demanded of no mechanic, and commands half its wages.

Those who, like Henry Ford, can afford to pay mechanics' wages for help can get all they want.

Many people go to the country without plan, preparation, or vocation, to make a living. They usually start to build a bungalow but seldom get further than the bungle. Don't build anything without plan. Get a comfortable house proof against cold and heat as soon as possible and, above all, well ventilated. At present the air in the country is good, because the farmers shut all the bad air up in their bedrooms.

They say

"The farmer works from sun to sun For the summer's work is never done."

We might add, it's never even half done--naturally. A donkey engine can work like that, but then it hasn't any brains. No man can work from sun to sun all summer and think at all or be good for anything at the end of it.

Above all things don't work long hours, even in learning, with the idea of saving that way. All up-to-date employers are agreed that an eight-hour day produces more and better results than a ten-hour day and that a twelve-hour day brings sheriffs and suicides instead of profits.

That's just as true of the individual worker as it is of the factory "hand." Yet most men and a few women proudly say that they "work like a horse" (it's usually not true). They don't; a horse won't work and can't work over eight hours a day steadily. Neither can you: you may keep buzzing around much longer--but the best work requires the best conditions and the best hours. You think, or you flatter yourself that you think, that it is necessary; but nothing is necessary that is stupid and wrong. It is hardly too much to say that when we are tired out or ill either we have been doing the wrong thing or doing it wrong.

There is besides, as an anti-rusticant, railroad discrimination in favor of long hauls, but the main reason that the small farms of the Eastern Coast are less settled than those farther west is the great difficulty in getting farm loans or loans on farm buildings. New York companies and others in the great cities will loan on farms west of the Alleghenies, but even the otherwise excellent eastern Building Loan Associations usually restrict themselves to places within twenty-five miles of a city. The

Jewish Agricultural and Industrial Aid Society will help approved Jewish farmers to buy and build: and there is a Federal Land Bank in Springfield, Mass., which lends to some Farmers' Associations, of which some four thousand are already formed. It is hoped that the State Land Bank of New York City may improve the situation in New York for Farmers' Organizations, but "generally nearly all available funds of the local banks seem to be drawn off for investments in Wall Street."

However, it is not to be forgotten that this difficulty is reflected in the lower prices of eastern Land.

One more thing that keeps many people from the country and drives some people back to the city is the mosquito (of course there are mosquitoes in town, but we are not out as much, so we notice them less). Mosquitoes breed or rather we breed them, in still water in which there are no fish, in pools, hollows in trees, wells, etc., and above all in old tin cans. They can no more breed without water than sharks could.

Mosquitoes do not breed in grass, but rank growths of weeds or grass may conceal small breeding puddles, and form a favorite nursery for Mamma Skeet. A teacupful of water standing ten days is enough for 250 wrigglers; their needs are modest.

Different species of mosquitoes have as well-defined habits as other birds and are classified as follows: Domestic, Migratory, and Woodland.

The common domestic or pet species breed in fresh water, usually in the house yard, fly comparatively short distances, and habitually enter houses. They winter in cellars, barns, and outhouses. Some of them are conveyors of malaria.

The Migratory Species breed on the salt marshes, fly long distances, do not habitually enter houses, and are not carriers of diseases so far as known.

Certain varieties of Woodland Mosquitoes breed only in woodland pools, appearing in the early spring, and travel a greater distance than the domestic species. They are not usually troublesome indoors.

It has been proved that malaria is transmitted only by certain species of Anopheles, one of which is the domestic mosquito. Eliminate this one species of mosquito and the disease will disappear as a direct consequence. So if you hear that pretty little song in the house, don't swear, thank the Lord that effects always follow causes. You need never be without a bite in the house if you have a nice cesspool handy for Sis Mosquito, for each one will have a first-class feed with you every second or third day.

They are needless and dangerous pests or pets. Their propagation can be prevented by draining or filling wet areas, by emptying or screening water receptacles, and by spraying with oil where better measures are not available. Oil should be sprinkled in any cesspools, sewers, and catch basins, rain barrels, water troughs, roof gutters, marshes, swamps, and puddles that cannot be done away with. All ponds and large bodies of water should have clean sharp edges, because in shallow, grassy edges larvae of the malarial species are commonly found. Large ponds with clean edges, inhabited by fish or predatory insects, are safe; smaller ponds, if wind swept, and all ponds in the "ripple area" are safe. All rain pools, stagnant gutters, overgrown edges of large ponds, and all receptacles holding water not constantly renewed, are dangerous. You raise most of your own mosquitoes.

Now a word specially concerning this revised edition.

The farm papers are supported mainly by men with large acreage, it is the rise in value of these acres more than the rise in farm products that has pulled the land-owning farmers out of the hole that they were in up to about the year 1900. Farmers' knowledge, liking, and equipment was for big fields, half cultivated, and at first they did not like to hear that they had been wasting so much of the labor that had bent their backs. Nor did they want to hear that it would have been far more profitable to them to have cultivated a few acres and left the goats and hogs or sheep to attend to the rest as wild land until the long-expected settlers came along to buy the land at dreamland prices.

Consequently, all the faults in the book there were, and some more besides, have been picked out by these critics. It is surprising as well as a notable compliment to the agricultural experts who revised the first edition that, with one exception, no material error or omission has been pointed out.

The more so because there is absolutely no limit to the advances in methods and results in doing things, and in growing things, all born of intelligent toil. Your suggestions may help the world to better and bigger things. If you will listen at the 'phone you may sometime hear a conversation like this:

"Hello, this is Mrs. Wise, send me two strawberries, please." "You'd better take three, Madam, I've none larger than peaches to-day." "All right; good-bye."

You may sometime see that kind of strawberry in New Jersey at Kevitt's Athenia, or Henry Joralamon's, or in the berry known by various names, such as Giant and different Joe's. But lots of people have failed in their war garden work even on common things; lots more ought to have failed but haven't--yet. Years ago, we, the book and its helpers, started the forward-to-the-land movement which has resulted in probably two million extra garden patches this war year. I have had carloads of letters, at least hand carloads, about the book, but not one worker who even tried to follow its counsels has reported failure.

So don't let us have a wail from you because your "garden stuff never comes up." Of course it doesn't; you have to bring it up, just like a baby. That's what I've been crying for long years in the wilderness ever since the first edition of this book. The Three Acres may be bought on credit but eternal vigilance is the price of Liberty and crops. To raise good crops costs time and attention and sweat of body and of brains.

Here is a chunk of wisdom out of the excellent Garden Primer (which you can get free by asking me for it):

"One hour a day spent in a garden ten yards long by seven wide will supply vegetables enough for a family of six"; but the value of this remark lies in the application of it. If you figure a bit on that you will find that ten minutes a day will provide enough for one person, but six hours once a week won't do. Six hours a day will bring up a baby; but two days a week is criminal neglect for the other five days. If you once let the weeds get a good start, say after a rain, they will make even the angels swear. It's regular attention that the baby and the garden and your education and your best girl will require.

If you want more minute instructions about how to grow each vegetable, put in words that anybody can understand without getting a headache or a dictionary, look up "The Garden Yard" by the Author. It is in nearly all libraries now, and it is the only book that makes perfectly plain everything that a plain man needs to know about growing plain things

So there is little to add in this new edition except to reinforce what was not strong enough. In the present jumping market to revise the prices quoted would be absurd, but it may be noted that, as in the prices of 'cowers, the minimum prices are still about correct, but the maximum prices have jumped almost out of sight. Every year there are more and more very wealthy people who will pay nearly any price for the very best. The world seems to be dividing into those who have to count their pennies and those who couldn't count their thousands. Of course, where war has prohibited the importation of the strong bulbs and roots needed for forcing flowers, the prices are about what any one who has any chooses to ask. Monopoly can always get its own price.

This New Edition does not attempt to bring prices quoted up to date. In these times not even a stock exchange telegraph ticker can do that. Prices of goods in general have advanced at least 80 per cent. By the day that this book is off the press they may have decreased, or more likely advanced some more. The next day they may slump. Prices of labor advance more slowly and do not slump so fast. Wages of men gardeners have risen perhaps 50 per cent in the last ten years, but women and children have learned to do much of the work. They do the work cheaper because most of them have some one on whom they can partly depend for support.

Similarly, when an example of total product given in the earlier edition is still typical and has stood investigation, it is not discarded in favor of a more modern instance.

It would have been easy to have revised all the figures, but of little advantage to our readers. For example, it is encouraging to the citizen to know that the average wheat yield per acre has increased more than two bushels since the first edition of this book, but it would not help the garden maker. The increase of possible products tends to counterbalance the increased cost of labor. So only the musty parts have been cut out of the book, which is more needed now than ever.

CHAPTER I
MAKING A LIVING--WHERE AND HOW

By thought and courage, we can help ourselves to own a home, surrounded by acres of fruit and vegetables, flowers and poultry, and learn the best methods so as to insure success.

In olden times any one could "farm," but it is necessary to-day to teach people to obtain a livelihood directly from the earth. Scientific methods of agriculture have revealed possibilities in the soil that make farming the most fascinating occupation known to man. People in every city are longing for the freedom of country life, yet hesitate to enter into its liberty because no one points the way.

Most sociologists are agreed that the great problem of our day is to stop the drift of population toward the cities. Seeing the overcrowding, the want and misery of our great towns, the philanthropist chimes in with "Get the people to the country, that is the need."

But there is no such need. Man is a social animal, he naturally goes in flocks, he earns more and learns more in crowds. To transport him to the country, even if he would stay, which happily he won't, would be to doctor a symptom. As in typhoid, what is needed is not to suppress the fever, that is easy, but to remove the cause of it.

It is not the growth of the cities that we want to check, but the needless want and misery in the cities, and this can be done by restoring the natural condition of living, and among other things, by showing that it is easier and making it more attractive to live in comfort on the outskirts of the city as producers, than in the slums as paupers.

We know already that the natural and healthy life is, that in the sweat of our faces we should eat bread. We observe that everything we eat or use or make comes from the earth by labor; but no one knows how abundantly the Mother can supply her children. It is well said that no man yet knows the capacity of a square yard of earth.

The farmer thinks that he has done well if he gets a hundred and fifty or two hundred bushels of potatoes from an acre; he does not know that others have gotten 1284 bushels.

("Mr. Knight, whose name is well known to every horticulturist in England, Once dug out of his fields no less than 1284 bushels of potatoes, or thirty-four tons and nine hundreds weight (about 34 bushels to the ton), on a single acre; and at a recent competition in Minnesota, 1120 bushels, or thirty tons, could be ascertained as having been grown on one acre." P. Kropotkin's "Fields, Factories and Workshops," page 114.)

Let us realize what an acre means. An acre is a square about 209 feet each way, 4840 square yards of land. A New York City avenue block is about 200 feet long from house corner to house corner. It has eight city lots 25 X 100 in its front; about double that space (17-2/5 lots) makes an acre.

An ordinary one-horse cart holds twenty bushels, so then a full crop of potatoes from that space would fill 56 carts.

To raise potatoes as an ordinary farmer raises them, requires him to go over the ground not less than a dozen times, plowing, harrowing, marking, planting, cultivating, three times weeding, three times for bugs, and digging; it would pay him to go over it much oftener.

If he plants his rows of potatoes three feet apart, to allow for horse cultivation, he has 69 rows of 200 feet each; which makes him walk at least thirty-three miles over each acre. If he has a twenty-acre lot in potatoes, he walks each year more than 650 miles over the field and gets, let us say, 150 bushels of poor potatoes per acre, or 3000 bushels off his twenty-acre field.

Now suppose he cultivates the soil, instead of just "raising a crop," and gets 600 bushels of fine potatoes to the acre, he need plant only five acres, walk only 200 miles, and, because his potatoes are choice and early, get many times the price that his pedestrian neighbor gets. It is much easier to grow 200,000 lb. of feed on one acre than to grow them on ten acres.

To cultivate is to watch the soil as you would watch your cooking and to tend the crop as you would tend your animals. The crop is as alive as the stock and as easily gets sick.

If an ordinary farmer rents 60 acres at $5.00 per acre, a moderate rent for good land, he pays out in cash $300, besides farm wages. If he buys it, his interest and taxes will amount to nearly as much; but if he tills but five acres intelligently, he can get as much out of it as out of an ordinary farm, and even if his rent be as high as $30 per acre for well situated land, he is $150 to the good; besides, doing the work himself, he has no drain of capital for wages.

Large barns and shelter for help being unnecessary, he can live in a cheap shack till he accumulates enough for proper buildings. Many of the successful vacant lot farmers live in a tent or in shanties made of old boxes and such like.

Of course, if we have the knowledge and ability and the capital and can give it the attention, it is more profitable to cultivate on a large scale than on a small one, because in that case each worker necessarily produces more than he gets as wages--and we pocket the difference.

Most American farmers are holding land that somebody ought to pay them a bonus for working, else they must come out of the little end of the horn. They get poor or poorly situated land, because it costs less, and then put three or four hundred dollars' worth of labor and money a year into the land and take out four or five hundred dollars' worth of crops.

The farmer thinks he must have big fields to feed his cattle, and that he must have cattle to keep the big fields fertilized, so he raises hay.

In that he makes two mistakes; hay, like most other low-priced crops, is risky--the cost of harvesting is high and the margin of profit small. A week of wet weather at cutting time or the impossibility of getting enough men and machines in the week when it should be cut, may make a loss.

But the scientific dairy man does not take that risk, nor let his cattle use up this fodder by wandering over the fields in search of tid-bits of grass or clover, or, goaded by the flies, trampling more grass than they eat and wasting their manure.

He keeps the cows in cool sheds, feeds them on cut fodder, and saves every ounce of the manure.

The modern cow is a ruminating machine for producing milk and cares little for exercise and needs little. To exploit the cattle as employers exploit the factory hands, he gives the cows a cool, shady place and food, and they stand there all day long to their profit and his.

(United States Agricultural Bulletin No. 22 says: "The New Jersey Experiment Station has been conducting a practical trial in soiling dairy cows for a number of years past, and finds that complete soiling is entirely practicable, i.e. that green foliage crops may serve as the sole food of the dewy herd, aside from the grain ration, without injury to the animals and with a considerable saving in the cost of milk.

"Under the soiling system a large number of animals can be kept upon a given acreage and by allowing open-air exercises in a large yard or pasture the practice has been demonstrated as entirely feasible for dairy animals.

"One acre of soiling crops produced sufficient fodder for an equivalent of 3 cows for six months. Rye, corn, crimson clover, alfalfa, oats and peas, and millets have been found to furnish food more economically than any other green crops in that locality. A grain rotation was always fed in addition to the soiling crops.")

Although we can feed a cow on less than an acre by raising forage crops, she needs to be milked every day at regular hours, and the milk, as well as the cans and the cow, need to be cared for--and she cannot wait.

The stock-raiser has a different proposition; he needs fields and grass; but if time and available labor is limited, we had better specialize on the garden--unlike the farmers.

The farmers are not to blame that they do not usually cultivate the land intelligently. They are mostly cut off from the educational advantages of the cities by distance and by bad roads.

Usually, that is because, desirable land being held at speculative prices, they are forced to places where the farm itself is worth less than the good improvements on it cost. Sometimes it is because, also, the land is poor or worn out; more often because it is thoughtlessly managed, nearly always because the land-hungry farmer has taken ten times as much land as he needs for farming. In the hope of a rise that often does not come, nearly all have bought more land than they can take good care of with limited capital and scarcity of help.

In addition, the farms have held out such poor prospects of fortune that the smarter and more enterprising boys and girls have left them for the towns, leaving behind the duller and more conservative to the mercy of the railroads and other monopolies. What wonder, then, that the overworked and struggling farmer finds little chance to study, or to investigate and invest in fertilizers or even in modern methods of agriculture.

No wonder farming does not pay if a "farmer" means a stupid man with neither training for, nor knowledge of, his business. Those who have the knowledge seldom have the experience and those who have the experience seldom have the knowledge.

The bonanza farms of the West are other samples of great areas of the most productive land in the United States being used most unscientifically. By the methods used, the land produces less per acre than land in the East which is not so good. Accordingly, we find that the bonanza farm plan, where great areas of wheat are worked by machines with labor employed only in the seed time and harvest, is rapidly breaking up. As the land becomes valuable and is taxed, such wasteful, wholesale methods do not pay as well as it pays to rent or sell the land to farmers, who each for themselves attend to details of the business. Consequently, most of those farms are being sold off. The whole amount of wheat ever raised on them, however, is small compared to the rice, millet, and wheat raised in China, India, and Russia, and is insignificant compared to the amount of produce grown on the myriad little farm plots.

A comparison of productions as taken from the 12th and 13th United States Censuses in the bonanza farm states shows that the yield of wheat was:

while New England shows 23.5 bu. per acre.

In 1899 In 1909

Minnesota 14.5 bu. per acre 17.4 North Dakota 13.5 bu. per acre 14.3 South Dakota 10.5 bu. per acre 14.6

By 1917 these largely increased, but the differences remain.

"The average extent of land tilled by one family in Japan does not exceed one hectare" (2.471 acres), less than two and a half acres. ("Japan in the Beginning of the Twentieth Century," page 89. Published by the Department of Agriculture and Commerce of Japan.)

"Farm households contain on an average 5.8 persons, of whom two and a half persons per family may be regarded of an age capable of doing effective work."

"So that here we have more than one person working on each acre and each acre supporting more than two persons, notwithstanding that their 22,000,000 tenant farmers pay sometimes four fifths of their product as rent." (Same, page 103.)

Denmark, one of the best agricultural countries and probably one of the happiest communities on earth, reported

1,900 farms of 250-300 acres, 74,000 farms averaging 100 acres, 150,000 farms averaging 7 to 10 acres, 1,050 cooperative dairies, and so on.

And so impressed has the ruling class there become with the advantage of this that the Government will supply the poor worker nine tenths of the means necessary to buy a small farm.

Says Kropotkin, "the small island of Jersey, eight miles long and less than six miles wide, still remains a land of open field culture; but, although it comprises only 28,707 acres (nearly 45 square miles), rocks included, it nourishes a population of about two inhabitants to each acre, or 1300 inhabitants to the square mile, and there is not one writer on agriculture who, after having paid a visit to this island, does not praise the well-being of the Jersey peasants and the admirable results which they obtain in their small farms of from five to twenty acres--very often less than five acres--by means of a rational and intensive culture.

"Most of my readers will probably be astonished to learn that the soil of Jersey, which consists of decomposed granite, with no organic matter in it, is not at all of surprising fertility, and that its climate, though more sunny than the climate of the British Isles, offers many drawbacks on account of the small amount of sun heat during the summer and of the cold winds in spring."

("The successes accomplished lately in Jersey are entirely due to the amount of labor which a dense population is putting on the land; to a system of land-tenure, land-transference, and inheritance very different from those which prevail elsewhere; to freedom from State taxation; and to the fact that communal institutions have been maintained down to quite a recent period, while a number of communal habits and customs of mutual support, derived there-from, are alive to the present time." (Fields, Factories and Workshops.")

"It will suffice to say that on the whole the inhabitants of Jersey obtain agricultural products to the value of $250 to each acre of the aggregate surface of land." (Same, page 113.))

In a small plot the character of the soil is of little consequence. We hear of one garden in New York City on the roof of a big building where the janitor smuggled up the needed soil in baskets.

The school gardens in New York City, some in a space as small as a hearth rug, one yard by two, show how to use a very small patch of land to the best advantage. Nor need it take more time than you can afford.

"Some of the cultivators of city lots on Long Island who kept count of the number of days they worked, show the surprising conclusion that they earned, not farm wages (seventy-five cents a day with board and lodging for the worker), but mechanics' wages (four dollars per day) for every working day; as, for instance, a stone-cutter, assisted by his two boys, worked fifty hours and made $120.23." ("Cultivation of Vacant Lots, New York," page 12); and four city lots is a very little farm.

But though one may not own even a little farm, almost any one who wants to can have a home garden--it needs but a small plot of land. Nor need we be discouraged because acquaintances who play at gardening tell us that their vegetables cost them more than if they bought them.

They naturally would, with thoughtless methods of cultivation, with the selection of crops and the purchase of seeds left to an uneducated man who does all his work the way he saw his grandfather do it.

Nor are we to be discouraged even by the "gentleman farmer" who runs a model farm, a model of how not to do it, for, notwithstanding its large capital, it seldom pays.

I am passing such a farm now as I write in the train--it is surrounded by a cut stone wall. Do you suppose the owner business would pay if it were run in the same way that his farm is run? We know the story of the white sparrow to find which would bring luck to the farm--but it was out only at daybreak; the farmer got up each morning to find the sparrow and found a lot of other things to attend to, which did bring luck to the farm. I don't think the owner of that wall worked at it, at daybreak.

The time is not far distant when the builders of homes in our American cities will be compelled to leave room for a garden, in order to meet the requirements of the people In the mad rush for wealth we have overlooked the natural state, but we see a healthy reaction setting in. With the improvements in steam and electricity, the revolutionizing of transportation, the cutting of the arbitrary telephone charges, it is becoming possible to live at a distance from our business. May we not expect in the near future to see one portion of our cities devoted entirely to business, with the homes of the people so separated as to give light, sunshine, and air to all, besides a piece of ground for a garden sufficient to supply the table with vegetables?

You raise more than vegetables in your garden: you raise your expectation of life.

Life belongs in the garden. Do you remember--the first chapters of Genesis show us our babyhood in a garden--the garden that all babyhood remembers, and the last chapter of the Apocalypse leaves us with the vision of the garden in the Holy City, on either side of the river, where the trees yield their fruits every month and bear leaves of universal healing. Just so will it be in our holy cities of the future--the garden will be right there "in the midst."

CHAPTER II
PRESENT CONDITIONS

Up to the Civil War and for some years after, our people were almost wholly agricultural. National activity contented itself with settling and developing the vast areas of the public lands, whose virgin richness cried aloud in the wilderness for men.

The policy of the government, framed to stimulate rapid occupation of the public lands, had attracted hordes of settlers over the mountains from the older states, and immigration flowed in a steady stream into the valleys of the Ohio and the Mississippi.

A system had grown up in the South almost patriarchal, based upon cultivation by slave labor of enormous areas devoted exclusively to cotton. In the North, New England had developed some few centers of industry, drawing their support from the manufacture of the great Southern staple. New York, Boston, and Philadelphia were growing as outlets for foreign commerce, but as yet manufacturing flourished but feebly and in few localities.

Such manufacturing and commercial enterprises as existed had been laboriously built up by long years of honest working. The free lands of the government, by giving laborers an alternative, kept up wages, forcing employers to bid against each other for labor; and monopoly thus being checked, individual equality was possible.

The mineral resources of Pennsylvania and Ohio were all but unsuspected, and the calm of a people devoted to the peaceful pursuits of agriculture rested over the country.

Railroads were few and inefficient: telegraph lines but in their infancy. Intercourse among the people, outside of a narrow fringe on the Atlantic coast, was cumbersome, and impeded by many obstacles. Primitive conditions everywhere prevailed, and communities brooded in silence, growing stragglingly in sluggish indifference, content with coarse food and coarser living.

Such, in general, were the conditions up to 1861. Then came the storm of shot and shell, the rain of blood, the elemental rage of passion called the Civil War. There was a total upset of business. Such periods of hard times as had occurred prior to that time had been caused by the tinkering of untrained minds with the money system or by land speculation, and not by lack of access to the riches of nature. After four years our people awoke, as from a nightmare, to find the old life swept away forever. In the South, the Confederates, bitter and sullen, groping amid the ruins of their institutions, sought to find some substitute for the agricultural despotism exercised for generations by their slaveholding families. In the East, the first families of the Revolution, secure in their preeminence, assumed again the manufacturing-banking-social prestige. The far West was still almost unknown, and remained in possession of the buffalo and the Indian. Settlers poured, in increasing numbers on to the unappropriated lands still left in the states of the central West, and the center of political power shifted rapidly to this fertile region.

Already men of keen insight foresaw a time when oil, timber, coal, and iron must become the stay of a vastly expanding industrial system, and bent their energies to secure the chief sources of supply. From the nature of their work the men who built railways first became aware of the riches of nature, and aided by an enormous public sympathy with their efforts, monopolized all the natural opportunities of value. Coupled with industrial development was the gradual appropriation of the land. The time soon arrived when the late comers either stayed in the manufacturing centers at the railways terminals or were pushed farther and farther away from the centers. As the landowning families multiplied, the young men were confined to the same choice. Forced off the land, the tendency has been to crowd the brainiest blood of America into the cities. In addition, the competition of the new Western lands, brought into use by railway development, has exiled the youth of New England, who found in their rocky acres no incentive to toil. They, too, joined the ever-increasing flow to the cities, and entered into the savage competition of our great towns.

In our time the pendulum has swung to its extreme. At every depression of business, armies of the unemployed perish in sight of the land they abandoned in the hope of a brighter future. Their children have forgotten the traditions of the soil, and the energies of our people must now be concentrated to reverse the aimless tide of human sufferers, which under stress continues to flow city-ward, and to send it to repeople the silent places whence it came. The fight will not be easily won. Changes in the national land policy are imperative. To give one generation privileges which enslave all who succeed it, is intolerable and will not be permanently endured.

It is easy to determine upon a policy in the quiet of the study; different is the problem of applying a comprehensive scheme to repeople the idle land. In the first place, where is the idle land? In all parts of our country it exists in abundance. Almost every state in the Union has lands which either have never been alienated, or which have reverted to the state through nonpayment of taxes. In the East, particularly, the competition of Western lands, aided by discriminating freight rates, now so notorious, has resulted in the abandonment to the mortgagee of vast areas in New York, Connecticut, New Hampshire, Maine, and to some extent in New Jersey. These are now largely resold.

Declining fertility and exorbitant and oppressive transportation charges have helped to keep these lands out of use, and some still lie idle and neglected, to excite the wonder of the social and economic student. To use the abandoned lands of the East, equal rates on agricultural products is a basic necessity.

The first step, now well under way, is railroad control by the Government. Equal access to transportation is as essential as equal access to land, for transportation is indeed an attribute of land.

Extending the inquiry westward, the coal and oil areas of Pennsylvania and Ohio are all controlled by a few hands. The original fertility of the farming areas of these states, together with the fact that they have been producing for only about a century, has enabled them to hold their own until recently, but now only the best located tracts are in maximum production, and this can he maintained only by the most advanced agricultural science. In spite of greater advantages, the crowded cities and deserted country districts are beginning to repeat in the fertile alluvial valleys of the interior, the tragic story of the East.

In the Mississippi valley, conditions seem better. Values of farming lands are increasing rapidly; the farms are rich and growing richer; food products are cheap and abundant; certain staples are produced in enormous quantities and sent to feed the cities of the East and the industrial population of Europe. The railroads transport these products nearly one thousand miles for the same prices as they charge in the East for transporting them one hundred miles. Wealth, activity, and political power concentrate at the inlet and outlet of the railway funnel, leaving vast areas of unused and unusable land between the terminals. Access to markets determines value. That is why the favored lands of Illinois, Iowa, Kansas, Michigan, and Wisconsin, one to two thousand miles from market, have risen in value to as high as three hundred dollars per acre, and the lands of New England, New York, and New Jersey go begging at twenty to sixty dollars per acre, unless they lie within the artificial prosperity of the cities.

Farther west in the irrigated regions of Colorado and Utah, restricted areas are held for special fruit crops, at prices ranging from three hundred to two thousand dollars and up, per acre. But here, again, monopoly, now a monopoly of natural opportunity, is a factor in creating prices; on this, however, the vast irrigation projects of the government, bringing into use larger and larger areas of these favored lands, were expected to exercise a check. Up to 1918 little has been sold. Their reclamation cost too much.

The willingness of the Southern planters to sell their lands, and so to release them for intensive cultivation, has partly turned the tide of immigration from the Eastern ports to the South, and the market garden system is reaching increasing areas. The development of factories to make cotton fabrics and to utilize the formerly wasted cotton seed by turning it into meal for cattle and other animals, as well as into the various food products, such as cotton-seed oil, cottolene, etc., has stimulated the use of the waste land around these budding factory centers, thus tending to encourage intensive use of small, well-located tracts.

With a climate much milder and more equable than that of the Northern states, with a potential fertility of soil, equally great under proper management, the South is making greater strides than any other part of the country.

The foregoing shows that in every section opportunities of getting the people to the land exist. Where a man should go is determined by a variety of things. If he be a newly arrived immigrant used to land work in Southern Europe, he would find his best chance in the South; if a German or Russian, or from any of the Northern European countries, he would find the beet-sugar sections of Michigan Colorado, or California more to his liking; if American born, without much knowledge of outdoor work, and feeling the need of social life, the cheap farms of New York, New Jersey, and New England would probably be most attractive.

Many persons write me that I say it is necessary to get good land near population or with cheap and assured transportation facilities--and that it must not cost more than it is worth for gardening. "I find," they say, "that such acres are held as 'lots' at wildly speculative prices" and they ask "Where can I find such land?" But this is a book on agricultural use of land. Why land costs too much and where the remedy lies are other questions, dealt with in my "Things as They Are."

However, probably the best chances now for intensive cultivation are in New Jersey, in the backwoods of the Middle states now made accessible by cheap autos--and in the South.

What can be undertaken with good prospects of success will be outlined in the following chapters.

CHAPTER III
HOW TO BUY THE FARM

Before the purchase of the land for a home in the country, some consideration ought to be given to probable increase in land values. Even if you are primarily interested in your early sales of produce, you will not object to reaping an additional profit from the presence of other people.

Inasmuch as density of population determines land values, it follows that vacant land near a large city at $100 per acre may be cheaper than similar land at a distance would be at $10 per acre. If you buy real estate, you become a silent partner who does nothing, but takes most of the profits of the business of others.

Some persons see so clearly that money is often easily gotten by investing in land, that sometimes they make mistakes, in trying to get in. It is as easy to be a lamb in the real estate market as it is in the stock market.

Foresight, judgment, and experience or luck are essential to success in real estate dealing, but help, at least in keeping out of danger, may be had by following a few simple rules, if one can command a little capital, borrowed or owned.

The following points, suggested by a professional land shark, will certainly be of interest and possibly of profit to the intending buyer. I believe myself that they contain the whole philosophy of land speculation.

For a sure profit buy low-priced land, keeping as near the "raw material" as possible; high-priced property is risky and expensive to carry. An acre which costs one or two hundred dollars, or ten dollars per lot, will cost but six to twelve dollars per year to carry and half a dollar for taxes, and if a stable does come next you, why, you can sell your land for a blacksmith shop.

Besides this, a ten-dollar lot, if restricted for residence or available for business, often advances to $100 in a year; one good house which some one else built near it may raise its value that much.

If the land *is* high priced, see that there is some kind of a building on it; even a shanty will usually bring in enough or save you enough by its use to pay the taxes; so you will have that working for you whilst you are away.

If possible, buy at auction and of reputable people who are not boomers, or at least buy at forced sale; that is how real estate is sold when it must be sold. Choose lots level with the curb and on high ground, lest the expense of grading and sewering eat up your profit.

Keep in mind that in buying land for speculation one really buys the opportunity to tax other people, by taking part of their earnings in the shape of rent or price. Do not then be deluded by boom schemes in inaccessible or desolate places; choose rather that land which in the natural course of events others must have in order to work or to live.

Home buying in small communities is safer than in the outskirts of a large city, because public improvements are much less costly. If you put $500 in a $5000 home and carry the balance on mortgage, an assessment of $1000 for streets or sewers, which helps the vacant lots, will probably put you out of business. Whether for use or speculation, buy in an established neighborhood or where the circumstances and neighbors are such that restrictions or expenditures will make its character sure. The increase in your land value depends first upon the presence, then upon the efforts, of others; it is by their labor you hope to profit.

Therefore, buy property on leading thoroughfares; except in a very small section devoted to the residence of millionaires, the price of residence property has a limit; even there the merest accident or the whim of fashion may destroy the value, but there is no telling what figure business property may reach.

Do not build unless you have to. It is rare that a building pays five per cent net on the value of the land and the cost of the house. "Who buys a house already wrought, gets many a brick and nail for naught." If, however, you can get a piece of ground in a growing neighborhood and live on it till you can sell at an advance, that is the safest, and surest of investments. It delivers you from the power of the landlord.

Lastly--in real estate--don't bite off more than you can chew.

Most of these rules apply to the purchase of suburban land. In farm buying, keep as close to your market as you can. See that railway facilities are all right; get land likely to be needed for other purposes. The best way to begin is by securing all information possible from state agricultural departments. Write to the industrial agents of important railroads traversing the section in which you want to locate. They have detailed information regarding land, markets, social conditions, etc.; get from the United States Agricultural Department a map showing the soil survey of the section of your choice. It must be borne in mind that personal aid is not to be expected from State Agricultural Departments, Bureaus of Immigration, railway companies, or any public agency.

From the big farm agencies run for profit you can get lists of thousands of properties for sale. Some State Agricultural Departments cooperate with real estate men in their own states, by referring inquiries for farms to them. Some states issue from time to time lists of "abandoned farms," but these change so constantly that they help but little except in the way of suggestion.

When you start farm-hunting take along a good map. Then you will know a few things on your own account. Verify railroad maps and "facts," as they are often biased. Don't waste your time wandering around a strange locality by yourself. The local real estate man knows more about his community than you can learn in five years. In trying to find out things for yourself you will waste in aimless journeys, undertaken in ignorance of real conditions, more time and money than a real estate man's commission amounts to.

The only way to form a correct idea of the production of any given section is to examine a particular farm in detail. Within well-recognized limits, all tile farms thereabouts will be found of similar character. Before spending money to look at land, learn all you can by correspondence. Whether it is more profitable in the long run to buy that good plot of land in a high state of cultivation with good buildings on it, at a high price, than to buy this exhausted piece of land with poor buildings or none at all, is a question for the individual to decide. It depends on your energy, grit, age, and how much money you have. It is much easier to take advantage of what the other fellow has done, than it is to build from the stump. You must bear in mind, however, that well kept land in a high state of cultivation seldom goes begging in the market. On the whole, if you have the capital to do it, you can make the biggest wages by buying rough or neglected land, and hewing it into shape.

If you have a knowledge of soils, you may be able to find land that will grow something that no one supposes it will grow. This will be particularly useful in the case of land thought to be valueless. The lands about Miles, Michigan, were considered sterile until some one found out that they would grow mint, a valuable crop, which made the land salable at high prices.

Get hold of a desirable bit of the earth. All that men wear or eat or use; everything--shelter, food, tools, and toys comes from the land by labor. Even the capital used to make more of those things is taken from the land. The employer and the capitalist are, at bottom, only men who control the land or its products, who own rights of way, mining rights, or the fee of valuable lands. Thousands have "made" money by finding unexpected products in their land or of their lands, oil, coal, mineral, plants; thousands more because their land was needed by some one else, and they were paid to get out of the way.

To speculate on these chances is risky business; to keep land that enables you to make good pay while you wait, is profitable.

CHAPTER IV
VACANT CITY LOT CULTIVATION

In this book, necessarily, we have to take much upon the reports of others, checking them by our own judgment and experience. The startling accounts of what has been done and is being done on plots of about a quarter acre to each family, however, can be easily re-verified by any one who will go or write to Philadelphia, or examine any present experiment or model gardens. These show what can be done even by unskilled labor, with hardly any capital, on small plots where the soil was poor, but which are well situated.

The directors say: "The first Vacant Lot Cultivation Associations were organized when relief agencies were vainly striving to provide adequate assistance for the host of unemployed. The cultivation of vacant city lots by the unemployed had already been tried successfully in other cities. The first year we provided gardens, seeds, tools, and instruction only, for about one hundred families on twenty-seven acres of ground. At a total cost to contributors of about $1800, our gardeners produced $46,000 worth of crops."

The applicant is allowed a garden on the sole condition that he cultivate it well through the season, and that he do not trespass upon his neighbors. He must respect their right to what their labor produces. A failure to observe these rules forfeits his privilege.

During twenty years, more than eight thousand families have been assisted, many old people who could no longer keep up the rapid pace of our industrial life, cripples whose physical condition held them back in the race for work, persons who on account of sickness or other misfortunes have been thrown out of the competition in modern business, and unfortunate beings who, though clear in mind and strong in muscle, have been forced to the ranks of the unemployed--these have all had an opportunity opened to them: opportunity to enjoy all of the fruits from nature's great storehouse which their own labor and skill might secure.

The war has forced France, Italy, and England similarly to utilize natural opportunities for subsistence in their enormous tracts of unproductive lands. In Mexico all proprietors will be required to designate what they propose to cultivate and the remainder will either be allotted temporarily for agricultural purposes to those desiring them or it will be cultivated under government management. There is no remedy like that for poverty.

The first man who applied for a vacant lot garden came to the Philadelphia office after the announcement in the papers, so weak and emaciated that the doctor was afraid the poor fellow would be unable to get out of his office without assistance. He was a widower with three girls and a boy, the oldest girl about seventeen.

He received a garden which contained only about one fifth of an acre. Later he observed that a part of another little farm was left untouched on account of being very rough, full of holes, and covered with stone and bricks. Part of this farm was below the street grade and subject to overflow, but it was larger than the others--nine tenths of an acre. He offered to exchange, saying he did not mind the extra work.

His offer was accepted. In a few days the stones and bricks had been thrown into the holes and covered with dirt. The low places had been filled in. It was a work in which the whole family joined. A small house was rented in the immediate neighborhood in lieu of their one room near the foul alleys of the city slum.

Every inch of the soil was utilized. A rosy hue took the place of the pale, wan cheek of a few months before. And now the harvest has come, and the winter's store can be enumerated. Thirty bushels of potatoes, four bushels of turnips, one bushel of carrots, thirty gallons of sauerkraut, fifteen gallons of catsup, five gallons of pickled beans, one hundred quarts of canned tomatoes, fifty quarts of canned corn, twenty quarts of beans, one thousand or more fine celery stalks, and many other things. Warm clothing has replaced the badly worn garments of nine months ago. A few pieces of furniture have been added. The boy has been provided with a small capital for his little business. ("Vacant Lot Cultivation," Reprint from N. Y. *Charities Review.*) Better labor would of course get even better results.

The personal benefits that have come to a few individual cases, are largely the same that all the gardeners enjoyed in New York and elsewhere.

An old colored woman--a grandmother--who had just been released from one of the hospitals where she had been treated for a long time for pleurisy, asked for a garden. It was more than a mile to the nearest plot, but she was quite willing to go even that distance if she could get a garden. At first, owing to her weakened condition, she was forced to work slowly and for short periods only, but a little assistance enabled her to get a garden started. The work proceeded so well that more land was added to her small holding, and most of her waking hours were now spent either in or near the garden, working among the tender plants or watching them grow. Before the season was half spent she had developed one of the best gardens in the whole plot. Her surplus produce became so large that she had to devote most of her time to gathering and selling it. Finally she rented a small shed on a prominent street and passers-by often stopped, and regular customers came to buy the freshly gathered produce, the supply being not only abundant, but of great variety.

One of the best gardens, from the standpoint of value of produce as well as for the varieties of products it contained and the artistic arrangement, was worked by a man who had but one arm. Many other successful and profitable gardens were cultivated by men and women of an age when we generally expect them to depend entirely upon others for support.

Many incidents were found where such habits as drinking and loafing around saloons and clubs and abusing the family have been checked on account of the gardener's time and attention being occupied in the little farm.

One of the workers came for work in a condition of mind and body which rendered his services almost worthless. He was scarcely able to carry on his work for a minute beyond what he was shown. Each new move had to be explained constantly, and even then he was often found doing the work in the wrong way only a few minutes afterwards. Before long, however, he began to see that his place had its responsibilities and that the work of Mother Nature depended on his doing his part and doing it well. By the time the crops were ready to gather and market he came to realize that the cost of production must come under the amount received from the sale of the produce so as to prevent loss. By the end of the season he had learned so to utilize his time and to organize his work and execute our plans that we were able to recommend him to a farmer who was looking for a handy man about the place.

In twenty years our Associations have made demonstrations of the following facts, each demonstration proving more clearly than the former ones:

First. That many people out of employment must have help of some kind.

Second. That a great majority of them prefer self-help, and many will take no other. Nearly all are able and willing to improve any opportunities open to them.

Third. That to open opportunities to them does not pauperize or degrade, but has the opposite effect of elevating and ennobling. It quickly establishes self-respect and self-confidence. The best and most effective way of helping people in need is to open a way whereby they may help themselves. The most effective charity is opportunity accompanied with kindly advice and a personal interest in those less fortunate than ourselves.

Fourth. That the offering of gardens to the unemployed with proper supervision and some assistance by providing seeds, fertilizers, and plowing accompanied with instruction, is the cheapest and easiest way of opening opportunities yet devised.

Fifth. That it possesses many advantages in addition to providing profitable employment; among others, that the worker must come out into the open air and sunshine; must exercise, and put forth exertion,--all of which are conducive to health, and, most important of all, he knows that all he raises is to be his own. This is the greatest incentive to industry.

The Vacant Lot Cultivation system is a school wherein gardeners are taught a trade (to most of them a new trade), farming, which offers employment for more people than all the other trades and professions combined: a trade susceptible of wide diversification and offering many fields for specializing. But little capital is required; any other field would require large outlay. Its greatest advantage, however, is that the idle men and the idle land are already close to each other--the men can reach their gardens without changing their domiciles or being separated from their families.

It was not until after several years that the full effect of the work was realized. A few gardeners each year from the beginning have, after one or two years' experience, taken small farms or plots of land to cultivate on their own account, or have sought employment on farms near the city; but the number is quite small compared to the whole number helped. Now more than ten per cent of those that had gardens previously have for the last two years been working on their own account. Out of nearly eight hundred gardeners, more than eighty-five either rented or secured the loan of gardens that season and cultivated them wholly at their own expense, and many others would have done so had suitable land been available. The number of gardens forfeited on account of poor cultivation or trespassing was only two out of 800 plots given out.

The first important advance was early in the spring of 1904, when it became known that a large tract of land that had been in gardens for several years would be withdrawn from use. A number of the gardeners came together to talk over the situation. One proposed that they form a club to lease a tract of land and divide it up among themselves. The plan was readily agreed to, and a nine-acre tract on Lansdowne Avenue was rented at $15 per acre per annum. Some sixteen families became interested' and Mr. D. F. Rowe, who had been one of the most successful gardeners, became manager They had the land thoroughly fertilized and plowed, and then subdivided. Some took separate allotments, as under the Vacant Lot Association's plan, and others worked for the manager at an agreed rate of wages per hour. The whole nine acres were thoroughly well cultivated, and a magnificent crop harvested.

As soon as there was produce for sale, a market was established on the ground and a regular delivery system organized which later attracted much attention. It was carried on by the children, of nine to twelve years of age, from the various families. Each child was provided with a pushcart. There were many and various styles, made from little express wagons, baby coaches, and produce boxes

The children built up their own routes, and went regularly to their customers for orders. They made up the orders, loaded them into their little pushcarts, charged themselves up with the separate amounts in a small book, and at the end of each day's sales each child settled with the manager and was paid his commission (twenty per cent of the receipts) in cash. These little salesmen and salesgirls often took home four to five dollars per week and yet never worked more than three to five hours per day. The work was done under such circumstances that to them it was not work but play. You can get the full report from the Philadelphia "Vacant Lot Cultivation Associations." It's interesting.

"The greatest value that our little garden has brought us," said a French woman, mother of a goodly number of rather small children, "has not been in the fine vegetables it has yielded all summer, or the good times that I and the children have had in the open air, but in the glasses of beer and absinthe that my husband hasn't taken." "Quite right, mother, quite right," came from a man near by. "The world can never know the evil we men don't do while we are busy in our little gardens."

Further, pillage of crops, which was always urged as an objection to raising fruits or truck on open grounds, has proved to be a baseless fear. Where any of the gardeners are allowed to camp or put up shacks on the patches, theft does not occur and various superintendents repeat that "the few and trivial cases of stealing from vacant lot plots or school gardens were almost all at the places that were fenced."

Perhaps our locks and bolts tend to suggest breaking in.

The Garden Primer issued by the New York City Food Supply Committee gives simple but incomplete directions for planting and tending a vegetable garden. For those who need that sort of thing, these are just the sort of thing they need. They will be useful if you do not follow them. The Primer tells you how to get some kind of parsnips, chard, spinach, common onions, radishes, cabbage, lettuce, beets, tomatoes, beans, turnips, peas, peppers, egg plants, cucumbers, corn, and potatoes.

Don't grow these things, unless it be for your own immediate use. Every one grows them and ripens them all at the same time. In many places these are given away or thrown away this year. Grow anything that every one wants and has not got, like okra, small fruits, etc.; you can get a much better return in cash or in trade than by spending your time "like other folks" who do not think.

So I refer to these directions for their instruction, and for your warning However, they give the following admirable injunctions.

"Help Your Country and Yourself by Raising Your Own Vegetables."

As we will likely have to send to Europe in coming years as much or even more food than we did last year, there is only one way to avoid a shortage among our own people, that is by raising a great deal more than usual. To do this we must plant every bit of available land. (Of course, we can't; the owners won't let us. Ed.)

If you have a back yard, you can do your part and help the world and yourself by raising some of the food you eat. The more you raise the less you will have to buy, and the more there will be left for some of your fellow countrymen who have not an inch of ground on which to raise anything.

If there is a vacant lot in your neighborhood, see if you cannot get the use of it for yourself and your neighbors, and raise your own vegetables. An hour a day spent in this way will not only increase wealth and help your family, but will help you personally by adding to your strength and well-being and making you appreciate the Eden joy of gardening. An hour in the open air is worth more than a dozen expensive prescriptions by an expensive doctor.

The only tools necessary for a small garden are a spade or spading fork, a hoe, a rake, and a line or piece of cord.

First of all, clear the ground of all rubbish, sticks, stones, bottles, etc. (especially whisky bottles).

Choose the sunniest spot in the yard for your garden.

Dig up the soil to a depth of 6 to 10 inches, using a spade or spading fork. (Deeper for parsnips and some other roots. Ed.) Break up all the lumps with the spade or fork.

If you live in a section where your neighbors have gardens, you might club together to hire a teamster for a day to do the plowing and harrowing for you all, thus saving a large amount of labor.

After your garden has been well dug, it must be fertilized before any planting is done. In order to produce large and well-grown crops it is often necessary to fertilize before each planting. Very good prepared fertilizers can be bought at seed stores, but horse or cow manure is much better, as it lightens the soil in addition to supplying plant food. Use street sweepings if you can get them.

The manure should be well dug into the ground, at least to the full depth of the top soil. The ground should then be thoroughly raked, as seeds must be sown in soil which has been finely powdered.

Lay out the garden, keeping the rows straight with a line. Straight rows are practically a necessity, not only for easier culture but for economy in space.

After you have marked all of your rows, the next step is opening the furrow. (A furrow is a shallow trench.) That is done with the hoe. (Best and quickest with a wheel hoe. Ed.) After the furrow is opened, it is necessary that the seed be sown and immediately covered before the soil has dried In covering the seeds the soil must be firmly pressed down with the foot. This is important.

In buying seed it is best to go to some well-established seed house, or, if that can't be done, to order by mail rather than to take needless chances. With most kinds of seeds a package is sufficient for a twenty-foot row.

Begin to break up the hard surface of the soil between the plants soon after they appear, using a hand cultivator or hoe, and keep it loose throughout the season. This kills weeds; it lets in air to the plant roots and keeps the moisture in the ground.

By constantly stirring the top soil after your plants appear, the necessity of watering can be largely avoided except in very dry weather. An occasional soaking of the soil is better than frequent sprinkling. Water your garden either very early in the morning or after sundown. It is better not to water when the sun is shining hot.

The planting scheme can be altered to suit your individual taste. For instance, peas and cabbage are included because almost everybody likes to have them fresh from their garden; but they occupy more space in proportion to their value than beets and carrots. Therefore a small garden could be made more profitable by omitting them altogether, or cutting them down in amount and increasing the amount of carrots, beets, and turnips planted; or any of the vegetables mentioned which may not be in favor with the family can be left out.

The kind of season we have would change the date of planting. In raising vegetables, as in everything else, one should use one's common (or garden variety of) sense. A good rule is to wait until the ground has warmed up a bit. Never try to work in soil wet enough to be sticky, or muddy; wait until it dries enough to crumble readily.

Gardening is not a rule of thumb business. Each gardener must bring his plants up in his own way in the light of his own experience and in accordance with the conditions of his own garden. A garden lover who has a bit of land will speedily learn if his eyes and his mind, as well as his hands, are always busy, no matter how meager his knowledge at the beginning.

There is plenty of land--if you can only get it.

Says Carl Vrooman, Assistant Secretary of Agriculture, in regard to the food problem:

"Millions of acres of farm land are being held out of use and other millions of acres are being cultivated on a wasteful and inefficient basis. Land values have risen at an unprecedented rate. They are based not upon what the farm will earn at the present time, but on an expectancy of what it will be worth in the future. The farmer's son or the tenant farmer, with little or no capital, cannot hope to acquire possession of a farm w hen the price of land is SO high that his earnings would not pay the interest on the investment. The result is that land remains idle or in the hands of tenants, and thousands of farmers' boys desert the country for the city.

". . . . What we need, and need badly, is a program of taxation which, without throwing additional burdens on the bona fide farmer, will place land now idle within the reach of men of limited means who possess the ambition and the ability to cultivate it."

You can see that poor ignorant people, women, boys, cripples, old men, often on less than 100 X 150 feet each, not only in Philadelphia, but as war gardeners in New York, and most other towns, have been able to support themselves by their work on the land. You can do much better.

To be sure, they had valuable land and often seeds free, but for such little pieces of land these are small items, and many of them had no certainty of having the land even for a second year, consequently they could not have hotbeds or any permanent improvement. You can make all these things.

Then what can you do? Only remember they had intelligent instruction and did the work themselves, and got the whole product; often the children helped-- they thought it fun. It does not pay to farm a small piece of land where all the workers have to be hired. Nor does it pay if one calculates merely to stick in seeds with one hand and pull out profits with the other.

CHAPTER V
RESULTS TO BE EXPECTED.

I f we get every one out on the farms, then there will be an over-production of farm products and a fall in prices."

True, but there are farmers who could do better in towns; what we want to do is to make it easy for people to get on the land about the cities, then it would be equally easy for those farmers who are better adapted for city life to get near the cities.

Under present conditions, where the worker is forced out fifteen or twenty miles from the town by the high price of land and the large amount of land required, the farmer is as much cut off from the city as the city dweller is cut off from rural life.

We need not be afraid to teach men better ways; there will always be plenty too stupid or too old or too isolated to learn; these will remain a bulwark against too sudden change.

Dr. Engel, former head of the Prussian Statistical Bureau, informs us that "Scientific farming succeeds because a given amount of effort, when more intelligently directed, produces greater results. Inasmuch, then, as the amount of food which the world can consume is limited, the smaller will be the number of farmers required to produce the needed supply, and the larger will be the number driven from the country to the city. It has already been observed that if 34 scientific methods were universally adopted in the United States, doubtless one half of those now engaged in agriculture could produce the present crops, which would compel the other half to abandon the farm." This is "Engel's Law."

This "argument" assumes that we are now utilizing all the land possible and that every one is fully supplied with food. But when we consider the great masses of people in the slums of all cities who are always underfed and whose constant thought is about their next meal; when we see hundreds of able-bodied men waiting in line until midnight for half a loaf of stale bread, surely it seems that there is a possibility of keeping all of the present farmers at work, if not of finding new fields for others, if we make our conditions such that there will be opportunities for every able-bodied worker to labor at remunerative employment.

Professor L. H. Bailey, a most industrious and accurate observer, says: "Dr. Engel's argument rests on the assumption that agriculture produces only or chiefly food; but probably more than half of the agricultural products of the United States is not food. It is cotton, flax, hemp, wool, hides, timber, tobacco, dyes, drugs, flowers, ornamental trees and plants, horses, pets, and fancy stock, and hundreds of other non-edible commodities. The total food produce of the United States, according to the twelfth census, was $1,837,000. The cost of material used in the three industries of textile, lumber and leather manufactories alone was $1,851,000,000.

"Dr. Engel thinks that the outlay for subsistence diminishes as income increases; but comforts and luxuries increase in intimate ratio with the income, and the larger part of these come from the farm and forest. Dr. Engel, in fact, allows this, for he says that 'sundries become greater as income increases.'"

We have already abundance of information about almost every county in the Union, published by Boards of Trade and land boomers, like the following about "Oxnard, Ventura County, the center of the famous lima bean district in California. For a year the returns from farm products alone, in this vicinity, are estimated at over $2,000,000. The sugar factory, which uses 2000 tons of beets every twenty-four hours, requires the yield of about 1900 acres every season. The beet crop is rotated with beans, and the factory's supply is kept good by systematic methods. Two thousand head of cattle are being fattened at the present time in the company's yard on the beet pulp. Much of the pulp is also sold to local stockmen, who value it highly for feed. The factory turns out 5000 bags of sugar every day." And again:

"Eastern farm lands steadily declined in price up to about 1902, so that Eastern land sold for less than Western land of the same quality and of like situation; but the tide seems at last to have turned, and much money is now being made in buying up cheap farms and especially in sub-dividing them for small cultivators."

That sort of thing is interesting; but it is not what a man wants to know--he is anxious to learn how much he can make and where and how to do it.

The man who seeks a comfortable living will do better to rent on long lease or buy a few acres convenient to trolley or railroad communication with a city; besides the returns which will come to the farmer from the use of a few acres, if he is the owner he will get a constant increase in the value of the land, due to the growth of the city. If the city grows out so that the land becomes too valuable to farm, he will be well paid for leaving.

(Although progress is continually forcing laborers back upon less desirable land, their loss, unless they are the owners, is the landowner's gain.)

The amount of product to be grown for one's own use depends on the size of the family and its fondness for vegetables.

"An area of 150X100 feet [about two fifths of an acre] is generally sufficient to supply a family of five persons with vegetables, not considering the winter supply of potatoes; but the acres must be well tilled and handled." (Bailey, "Principles of Vegetable Gardening.")

"The produce that could thus be obtained from an acre of land well situated would abundantly supply with nearly all the vegetables named, nineteen families, comprising in all 114 individuals."

In our garden we must know what we want and know how to get it.

(It is impossible to treat exhaustively of the various crops in a book of this kind. On onion culture alone there are four standard books, besides seven or eight recent experimental station bulletins.

"In a family garden 100 X 150 feet (which equals six New York City lots), the rows running the long way of the area, eight or ten feet may be reserved along one side for asparagus, rhubarb, sweet herbs, flowers, and possibly a few berry bushes. A strip twenty feet wide may be reserved for vines, as melons, cucumbers and squashes. There remains a strip seventy feet wide, or space for twenty rows three and one half feat apart. This area is large enough to allow of appreciable results in rotation of crops; and i! it is judiciously managed, it should maintain high productiveness for a lifetime." (Bailey, "Principles of Vegetable Gardening."))

"The things to be considered in the home garden are: (1) a sufficient product to supply the family; (2) continuous succession of crops; (3) ease and cheapness of cultivation; (4) maintenance of the productivity of the land year after year.

"The ease and efficiency of cultivation are much enhanced if all crops are in long rows, to allow of wheel-tool tillage either by horse or wheel-hoe."

The experience of the Vacant Lot Gardeners (Chapter IV) shows that if the land be near a large market where the product can be peddled or sold by the producers or by those (as in Mr. Rowe's case), with whom he directly deals, more than twenty-five dollars capital is not necessary, but Peter Henderson ("Gardening for Profit") estimates that to get the best results, $300 capital per acre is required for anything less than ten acres.

Where the land is favorably situated a fortune may be made in cultivation of a few acres--with brains.

Quinn says ("Money in the Garden") that he knows a large number of market gardeners worth from ten to forty thousand dollars each, none of whom had five hundred dollars to begin with.

If one has not enough money to get all that can be gotten out of his plot, it is best to put part of the land into clover to fit it for later use or to use it for raising grass.

Results undoubtedly come from hard work; but it is not necessary, in order to cultivate a little land successfully, that you should work all day on your hands and knees; if you can raise fruit or nuts, this is not needed at all.

But for vegetables a certain amount of it is necessary--when there is a large job of that kind of weeding to be done, you can hire Italians or other foreigners to do it better and cheaper than you can do it yourself. Those who will read this book can earn more with their heads than their hands; but when weeding is needed after a sudden shower and there is no one else, you must do some of it yourself; the weather will not wait for you to "get a man," and if you are not willing to do such things, your chances of success are greatly lessened.

Here is the experience of one who "got a man":

"My garden, to begin with, was in the most rudimentary condition, having been allowed to run to grass. After digging up a spot about ten feet square in the turf, taking the early morning for the work, I decided that it would require all summer to get the garden fairly spaded up, so I hired a stalwart Irishman to do the work for me, which he did in a week, charging me nine dollars for the job. As he professed to be also an expert in planting vegetables, I bought a supply of seeds in the city and intrusted them to him, assuring myself that once in the ground the rest of the work would fall to me; if I could not keep a garden patch fifty feet square clear of weeds, I had better abandon the business at once, and all hopes of making a living out of scientific gardening. The beginning was an unfortunate one. The weather happened to be first very wet, and then so dry and hot that my vegetables were unable to break their way through the baked earth. When my peas and beans still gave no signs after being in the ground for two weeks, I discovered that the whole work would have to be done over again. A Presidential campaign was beginning, which kept me in town often late at night, so that the chief labor of the garden fell to my faithful Irishman, who got far more satisfaction out of it than I did. The vegetables finally did come up above the surface, and many an evening I finished a hard day's work by pumping and carrying hundreds of gallons of water to pour upon potato plants, tomatoes, beans, and other things which a friend of mine, an expert in such matters, assured me were curiosities of malformation and backwardness. My Irishman told me that it was all for want of manure, and by his advice I bought six dollars' worth of manure from a neighboring stable, and had it spread over the ground. The bills for my garden were meanwhile mounting up. I had begun the spring with a garden ledger, keeping an accurate account of every penny spent, and hoping to put on the other side of the page a tremendous list of fine vegetables. The accounts are before me now, and I presume that every one who has been through the same experience has preserved some such record." (Naturally, if he began that way.) ("Liberty and a Living," by P. G. Hubert.)

If your idea of farming is to bury "some seeds" in untilled ground, regardless of suitability, and "wait till they come up," you will wait in vain for a decent crop.

Says Professor Roberts in the "Farmstead" (Macmillan), "Mushrooms sell at fifty cents per pound; maize for one half cent per pound. Why? Because anybody, even a squaw, can raise maize, but only a specially skilled gardener can succeed in mushroom culture."

But enough has been said to show that you must cultivate with brains. The Germans say, "What your head won't do, your legs have to."

"We'll have a little farm, A pig, a horse and cow And you will drive the wagon While I drive the plow,"

is very pretty. The horse and the pigs are practical, if you can take care of them yourself; pigs are good farm catch-alls. If you have to pay a man to do it, you had better hire your horses and buy your pork.

Two well-groomed, healthy cows, one calving in the spring and one in the autumn, can be made a source of profit, and of valuable manure, if you have land enough in a neighborhood where up-to-date parents are willing to pay ten to twenty cents a quart for pure milk for their infants or even for family use. But your land and your own baby's care and milk will probably be enough for you to attend to promptly and thoroughly every day--and night.

It is an age-old experience that if we take care of a little land, the land will take care of us. In Ferrero's "Grandezza e Decadenza di Roma" is an interesting account of Marcus Terentius Varro's "De Re Rustica." Varro wrote in the year 37 B.C., and as he was then eighty years old, he had seen the transformation of Italy from an agricultural to a manufacturing, trading community and the accompanying wreck of the old agricultural system, which, of course, he laments.

The growth of vast landed estates largely held by imperial favorites, as Pliny said, destroyed Italy. So fearful has the destruction been that it is only in our generation that the Campagna at Rome, which was once an intensely fruitful quilt of garden patches, has been reclaimed from the fever-smitten swamp to which vast landlordism had reduced it.

In the third book of "De Re Rustica," Varro recommends as his remedy, intensive cultivation close to the cities, and the breeding of "fancy stock," including pigeons' snails, peacocks, deer, and wild boars.

He tells how an aunt of his made 60,000 sesterces ($3000) in one year by raising thrushes for the Roman market, at a time when an excellent farm of about 200 acres only yielded 30,000 sesterces per annum. He quotes another case of one who made 40,000 sesterces per annum from a flock of one hundred peacocks, by selling the eggs and the young. Those old Roman women weren't so slow.

Ferraro calls Varro's work one of the most important for the history of ancient Italy and says historians have made a mistake in not reading it.

At the time of the migration of the barbarians (350 to 750 A.D.), the lot of each able-bodied man was about thirty morgen (equal to twenty acres) on average lands, on very good ground only ten to fifteen morgen (equal to seven or ten acres), four morgen being equal to one hectare. Of this land, at least a third, and sometimes a half, was left uncultivated each year. The remainder of the fifteen to twenty morgen sufficed to feed and fatten into giants the immense families of these child-producing Germans, and this in spite of the primitive technique, whereby at least half the productive capacity of a day was lost. (From "The State," by Franz Oppenheimer, p. 11.)

In the Orange Judd prize contest, merely for the clearest account of a garden, not for results at all, a number of the contestants raised produce at the rate of $150 to $400 per acre and over, even in semi-arid regions; for instance, L. E. Burnham says that he raised on his first garden of about one third of an acre in eastern Massachusetts, garden stuff which he sold to summer cottagers for $61.69.

This took about eight days' work, nearly all with a wheel hoe.

Remember about the present increased and changing prices and costs? At the present writing, 1917, the advances in costs and prices would probably average about three quarters, and those of common labor perhaps one third over those given in the text. In other respects, the instances and authorities, still pertinent, have been retained in this revision.

It would have been waste, not thrift, to get a new authority to tell us that straw makes the cleanest mulch for strawberries; that's the reason they were called strawberries; and they grew just the same way ten years ago.

L. E. Dimosh of Connecticut raised on one quarter of an acre $146.21, of which over $85 was profit.

In other cases the profits were $142 (Gianque, Nebraska) per acre; and over $295 (Dora Dietrich, Pennsylvania); with the rather exceptional profit at the rate of $570 (Mrs. Hall, Connecticut). Some showed a loss.

Some of the town or city lots yielded very high profits; one of a third of an acre gave a profit of $224.33 (Edge Darlington, Md.).

The summary "based upon the reports of five hundred and fifteen gardens in nearly every state and territory and in Canada and the provinces, may be considered accurate and reliable. Covering such a vast territory local conditions are avoided." It shows that "the average size of farm gardens was 24,372 square feet, or about half an acre, the average labor cost $26.34, the average value of product was at the rate of $170 per acre, and the net profit over $80 per acre."

To get results we must first learn and then teach what we know. The finest game in the world is to teach. No one ever knows anything thoroughly till he tries to teach it.

When you tell a person how to do a thing, he doesn't know how to do it himself. When you show him how to do it, still he doesn't know that he could do it himself. But when you get him to do it himself, then he knows.

Country boys will believe that early tomatoes can be raised by starting them in the house; but like the rest of us they don't know how to do it, and when spring comes and it is time to do such things, they are busy on the farm. There are several schools trying the experience of allowing the children to plant in window boxes in early April and are showing them how to do it. But as there is not room for all the children to plant in these window boxes, there is a new idea which originated in the country, where the children are engaged in the fall and the spring assisting their parents at agricultural work.

It was hard to get up any interest in school gardens, but it was all the more important that they should have agricultural instruction in the winter time.

At Berkeley Heights, N. J., we devised this simple plan, and it works. We made a number of wooden boxes, one foot wide, two feet long, so they will just fit on the ledge of a school desk. They are only three inches deep, with a bottom of tin, turned up at the edges, or of well painted pine, white-leaded at the joints. There is no drainage, since we discovered that if they are not watered too much, they do better without drainage. The holes usually made in the bottoms of flower boxes carry off a lot of plant food with the water that runs through.

Now, how to store these boxes when they are not in the sunny places near the windows? Why, we set up four posts of one-inch stuff at the four corners, so that the box looks like a kitchen table turned upside down. Now the boxes filled with earth and with the young plants growing can be stored at night, one on top of the other, by the wall of the schoolroom.

If it is going to be cold, and over Sundays, the pile of them can be covered with newspapers, which keep them from getting chilled and from drying up, or the boxes can be covered and carried home by the children. We found that for most plants nine inches is high enough for the posts, and that well-seasoned one-inch lumber is heavy enough not to warp if it is painted inside and out, and it is not too heavy to lift.

By the way, better paint the joints before the sides are nailed together. It makes them more water-tight. Four screws at the corners will make them still tighter.

The scholars raise lettuce, parsley, onions, and strawberries, and all kinds of small plants, as well as flowers, in the winter; and when the plants get too big or two crowded for the boxes, they are separated and transplanted into other boxes to be taken home.

This was so successful that we devised a big window box which is suited for home use also; it is just as wide as the window and half as long again as it is wide. But this box does not stand outside on the window sill; if it did, the plants would freeze. One end only rests on the inside window sill where it gets the sun; the end is supported by two legs of the same height that the window sill is from the floor.

When a nice warm day comes, the other end of the box is pushed out of the window and the sash closed down on it to keep it from falling out. A couple of cleats or nails in the window jamb help to hold it in place.

Of course, the box has to be watched and taken in if it turns cold, but it's astonishing how much can be raised and how much more can be learned out of season by the school desk boxes and the home window sliding boxes.

Try it and see for yourself.

The children can learn as much about some things from a box 2X1 ft. as they can from a children's garden. Here are a couple of samples of what the kids themselves in a city school think of it.

"DEPARTMENT OF EDUCATION

"*Office of the Principal of Public School No. 7*

"VAN ALST AVE., ASTORIA, QUEENS

"I inclose a few compositions that were written by some of our boys and girls of the Fourth Year. You will recognize the descriptions of your Garden Trays for classroom use Unfortunately the free space in the classroom is limited, so we have found it necessary to allow each pupil only part of a box.

"The children themselves are delighted, as you can see by their compositions.

"Very sincerely yours, (Signed)"

AGNES A. CORDING

"Asst. Principal."

P. S. No. 7

Grade 4 A--April 21, 1915.
Arthur Miller, Age 10
OUR GARDEN
At first we planted radishes then onions and lettuce and beans and sunflowers. Each one of us have 1/4 of a box. When we had finished that we brought them up to the front of the room and then watered them and went home.

Anna Duerr, Aye 8
MY GARDEN
I have a garden. It is a box. I have a quarter of a box for my very own. My garden has five rows. In the first there are radishes, in the second lettuce, in the third onions, in the fourth beans, in the fifth sunflowers. I hope my garden grows up.

Of course these are only preparatory for profitable work. We have cases in which $2000 has been recorded from sales in one year from one acre, and many cases in which at least $1000 worth of produce has been sold from an acre. These are sales, not profits.

Such results are not due to the boundless and fertile soil of the new world nor to small farming alone--they are due to intelligence.

Professor Ronna gives the following figures of crops per acre at Romford (Breton's Farm): 28 tons of potatoes (say 952 bushels), 16 tons of marigold, 105 tons of beets, 110 tons of carrots, 9 to 20 tons of various cabbages, and so on.

It was suggested to the Agricultural Department that it might fix standards of what is a good attainable crop.

On every golf links we have what is called a Bogie score posted up. That is a score that a certain mythical Captain Bogie, supposed to be an average good player, could make on those links. On one typical club-course, for instance, the Bogie score is 42. Though it has been done in 37, the ordinary player congratulates himself when he gets down to the Bogie score.

Now, if there were standards attainable to ordinary intelligent and good cultivation set in each section, it would enormously encourage farmers to reach them, which may be of great importance.

One of the heads of the Department replied as follows:

"'In regard to fixing a standard for each farmer to strive to attain, I think that a very good idea; but the standard for each crop in each particular locality would necessarily be somewhat different from that in every other locality. Persons who have had experience in experimental work keenly appreciate these points. The work which is done upon one soil formation under different climatic conditions in one season, does not necessarily find a duplicate in any other locality, and the experience is that what is accomplished in one year would not be duplicated on the same soil and under the same management again in several years, for the conditions under which agriculture is carried on are so many of them outside of the control of the operator that it is very difficult to predict results or to attain any fixed standard. This is necessarily so with an operation which has so many uncertain factors to deal with as agriculture. Humidity of the atmosphere and of the soil, the available plant food in the soil, methods of tillage, fertilizers used, recurrence of frosts, amount of sunlight, the altitude and latitude of different localities, all have a bearing upon crop production. It is, therefore, very difficult to fix any approximate standard or average production for any particular locality without basing it upon a long series of years. I think, however, that it is a subject worthy of agitation, and it might inspire agriculturists to better work were such an ideal fixed upon."

This indicates that each experiment station or progressive farmer or teacher of agriculture might advantageously establish the local "Bogie score" of what might fairly be expected.

We know how misleading averages are. The man who tried to wade across a stream whose average depth was two feet, was drowned. "The writer used to go to a fishing club of which Cornelius Vanderbilt was a member. One of the standard jokes there was that the thirty members are worth on an average over two million apiece, that is, Cornelius sixty millions, and the rest of us (comparatively) nothing. Which are you to be? A Vanderbilt among cultivators, or the other fellow who makes the 'average'?" ("Money Making in Free America," by the Author.)

But even making all allowances we see that we must cultivate much better than the "average," to make anything more than the farmer's hard living off the land. Peter Dunne tells us what kind of a grind that is.

"This pa-aper says th' farmer niver sthrikes. He hasn't got th' time to. He's too happy. A farmer is continted with his farm lot. There's nawthin' to take his mind off his wurruk. He sleeps at night with his nose against th' shingled roof iv his little frame home an' dhreams iv cinch bugs. While th' stars are still alight he walks in his sleep to wake th' cows that left th' call f'r four o'clock. Thin it's ho! f'r feedin' th' pigs an' mendin' th' reaper. Th' sun arises as usual in th' east, an' bein' a keen student iv nature he picks a cabbage leaf to put in his hat. Breakfast follows, a gay meal beginnin' at nine an' endin' at nine-three. Thin it's off f'r th' fields where all day he sets on a bicycle seat an' reaps the bearded grain an' th' Hessian fly, with nawthin' but his own thoughts an' a couple iv horses to commune with. An' so he goes an' he's happy th' livelong day if ye don't get in ear-shot iv him. In winter he is employed keeping th' cattle fr'm sufferin' his own fate an' writin' testymonyals iv dyspepsia cures." ("Mr. Dooley Says.")

CHAPTER VI
WHAT AN ACRE MAY PRODUCE

We have shown what an acre has produced. You must figure out for yourself what you can make your acres produce and what the product can be sold for.

All progress in agriculture has come heretofore through experiments, made mostly by uninformed and untrained men. What may not be done by practical learning and applied intelligence?

The wonderful recent advances have been made in just that way.

"The modern improved methods in agriculture, known collectively as intensive farming, have nearly all had their origin in the hands of truck farmers and market gardeners. No class of the rural population is more alert in utilizing the newest researches and discoveries in all lines of agricultural science, and none keeps in closer touch with the agricultural colleges and experiment stations." ("Development of the Trucking Interests," by F. S. Earle.)

Still, it is not advisable for the ordinary city dweller, however intelligent, without other means and without either experience or study, to cast himself upon a small patch of ground for a living; but if he can give it most of his time mornings and evenings, or if he sees, as many do, that he will be forced out of a position, it would be well for him seriously to consider intensive cultivation as a resource.

It would be the greatest blessing to our day laborers if they could secure an acre of land which they could till in conjunction with their other labor. If time and change 90 works upon society as to put the laborer out of a job, he will be safe in his acre home and can live from it and be happy and contented.

The time required to cultivate an acre is much less than is generally supposed.

The maximum time required seems to be that given in the University of Illinois

Experiment Station at Urbana, Bulletin 61, by J. W. Lloyd, at the rate of 140 hours (say 14 days) with one horse and 250 hours (say 25 days) for hand labor. With a great variety of crops, or with poor labor add one half to this time allowance. The results vary greatly.

An acre of northeastern Long Island will produce 250 to 400 bushels of potatoes at a selling price of fifty to seventy five cents per bushel, which wholesale, at those figures much below present prices, bring an income of $125 to $300 to the grower. The actual cash outlay in one instance was:

Seed Potatoes
$10.00
Commercial Fertilizer
13.00
Spraying for blight and pests
4.00
TOTAL
$27.00
250 bu. selling at the minimum price
$125.00
Less the cash outlay
27.00
Income to the grower from an acre
$98.00

A production of 400 bushels costs no more cash outlay per acre, while the income is big wages to the farmer.

If but one acre be grown and hand labor is used, the labor might cost an average of $40 per acre, with wages at $1.35 to $1.50 per day, and if the produce is shipped any distance by rail and consigned, it would cost $40 to $50 to pay selling charges, leaving you a profit of about $30 per acre on this crop. Other crops in the rotation might not be so profitable, hence it is not fair to figure an income on one. But, of course, in the above estimate, we are considering mainly the cases where the gardener does the work and earns the wages himself.

An acre will bear if devoted to each crop, of:

Blackberries, 10,000 qt., which at 7 cent a qt., would bring $700.00 Dewberries,

9,000 qt., say at 7 cent a qt. 630.00 Gooseberries, 250 bu. at $2.00 a bu. 500.00 Straw-berries, 8,000 qt. at 5 cent a qt. 400.00 Currants, 3000 plants yield 6000 bu. 200.00 Raspberries, per acre 200.00 to 600.00 Peaches, per acre 200.00 to 400.00 Pears, per acre 200.00 to 500.00 Apples, per acre 100.00 to 500.00 Grapes 100.00

Five, or even three acres will give a good living if this can be approximated:

An acre will produce in vegetables--either

Asparagus, 3000 bunches at 20 cent a bunch, would be $600.00 Cauliflower, 100 to 300 bbl. at $1.50, say 450.00 Onions, 600 bu. at 75 cent per bu. 450.00 Cab-bage Seed, 1000 lb., at 40 cent a lb. 400.00 Brussels sprouts, 3000 qt. at 10 cent a qt. 300.00 Celery, 600 bunches at 5 cent a bunch 300.00 Parsnips, 300 bu. at 1.00 a bu. 300.00 Lettuce, 9000 heads at 3 cent a head 270.00 Lima Beans, 50 bu. at $5.00 a bu. 250.00

We may hope to get from an acre, respectively in

Potatoes, 300 bu. at 75 cent a bu, would be $225.00 Cabbages, 20 tons at $10.00 a ton 200.00 Carrots and Beets, 200 to 400 bu 150.00 Tomatoes, 200 crates at 75 cent a crate 150.00 Early Peas, 50 bu. at $2000 a bu. 100.00 Turnips, 400 bu. at 25 cent a bu 100.00 Spinach, 100 bbl. at 50 cent a bbl. 50.00

Mr. D. L. Hartman, whose experience in the North is given on a later page, has since moved to Little River, Florida. He writes in 1917:

"I have recently sold the last strawberries of a small plot. Owing to a combina-tion of circumstances it produced, I think, the largest value per area of any crop I have ever cultivated. The main factors were high prices realized and heavy yield.

Area of plot, a trifle over one fifth acre. Total yield, 2295 quarts, total receipts, $ 4703.80.

First berries picked January 2nd; last berries picked June 26th; Variety, Bran-dywine.

"This shows a yield of 11,107 quarts per acre worth at the same rate, $3398.00.

"The fruit was all sold to stores in Miami (five miles distant) and brought an average you notice of 30-2/3 cents per quart for the crop, the highest bringing fifty cents per quart. The average price during the ordinary seasons is about twenty cents per quart. My ordinary average yield is less than half of this yield or about 5000 quarts per acre, and that is much above the average of most yields of other growers. The crop was started with northern plants, set just as for matted rows in the North, then early in November plants were dug up and set out in order in rows 12 inches apart and 8-1/2 inches apart in the row, leaving every fifth row vacant for paths. It is super close culture; one plant per square foot for the total area or a little more.

"I often think that if I were operating in the North again I would like to try strawberries the same way, except that I would do the transplanting September 1st instead of November 1st as here, since I would expect them to grow larger and of course I would plan to mulch them during the winter. It would take a lot of planting but I think it would insure a tremendous yield. I find that the digging and planting including watering of 1500 plants makes ten hours' work with elimination of all waste motion."

You will not get as good results as Mr. Hartman's average, unless you learn as much as he has learned; he has succeeded by well-directed work in different places and circumstances

The South and West are not the only places in the United States where a man can live on one acre of ground, by intensive culture and with irrigation. The Eastern and Middle States can present just as good, if not better, opportunities, especially where land in small tracts is available near the large cities.

The Farmers' Advocate (Topeka, Kansas) says of lands which ten years ago were among the much advertised "abandoned farms" of the eastern states: "All over the eastern states where farming twenty years ago was pronounced a failure under Western competition there has sprung. up this intensive cultivation. Violets are grown in one place and tuberoses by the acre in another. Celery is making one man's large profit near Williamsburg. Special fruits are cultivated. Currants are grown by the ton and sold by the pound, yielding a profit. This is in progress over the entire range of farming."

At Hyde Park, a little village three miles north of Reading, Pa., there is a small farm owned by Oliver R. Shearer, who may be said to be one of the most successful farmers in the United States. This farm contains 3-1/2 acres, only 2-1/2 of which are cultivated, but they yield the owner annually from $1200 to $1500. From the profits of his intensive farming, Mr. Shearer has paid $3800 for his property, which, besides the land, consists of a modern two-story brick house, with barn, chicken-yard, and orchard, the whole surrounded by a neat fence. He has also raised and educated a family of three children.

There are no secrets, Mr. Shearer says, about his method of farming. A study of conditions, the application of common-sense methods and untiring energy, he asserts, will enable others to do what he has done, but that most men would kill themselves with the work.

In an agricultural exchange a small farmer tells that he makes a living and saves some money from a ten-acre farm. Before he was through paying for his land, which cost $100 an acre, building his house, fences, and outbuildings, he went in debt $1300, having about the same amount to start with. He is near a good market, and in five years has paid off the debt, and has been getting ahead ever since. He raises poultry and small fruits, and says that it is a good combination, as most of the work with poultry comes in winter, while he can do nothing out of doors. He maintains that a ten-acre farm rightly managed will bring a good living, including the comforts and some of the luxuries of life, and says: "This I have fully demonstrated, and what I have done others may do."

Maxwell's Talisman says:

"E. J. O'Brien of Citronelle, Alabama, received $170 clear from an acre of cucumbers shipped to the St. Louis market. He was two weeks late in getting them on the market. He says those two weeks would have meant nearly double the net returns. He does not consider this an extraordinary return and hopes to do better next year."

"Professor Thomas Shaw writes of a plot of ordinary ground in Minnesota comprising the nineteenth part of an acre, which for years kept a family of six matured persons abundantly supplied with vegetables all the year, with the exception of potatoes, celery, and cabbage. In addition, much was given away, more especially of the early varieties, and in many instances much was thrown away."

"In the market-gardens of Florida we see such crops as 445 to 600 bushels of onions per acre, 400 bushels of tomatoes, 700 bushels of sweet potatoes; which testify to a high development of culture."

We select from Bailey's "Principles of Vegetable Gardening" the following general estimates:

Beets-- Average crop is 300-400 bushels per acre.

Carrots-- Good crop is 200-300 bushels per acre.

Cabbage--8000 heads per acre.

Potatoes--The yield of potatoes averages about 75 bushels per acre, but with forethought and good tillage and some fertilizer the yield should run from 200 to 300 bushels, and occasionally yields will much exceed the latter figure.

Rhubarb--From 2 to 5 stalks are tied in a bunch for market, and an acre should produce 3000 dozen bunches.

Salsify--Good crop 200-300 bushels per acre.

Onions--A good crop of onions is 300-400 bushels to the acre, but 600-800 are secured under the very best conditions.

The price per ton for horseradish varies from ten to fifty dollars, and from two to four tons should be raised on an acre, the latter quantity when the ground is deep and rich and when the plants do not suffer for moisture.

Averages are very misleading and it would be better to pay little attention to them. They are like the average wealth possessed by a class of twenty schoolchildren. The schoolmaster who had $20 asked what was the average wealth of each, if the total wealth of the class was $20. The brightest boy answered, "One dollar." The schoolmaster asked Tommy at the foot of the class if he did not think they would be a prosperous class. He answered, "It depends on who has the 'twenty.'"

But, all the more, good averages imply some wonderful yields. The following are actual averages in the United States Twelfth and Thirteenth Census Report, respectively.

Flowers and plants, $2014 and $1911; nursery products, $170 and $261; sugar cane, $87 (4 tons per acre) and $5540; small fruits, $81 and $110; hops, $72 (885 lb. per acre) and $175; sweet potatoes, $37 (79 but per acre) and $55; hemp, $34 (794 lb. per acre) and $54; potatoes, $33 (96 bu. per acre) and $45; sugar beets, $30 (7 tons per acre) and $54; sorghum cane, $21 (1 ton per acre) and $23; cotton, $15 (4-10 bale per acre) and $25.70 flaxseed, $9 (9 bu. per acre) and $14; cereals, $8 and $11.40.

Specialties, however, often do much better. For example, R. B. Handy, in Farmers' Bulletin No. 60, United States Department of Agriculture, tells us that a prominent and successful New Jersey grower says:

"I cannot give the cost in detail of establishing asparagus beds, as so much would depend upon whether one had to buy the roots, and upon other matters. Where growers usually grow roots for their own planting the cost is principally the labor, manure, and the use of land for two years upon which, however, a half crop can be had.

"The cost of maintaining a bed can only be estimated per acre as follows:

Manure (applied in the spring) $25.00 Labor, plowing, cultivating, hoeing, etc 20.00 Cutting and bunching 40.00 Fertilizer (applied after cutting) 15.00

Total $100.00

"An asparagus bed well established, say five years after planting, when well cared for should, for the next ten or fifteen years, yield from 1800 to 2000 bunches per annum, or at 10 cents per bunch (factory price) $180 to $200."

"If the rent, labor, etc., for a crop of asparagus is $200 per acre, and the crop is three tons of green shoots at $100 per ton, on the farm, the profit is $100 per acre. If we get six tons at $100 per ton, the profit, less the extra cost of labor and manure, is $400 per acre." ("Food for Plants," by Harris and Myers, page 19.)

Around Bethlehem, Indiana, the farmers raise hundreds of tons of sunflower seed every year, and the industry pays better than anything else in the farming line. A good deal of the seed is made into condition powder for stock, occasionally some is made into so-called "olive oil" which is said to surpass cotton-seed oil. Large quantities are used for feeding parrots and poultry, or consumed by the Russian Hebrews who eat them as we would eat peanuts.

A careful investigation made in 1898 of the value of certain productions taken from farms in New York State shows that the culture of apples is very profitable. From twenty adjoining farms in one neighborhood in western New York, the report gave an average annual return of $85 per acre at the orchard, covering a period of five years. Another report gave an average of $110 annual income per acre for three years, and these results were obtained where only ordinary care was given to the orchard. But note this.--

One orchard, where the trees had been well sprayed to protect the fruit from insect injuries, and the soil well cultivated and properly fertilized, gave a return in one year of $700 per acre, and for three years an average income of $400 per acre.

One man bought a farm of 100 acres in Central New York with a much-neglected orchard upon it of 30 acres, paying $5000 for the whole. He cultivated the orchard, pruned and sprayed the trees thoroughly, and in seven months from the time he purchased the farm, sold the apple crop from it for $6000 cash.

"Peanuts: Culture and Uses," by R. B. Handy in Farmers' Bulletin No. 25 of the United States Department of Agriculture says:

"According to the Census the average yield of peanuts in the United States was 17.6 bushels per acre, the average in Virginia being about 20, and in Tennessee 32 bushels per acre. This appears to be a low average, especially as official and semiofficial figures give 50 to 60 bushels as an average crop, and 100 bushels is not an uncommon yield. Fair peanut land properly manured and treated to intelligent rotation of crops should produce in an ordinary season a yield of 50 bushels to the acre and from 1 to 2 tons of excellent hay. (Of course better land with more liberal treatment and a favorable season will produce heavier crops, the reverse being true of lands which have been frequently planted with peanuts without either manuring or rotation of crops.) Besides the amount of peanuts gathered, there are always large quantities left in the ground which have escaped the gathering, and on these the planter turns his herd of hogs, so that there is no waste of any part of the plant."

Tobacco is a paying crop if the soil is just right. Two thousand pounds per acre can be raised on favorable sites. Connecticut tobacco brings, in ordinary times, from twenty to thirty cents a pound; from four to over six hundred dollars being the possible return.

Some Connecticut soils raise Sumatra tobacco equal to the imported crop that sells in this country at fancy prices. The Department of Agriculture claims that the Cuban type of tobacco can be closely approximated in Pennsylvania and Ohio. But it must be remembered that the soil is of paramount importance in tobacco raising. The Department has prepared soil maps of most of the important tobacco districts of the United States. If you think your land may be suited to tobacco, apply there for information. You may make your land invaluable.

D. L. Hartman, *Rural New Yorker,* gave the following facts and figures: "During last season the sales from one acre of early tomatoes amounted to $454, and from a trifle more than two and one half acres, including the acre of 'earlies,' the remainder mid-season and late plantings, the total sales amounted to over $900. From a little less than one acre and a half $555 worth of strawberries were sold, while the returns from early cabbages during the last few years have been at the rate of about $300 per acre. These statements are not made in the spirit of challenge. The results are gratifying to me, because larger than anticipated; but much greater values can be and are produced. In fact, the limit of value that may be grown on an acre of land no one can tell. I have a small plot of ground containing less than one sixth of an acre, planted one year with radishes and lettuce, followed by eggplant and cauliflower, and the next year to radishes alone, followed by egg-plant, and each year the total sales amounted to over $200, at the rate of $1200 per acre. Greatly exceeding even this was a smaller plot, measuring 20 X 65 feet, last year, planted first to pansies, plants sold when in bloom, followed by radishes, of which one half proved to be a worthless variety (it lay idle long enough to have produced another crop of radishes), then half was planted to late lettuce, the other half being sown for winter cabbage, plants yielding no cash return. Yet the total sales for the season from this small plot, less than one thirty-second of an acre, was $86.78 at the rate of the surprising sum of $2780 per acre, and could easily have been raised to the rate of $4,000, and that without the use of any glass whatever, Truly the possibilities of the soil are unknown."

The cooperative features used by Northeastern Long Island intensive farmers are worthy of imitation. In the community of Riverhead a club buys at wholesale rates commodities which the farm and household require. The club does a large business, and has a high rating in the commercial agencies. In another instance at Riverhead an association markets the crop of cauliflower, sending cars of such produce to Cincinnati and Chicago. These are the best forms of cooperation.

"In the market-gardening sections the banks show prosperity. In the towns of Riverhead and Southold there are savings banks with deposits of $4,000,000 each, and five business banks which are doing a thriving business. In this stretch of thirty miles on eastern Long Island the farms are mostly free from encumbrance of any kind.

" It should be noted, however, that their towns have the open Sound with its bays which furnish open ways for transportation and an unowned field for work." (From circular of the Long Island Guild of New York City.)

CHAPTER VII
SOME METHODS

We must not put all our time into one crop unless we are rich enough to do our own insurance; for drought, or damp; or accident, ill-adapted seed, or general unfavorable conditions may make failures of one or more crops. But in variety and succession of crops is safety and profit. In order to succeed, crop must be made to follow crop, so that the ground is used to its full capacity. To leave it fallow for even a week is to invite weeds and to lose much of the advantage of tillage, as well as so much time.

In the North, seeds of many kinds should be sown from the first of March to the first of August; in the South they should be sown m every month.

By following the simple time tables for planting you will find work ready and crops maturing and ready for sale in every month in the year.

There is an admirable table of the time to plant, given in "How to Make a Vegetable Garden," though it does embrace some weird vegetables, explaining, for instance, that pats-choi is used like chards, and that "Scolymus is sowed like Scorzonera."

One can live while waiting for the crops to come up, for many crops mature rapidly.

Specialties give employment only during a few months of each year and bring returns only at periods of the year, but the returns can be made almost immediate and the work almost continuous.

Long Island and Jersey farmers in marketing their crops sell

Spinach and Radishes in April Peas, Early Onions, and Lettuce in May Asparagus and Strawberries in June Tomatoes, Cucumbers, and Cabbage Seeds in July Early Potatoes, Peaches, and Beans in August Onions and Potatoes in September

Celery in October Cauliflower in November Cauliflower and Brussels Sprouts in December Cauliflower and Brussels Sprouts in January Brussels Sprouts in February Brussels Sprouts in March

This order of crops can be varied to suit conditions.

"The old practice of growing vegetables in beds usually entails more labor and expense than the crop is worth; and it has had the effect of driving more than one boy from the farm. These beds always need weeding on Saturdays, holidays, circus days, and the Fourth of July. Even if the available area is only twenty feet wide, the rows should run lengthwise and be far enough apart (from one to two feet for small stuff) to allow of the use of the hand wheelhoes, many of which are very efficient. If land is available for horse tillage, none of the rows should be less than thirty inches apart, and for late growing things, as large cabbage, four feet is better. If the rows are long, it may be necessary to grow two or three kinds of vegetables in the same row; in this case it is important that vegetables requiring the same general treatment and similar length of season be grown together. For example, a row containing parsnips and salsify, or parsnips, salsify, and late carrots would afford an ideal combination; but a row containing parsnips, cabbages, and lettuce would be a very faulty combination. One part of the area should be set aside for all similar crops. For example, all root crops might be grown on one side of the plot, all cabbage crops in the adjoining space, all tomato and eggplant crops in the center, all corn and tall things on the opposite side. Perennnial crops, as asparagus and rhubarb, and gardening structures, as hotbeds and frames, should be on the border, where they will not interfere with the plowing and tilling." ("Principles of Vegetable Gardening," page 31.)

Usually where large acreages are worked there is a tendency to devote a greater portion of tile land to one crop and sometimes a failure in this crop will mean ruin to the farmer, whereas, where small areas are used, there is generally a diversity of the higher-priced crops and a failure in one is not so likely to be disastrous.

To get the greatest production from the soil two crops can be grown in the same soil at the same time--one of which will mature much earlier than the other, thereby giving its place up just about the period of growth when the second crop would need more room. This is known as companion cropping.

"In companion cropping there is a main crop and a secondary crop. Ordinarily the main crop occupies the middle part and later part of the season. The secondary crop matures early in the season, leaving the ground free for the main crop. In some cases the same species is used for both crops, as when late celery is planted between the rows of early celery.

Following are examples of some companion crops:

Radishes with beets or carrots. The radishes can be sold before the beets need the room.

Corn with squashes, citron, pumpkin, or beans in hills. Early onions and cauliflower or cabbage. Horseradish and early cabbage. Lettuce with early cabbage."

("Principles of Vegetable Gardening," page 184.)

If fruit trees be planted, vegetables may be grown in rows. As soon as the early vegetables mature they are removed, and a midsummer crop planted. These are followed by a fall or winter crop.

Radishes, lettuce, and cabbage grow at the same time and on the area formerly used for one crop. Early potatoes and early cauliflower are followed by Brussels sprouts and celery, two crops being as easily grown as one by intelligent handling. The best beans are grown among fruit trees.

The principles of "double-cropping" are summarized by Professor Thomas Shaw, in *The Market Garden.*

"Onion sets may be planted early in the season and onion seeds may then be sown. Between the rows cauliflower may be planted. Later between the cauliflower, two or three cucumber seeds may be dropped. The onion sets up around the cauliflower may be taken out first, and the cauliflowers in turn may be removed in time to let the cucumbers develop.

"Midway between the rows of onions grown from seeds, we can plant radishes, lettuce, peppergrass, spinach, or some other early relish, which will have ample time to grow and to be consumed before harm can come to the onions from the shade of any one of these crops. When the onions are well grown, turnips can be sown midway between their rows."

So we get two crops of onions, besides cauliflowers, cucumbers, and turnips off the same place. Weeds won't have much chance in soil treated like that.

"Multum in Parvo Gardening" (Samuel Wood) claims L 620 ($3100) from one acre by the expenditure of considerable capital in growing fruit against brick walls--it cost over $3100 to prepare the land, of which the walls cost $2300. In this system the fruit trees are pruned and trained till they look like firemen's ladders.

"In the suburbs of Paris, even without such costly things with only thirty-six yards of frames for seedlings, vegetables are grown in the open air to the value of L 200 per acre." ("Fields, Factories and Workshops," page 80.)

"At the present time, for fully 100 miles along the Rhone, and in the lateral valleys of the Ardeche and the Drome, the country is an admirable orchard, from which millions worth of fruit is exported, and the land attains the selling price of from L 325 ($1625) to L 400 ($2000) the acre. Small plots of land are continually reclaimed for culture upon every crag." (Same, page 133.)

In California we hear (from George P. Keeney) that while good truck and fruit lands usually sell for $25 to $350 per acre, the land with full-bearing fruit or nut trees often sells at $1000, and even up to $2000 per acre. There is no reason why any intelligent persons should not make their land increase in the same way.

The London Daily News reports that in one year, which was not a good season for all crops, on a half acre of land, Mr. Henry Vincent, of Brighton, England, raised the following products:

2660 cabbages, 70 bushels spinach, 950 cauliflowers, parsley, 1460 lettuces, 660 broccoli, 16 bushels potatoes, 19-1/4 bushels Brussels sprouts, 106-1/2 gallons peas, 120 gallons artichokes, flowers, 267 vegetable marrows, 2976 carrots, 264 bundles radishes, 14 gallons French beans, 12 gallons currants' 95-1/2 punnets mustard, 27 pounds mushrooms, rhubarb, 948 bushels sprout tops, 38 dozen leeks, 1150 plants, 11-1/4 gallons broad beans, 97 bundles sea-kale, 978 bundles of asparagus-kale, 504 beet roots, 2913 gallons gooseberries, 219 bundles mint, 20 bundles sage, 18 bundles of fennel, thyme, besides one cartload of stones.

Mr. Vincent explains how he came to go into intensive cultivation: "A few years ago the doctors said if I did not go out more I could not live. Very well, just at that time there was an outcry about the land not paying for cultivation. I could not understand this, for as a boy at seven years of age I had to go out to farm work, therefore I never went to school. Anyhow I thought something was very wrong if the land would not pay; so, to compel myself to go out in the fresh air, I took an allotment on the Sussex Downs to work in the early morning before my daily duties began. I might say that I am a waiter, and have been in my present situation forty years, so you can understand I could not know much of land or garden work I could not see my way clear in the few spare hours I get to take more than half an acre of land to garden early, especially as I started knowing practically nothing about such work, but I can manage to do my half acre all alone.

"My garden is situated on the Brighton Race Hill ridge, and twelve years ago it was but four inches of soil on chalk, but I now have a foot of soil on the whole of the half acre, and year by year my profits increase.

"Yes, get the men to stop on the land in this country. We ought not to have workhouses. Every man could live, and live well, if he could get the land, and would work it as it should be worked.

"Farmers and landowners grumble because the land does not pay. Now for the fault. It is quite evident it is not the land, therefore, it must be the fault of the man. Very well, get the land from these landed proprietors, by sale preferred, and let it out to men, not by 1000 acres, as no man can farm well a thousand acres in England; let the farms be greatly reduced, and then the land can be treated as it should be. Most of us have children, and we all know how we love and treat them. Treat the land in the same manner, feed it, and keep it clean, and you will have no cause to complain. The land of old England is as good as it ever was.

"I have serious thoughts of opening a kind of school for people who would like to make $500 a year on an acre. It is to be done, and done easily. I do know that one man alone can manage two acres, and at the end of this year I shall be able to tell how much more he can manage alone, so under my system one can gain L 4 a week off two acres and do all one's self.

"If the land will produce over one hundred pounds per year per acre, is it not wrong for a man to have, say, 500 or 1000 acres which in no way can he properly manage; as, in the first place, he cannot feed such an acreage, let alone keep it clean and gather in his crops?"

In truth, what an acre may produce depends on time, place, and circumstances The product of the best acre of land so situated that its product could be sold at retail in a near-by market, and which has been cultivated under the best management for a term of years, would provide a very comfortable living. The product of other acres, measured by what they produce to the cultivator in living, declines through various grades down to almost nothing on the acre far from railroads or difficult of access.

While in quantity and quality the least favored acre could be made to produce as much as one best situated, yet, almost none of its production would be available to sell, while the product of the favorably located acre could be sold as rapidly as grown.

CHAPTER VIII
THE KITCHEN GARDEN

The aim of the kitchen garden is to provide an abundance and variety of food for the family. As the object of the cultivator is to get the largest product for his labor, he ought to produce all that he can consume on the least possible area. Though one may go into mushrooms or frog raising as a money crop, the kitchen garden is the first indispensable and should first be given attention.

For a garden choose a piece of land with a southern exposure, sheltered on the north and west by woods, buildings, hedge, or any kind of a windbreak. This arrangement will give the earliest garden, for it gets all the sun there is. By running the rows north and south, the rays of the sun strike the eastern side of the row in the morning, and the western side in the afternoon.

The best time to take hold of a piece of land is in the fall, because then it can be plowed ready for the spring planting. The alternate freezing and thawing during the winter breaks up the sod and the stiff lumps thrown up by the plow, so rendering the soil pliable and easily worked. This is especially true of land that has been reclaimed from the forest, or which has not been farmed for many years.

Before the plowing is done, the land for the garden should be manured at the rate of twenty-five large wagon loads to the acre. If you can get a suitable plot that has been in red clover, alfalfa, soy beans, or cowpeas for a number of years, so much the better. These plants have on their roots nitrogen-fixing bacteria, which draw nitrogen from the air. Nitrogen is the great meat-maker and forces a prolonged and rapid growth of all vegetables.

After manuring and plowing, harrow repeatedly with a disk or cutaway harrow until the soil is as fine as dust. Then you have a seed bed which will give the fine roots a chance to grow as soon as the seeds sprout. Too much stress cannot be laid upon the importance of thoroughly working the soil at this time. Every stone, weed, or clod that is left in the soil destroys to that extent the source from which the plants can get their food.

A quarter-acre garden, which is big enough to supply the whole family with a succession of vegetables for summer and fall, as well as some potatoes and turnips for winter, will take a diligent workman about four days to dig over and three days to plant. The four days' work of digging will need to be done only once. The time spent upon planting succession crops will depend upon the amount of the garden reserved for rotation. The part kept for lettuce, radishes, spinach, beets, Swiss chard, peas, string and wax beans may be digged over in a favorable season for three successive plantings, while the part devoted to early potatoes would need to be digged only twice--once when the planting is done, and again when crop is gathered and the ground be prepared for a crop of late cabbage or turnips. A planting table for vegetables, which is complete and comprehensive, is distributed free by the National Emergency Food Garden Commission at Washington, D.C.

It is far more important to plant seeds at the proper depth than that they should be planted thinly or thickly, for if they are planted too thin, it makes a sort of advantage by giving the individual plants ample room to develop to large size; and if planted too thick, the evil can easily be remedied by thinning or transplanting.

After the seeds come up, the size of almost all the vegetables can be increased by transplanting, in favorable soil, which gives each plant room for complete development.

It is too expensive to risk part of the land being unused or half used on account of seeds dying, or to put in so many seeds in order to insure growth that they will crowd one another. Where possible, therefore, seeds should be sprouted and planted, not "sown."

Lima beans planted on edge with eye down will come up much sooner than if dropped in carelessly so they have to turn themselves over. In a small garden the time saved by such planting will repay the extra trouble.

In some things like onions and radishes, however, it is better to sow them thick, and then thin them out, so as to get the effect of transplanting without so much labor. In others, like lettuce and all the salad plants, transplanting gives new life and energy and develops the individual plants in a way that will astonish those not familiar with what free development means.

It is wise to plant corn after lettuce and radishes are gathered, and more lettuce, corn, or salad, after the beans are picked. Then late crops, cabbage, cauliflower or spinach, can go where early corn grew, so that the small patch may earn your living and pay big dividends.

Do not let two vegetables of the same botanical family follow each other. For instance, lima beans should not follow green beans or peas, as all the family draw about the same elements from the soil, and are likely to have the same insects and diseases.

Do not plant cucumbers, squash, or pumpkins too near each other, as they will often inter-impregnate and produce uneatable hybrids.

Decide what you are going to do with your crop before you plant it, whether to sell it, at wholesale or at retail, to eat it, or to feed it to stock.

C. E. Hunn, in the Garden Magazine, gives the following arrangement: "For the beginner who wants to get fresh vegetables and fruits from May until midwinter, a space 100 X 200 feet is enough.

"1. Plant in rows, not beds, and avoid the backache.

"2. Plant vegetables that mature at the same time near one another.

"3. Plant vegetables of the same height near together--tall ones back.

"4. Run the rows the short way, for convenience in cultivation and because one hundred feet of anything is enough.

"5. Put the permanent vegetables (asparagus, rhubarb, sweet herbs) at one side, so that the rest will be easy to plow.

"6. Practice rotation. Do not put vines where they were last. Put corn in a different place. The other important groups for rotation are root crops (including potatoes and onions); cabbage tribe, peas and beans, tomatoes, eggplant and pepper, salad plants.

"7. Don't grow potatoes in a small garden. They aren't worth the bother.

"By training on trellis or wire, the smaller fruit plantings can be made much closer.

"If fruits are wanted in the garden, plant a row of apple trees along the northern border, plums and pears on the western sides, cherries and peaches on the eastern side. Next the apple trees run a grape trellis; and then in succession east and west, run a row of blackberries, raspberries, gooseberries, and currants. These rows, with the apple trees, form a windbreak, and besides adding to the income, protect the vegetables. Next to the bush fruits, between them and the ends of the vegetable rows, put rhubarb, asparagus, and strawberries."

Insect pests must be watched for and their destructive work checked. Ashes, slaked lime, or any kind of dust or powder destroy most insects which prey on the leaves of plants. The reason for this is that the dust closes the pores through which the insects breathe. It should therefore be applied when the leaves are dry.

Cutworms can be destroyed by winter plowing. Rotation of vegetables will reduce the damage from insects, because each family has its peculiar bugs. By constant change to new soil, the pests have no opportunity to get a foothold.

With bugs, as with boys, only those who are interested in them and therefore understand them can manage them. It is fun to study the insects--and it pays.

Here's another use of "land." Maybe a pool in your garden or a dam in a little brook in it may help out your home garden bank account. Of course a pond a few square yards in extent will give even better returns if you can sell its produce at retail near by.

W. B. Shaw, a seventy-year-old veteran who lost his right arm during the Civil War, lives in Kenilworth, D. C., and clears $1500 an acre every year out of mud puddles--if mud puddles can be measured by the acre.

Mr. Shaw is a pond lily farmer, and despite his lack of his good right arm, he poles his boat about his mud puddles and gathers in the pond lilies. His is not exactly a "dry farm" and neither wet nor cloudy weather bothers him. Furthermore, the demand for his pond lilies in Baltimore, Washington, Philadelphia, and even New York, and Chicago, is greater than he can supply.

Mr. Shaw secured this swamp for almost nothing, as it was considered worthless. He divided it into fifteen pools with little dams between them, and rollers on the dams to enable him to drag his boat from one to the other. From May to late in September he is busy every morning gathering lilies. His average is about 500 a morning, which he ships in little galvanized iron tanks with wet moss.

Many school children know how to get results on a little land. Mr. Mahoney, Superintendent of the Fairview Garden School, Yonkers, New York, estimates that the total value of produce grown on the 250 gardens, composing the school plot, in all about one and one quarter acres of land, was $1308, or at the rate of more than a thousand dollars per acre. When it is taken into consideration that all the labor was done by boys ranging in age from eight to twelve years, this result is truly astonishing.

What may not adult skilled labor produce when applied freely to the land.

CHAPTER IX
TOOLS AND EQUIPMENT--SPECIALIZED CROPS

To subdue the land with an ax, a plow and a spade is possible; millions of acres have been so subdued. This method, however, is the most expensive of all, as in our times, markets won't wait, and the man who wants to get on must produce as quickly as possible. To do so, he must have the best tools. They will pay for themselves many times over in a single year. For the farm, the following list, in addition to a well-stocked tool chest (hammer, saw, plane, ax, etc.) covers the indispensible:

1 team horses (these may be hired) $200.00 1 walking plow 10.00 1 disk or cutaway harrow 25.00 1 farm wagon 50.00 1 cultivator (two horse) 25.00 1 one-horse cultivator 8.00 Shovels, pick, mattock or grubbing hoe 10.00 Work harness for two horses 25.00

TOTAL $353.00

These things you must have to get the land in proper shape for seeds or plants; but special crops require special tools. A scythe is good to keep weeds away from fences. A sickle is handy to keep down grass. To reduce living expenses, a cow for $60, and fifty hens at fifty cents each, say $25, will supply a large family with milk and eggs. Most people make the mistake of buying too many things and these poorly selected. It is better to have too few tools than too many, for tools are often dropped where last used, and so are lost. Then if money is scarce, you may not be able to make a shelter for your machines and tools, and they will rust through the winter. Many farmers, through neglect, have to replace their tool equipment every four or five years, but with attention and care, the original equipment, even to the team, ought still to be in use twenty years after their purchase. I know many instances where this is true. The above equipment is the minimum for beginning work. The character of additions to it will depend much upon the crops which you select as the money getters.

For general market gardening and the kitchen garden too, the following tool list, together with the above, will include everything absolutely necessary.

Wheel hoe $6.00 Spade and fork, each $1.00 2.00 Push hoe .65 Watering can .60 Rake and common hoe 1.00 Bulb sprayer .25 Trowel .10

TOTAL $10.60

The wheel hoe is a great saver--of backache, especially to the beginner; as Warner says, "at the best you will conclude that for gardening purposes a cast-iron back with a hinge in it is preferable to the ones now in use."

The dibble, an old tool handle, or a bit of broomstick sharpened, and garden lines to get the rows straight, labels, tomato supports, plant protectors and stakes earl all be homemade out of old material. The full outfit would include the following:

Roller $8.00 Wheel-hoe with seeder 8.50 Sprayer 3.75 Wheelbarrow 4.00 Crowbar 1.50 Weeder .35

For such crops as admit of horse cultivation a horse hoe will save a great deal of time.

The weeder is a cousin to the push hoe and has a zigzag blade for cutting off young weeds which are just starting above ground. It is pushed backward and forward and cuts both ways. It is very good for soft ground; on a harder patch use the push hoe.

A market garden is really a big kitchen garden, from which the cultivator supplies not only his own family, but his neighbors, the public. To run a successful market garden for profit, land suitably situated near transportation and markets, a large supply of stable manure, hotbeds for raising plants, crates for shipping, wagons for delivering, and a complete outfit of tools are necessary. You must raise all sorts of vegetables and salad plants in quantities sufficiently large to justify you in giving your whole time to the work. An acre devoted to general market gardening could be attended to by two men with some extra help for marketing.

To get a place fully established on new, rich land requires two or three years. On worn-out land it would take longer to build it up to the high fertility needed for maximum production. Crops like asparagus and rhubarb take two years to establish on a remunerative basis. If bush fruits are raised, three years are required to get maximum results. So in starting, land should be bought outright or leased for ten years.

In market gardening for profit, one acre might be devoted to vegetables, one acre to small fruits; strawberries, raspberries, blackberries, currants, gooseberries, etc. and one acre kept for buildings, poultry, etc. An energetic man could clear one thousand dollars a year besides his living, after he got a start, and be absolutely independent; that is, unless some predatory railroad corporation could confiscate his profits before his product reached the market.

Some persons are just naturally so successful with plants that if they stuck an umbrella in the ground we should expect to see it blossom out into parasols--but they don't know why it does, and they can't teach any one else how to do it.

Any fool can sneer at "book farming" or at anything else, but you can hardly succeed without the best books by practical men. Do not let some experienced ignoramus talk you out of experimenting under their guidance. You will learn little without experience, and unless you have the grower's instinct, you will learn less without books.

Don't be hypnotized by long experience or by success. Hardly anybody knows his own business. You must have noticed that few of the people you buy of or sell to, know any more of their goods than you do.

It is just the same with trades. Hardly a barber knows that he should not shave you against the grain of the skin. Even the cat won't stand being rubbed up the wrong way; but the barber never thought of that.

We lawyers and the doctors are supposed to be thorough in our own field--I said lately to one of the ablest men at the New York Bar, "About one lawyer in a hundred knows his business." He said, "That is a gross overestimate." Shortly after I talked with three Judges, one of the City Court, one of the Supreme Court, and one of the United States Circuit, and they each agreed that my friend's remark was about true, and that in most cases litigants would do as well without lawyers as with them.

If that is true, what chance is there that an uneducated man who has "raised garden sass ever since he was a boy, and seen his father do it before him," can teach you correctly?

Men learn very slowly by experience, because no two experiences are exactly alike, unless they perceive and apply the principles under the experience.

An intelligent man accustomed to investigation can learn more about a specialty in a week's study than an untrained practitioner can believe in a year.

What the untrained teacher can tell us is of little account; what he shows us is another matter.

Therefore get help who know that they don't know anything about a garden and who consequently will do with a will exactly what you tell them to do; such labor is cheap--why should you pay extravagant prices for skill to a man who has succeeded so poorly that he can only earn day's wages? You can get much better knowledge at less cost from a book. Study and put your knowledge into practice yourself, where you see promise of a profit.

Almost every crop can be made a specialty. In proportion as special crops are profitable when conditions are right, so are they sources of loss when things go wrong. If, after your first season in the country, some special crop takes your fancy, give extra space and time to it the second year and see if you are successful in handling an eighth or a quarter acre. If so, you may extend your operations as rapidly as purse and market permit.

Before concentrating upon any crop as the chief source of income, a careful study must be made of all the conditions surrounding its production; a crop is not produced in the broad meaning of that term until it is actually in the hands of the consumer.

Potatoes, for instance, are grown by the hundred acres in sections adapted to their growth, and special machinery costing hundreds of dollars is used in planting, cultivating, and harvesting the crop. The good shipping and keeping qualities of the potato enable it to be raised far from markets and so brings into competition cheap land worked in large areas, with large capital. In spite of this, however, the small cultivator can usually make money if he can sell his potatoes directly to the consumer.

If your land is so situated that you can put your individuality into the crop and can control all the circumstances, preparation of land, planting, cultivation, harvesting, and marketing, your chances of success are immeasurably increased. As soon as any important part must be trusted to some one beyond your control, danger arises. Assiduous care in planting, cultivating, and packing will avail nothing if the product falls into the hands of transportation companies or commission merchants indifferent as to what becomes of it. It is therefore better to be quite independent, sell your own crop, and have the whole operation in your own hands from the very beginning.

Generally speaking, seed growing for the market is a highly developed special business which is usually carried on by companies operating with large capital, able to employ the best experts, and to avail themselves of all the advantages of scientific methods in culture, regardless of expense. So uncertain is the business, that even with all these facilities, they rarely guarantee seeds. It is obvious that the amateur has little chance of succeeding in such a difficult business. Nevertheless, he will be able after a few seasons of increasing experience to gather seeds from selected plants and so furnish his own supply. It must be borne in mind, however, that plants can be improved by cross breeding and that by keeping a variety too long on the same ground its quality deteriorates, and the plant tends to revert to the type natural to it before domestication.

When land is cropped every season, the nitrogen, potash, and phosphorus removed from the soil must be replaced in some form, otherwise you have diminishing returns, while the expense for labor is the same. In farming small areas for specialties you cannot easily invoke the principle of rotation by enriching the land with legumes, to be plowed under while green, the bacteria on the roots of which gather nitrogen from the air, but you must get stable manure or buy chemical fertilizers to maintain the fertility.

Special crops divide themselves naturally into two classes: those raised for immediate shipment to market, and those to be hauled to canneries. The first type are generally prepared in a more expensive way, and need more care and attention. Each class requires its own special forms of packing to conform to market peculiarities fixed by the taste of consumers.

For the cultivation of all specialties, many items of preparation are identical. Land must be well drained, it must contain a sufficient amount of humus, or decaying vegetable matter, to make it loose and porous; it must be free from sticks and stones or any foreign matter likely to impede cultivation or obstruct growth. The proper formation of a seed bed is a prime prerequisite to successful cropping. After the land is manured and plowed it should be gone over in all directions with a disk and smoothing harrow, until it is of a dustlike fineness.

In thorough cultivation before the crop is planted, lies the secret of many a success, and in its neglect the cause of many failures. Intelligent handling of crops is in a large measure knowledge of the influence of wind and rain, sunshine and darkness, on the particular nature of the plant Delicate plants, for example, ought to be grown where buildings or forests break the force of prevailing winds. Sheltered valleys in irrigated sections have proved the best for intensive cultivation. For thousands of years in China and Japan the conditions of successful intensive cultivation have been well understood, and to-day the most efficient gardeners are the Chinese. In some parts of Mexico, for the same reasons, intensive cultivation has reached a high development. In our own West we are catching up on vegetables and fruits.

CHAPTER X
THE ADVANTAGES FROM CAPITAL

We have seen what a worker with very little money can do and how he can succeed. A small capital, however, can be used to increase the returns to as great advantage on a small farm as large capital can be used on a large farm and with much less risk.

Stable manure is still the favorite article with the masses of gardeners. One ton of ordinary stable manure contains about 1275 pounds of organic matter, carrying eight pounds of nitrogen, ten pounds of potash, and four pounds of phosphoric acid.

When thoroughly rotted, the manure acquires a still larger percentage of plant food; it is more valuable, not only for that reason, but also on account of its immediate availability. Further, the mechanical effect of this manure in opening and loosening the soil, allowing air and warmth to enter more freely, adds greatly to its value.

It is easily gotten and often goes wholly or in part to waste. On the outskirts of some towns may be seen a collection of manure piles that have been hauled out and dumped in waste places. The plant food in each ton of this manure is worth at least two dollars--that is the least Eastern farmers pay for similar material, and they make money doing it. Yet almost every liveryman has to pay some one for hauling the manure away. This is simply because farmers living near these towns are missing a chance to secure something for nothing--because, perhaps, the profit is not directly in sight. But from most soils there is a handsome profit possible from a very small application of stable manure.

While writing this, I saw a man in New Rochelle, N. Y.; dumping a load of street sweepings into a hole in a vacant lot. It would have been less wasteful to have dumped a bushel of potatoes into the hole.

Commercial fertilizers are coming more and more in use by market gardeners, and with reason. If we examine a good fertilizer, analyzing five per cent available nitrogen, six per cent phosphoric acid, and 8 per cent potash, we shall find that one ton of it contains, besides less valuable ingredients: 100 lb. nitrogen, 120 lb. phosphoric acid, 160 lb. potash.

Such fertilizers probably retail at forty to sixty dollars per ton, and are fully worth it. All this plant food, and perhaps one half more, can be drawn in a single load, while it will take ten such loads of stable manure to supply the same amount of plant food.

There is no reason to be afraid of too much fertilizer, provided it is evenly distributed and thoroughly mixed through properly prepared soil. Stinginess in this item is poor economy.

Nitrogen is the most essential food for plant growth. It is an important element of plant food in manure. In ordinary manure most of the value is due to the nitrogen, although phosphoric acid and potash are also present. It is found in the most available form in nitrate of soda. Nitrate of soda will benefit all crops, but it does not follow that it will pay to use it on all crops. Its cost makes it unprofitable to use on cheap crops; but on those that yield a large return nitrate of soda is a very profitable investment.

"It is shown in the experiments conducted with nitrate of soda on different crops that in the case of grain and forage crops, which utilized the nitrate quite as completely as the market garden crops, the increased value of crops due to nitrate does not in any case exceed $14 per acre, or a money return at the rate of $8.50 per 100 pounds of nitrate used, while in the case of the market-garden crops the value of the increased yield reaches, in the case of one crop, the high figure of over $263 per acre, or at the rate of about $66 per 100 pounds of nitrate." (New Jersey Agricultural Experiment Stations, page 8, No. 172.)

Professor Voorhees, of the same station, experimented with tomatoes, with these results:

Manure and Fertilizer Used Cost Per Acre Value of Crop

No manure $271.88 30 tons barnyard manure $30.00 291.75 8 tons manure and 400 lb. fertilizer 15.00 317.63 160 pounds nitrate of soda alone 4.00 361.13

Such common crops as tomatoes, cabbage, turnips, beets, etc., in order to be highly profitable, must be grown and harvested early; any one can grow them in their regular season; their growth must be promoted or forced as much as possible, at the time when the natural agencies are not active in the change of soil nitrogen into available forms, and the plants must, therefore, be supplied artificially with the active forms of nitrogen, if a rapid and continuous growth is to be maintained.

It is quite possible to have a return of $50 per acre from the use of $5 worth of nitrate of soda on crops of high value, as, for example, early tomatoes, beets, cabbage, etc. This is an extraordinary return for the money and labor invested; still, if the increased value of the crop were but $10, or even $8, it would be a profitable investment, since no more land and but little additional capital was required in order to obtain the extra $5 or $8 per acre.

The results of all the experiments conducted in different parts of the country and in different seasons, show an average gain in yield of early tomatoes of about fifty per cent, with an average increased value of crop of about $100 per acre. The rest of the report shows similar results with other crops. (New Jersey Agricultural Experiment Station, Bulletin 172.)

Joseph Harris says, "Some years ego we used nitrate of soda cautiously as a top dressing on the celery plants. The effect was astonishing. The next year, having more confidence, we spread the nitrate at the time we sowed the seed, and again after the plant came up, and twice afterward during a rain.

"Instead of finding it difficult to get the plants early enough for the celery growers who set them out, they were ready three weeks before tile usual time of transplanting.

"At the four applications, we probably used 1600 lb. of nitrate of soda per acre, and this would probably furnish more nitric acid to the plants than they could get from five hundred tons of manure per acre, provided it had been possible to have worked such a quantity into the soil. Never were finer plants grown. As compared with the increased value of the plants, the cost of the nitrate is not worth taking into consideration."

As a means of fertilization without the use of artificial fertilizer, soil inoculation has come. It has grown out of the discovery of the dependence of leguminous plants on bacteria which live on their roots. The discovery is one of the most important of those made in modern agriculture.

It has received its greatest impetus in America, under the experiments of Professor Moore of the United States Agricultural Department.

The Department supplied free to farmers the bacteria for inoculation. Now they supply it only for experimental purposes. A laboratory has been fitted up for the work. The method is to propagate bacteria for each of the various leguminous plants such as clover, alfalfa, soy beans, cow peas, tares, and velvet beans. All of these plants are of incalculable value in different sections of the country as forage for farm animals. In the West, alfalfa is the main reliance for stockraisers. The farmers of the East are trying to establish it, but meet with difficulty chiefly for want of the special bacteria which should be found on the roots.

The function of these bacteria is to gather the nitrogen of the air and supply it as plant food. Without the bacteria the plant can get only the nitrogen which is supplied from the soil in fertilizers. With the aid of the bacteria the growing plant can derive the greater part of its food from the air.

Here is one of the results of the use of inoculated seed as reported by the United States Agricultural Bulletin No. 214.

G. L. Thomas, experimenting with field peas on his farm near Auburn, Me., made a special test with fertilized and unfertilized strips, and stated that "inoculated seed did as much without fertilizers of any kind, as uninoculated seed supplied with fertilizer (phosphate) at the rate of 800 pounds and a ton of barnyard manure per acre."

This seems to be only in its infancy. The Department warns us that nitrogen inoculation is useless where the soil already has enough nitrogen and where other plant foods are absent.

The experiments are most important, and we are probably on the eve of as great advances in agriculture as in electricity, but the human race has a great love for "inoculation," and indeed for all unnatural processes.

You remember the story of the wonderful coon that Chandler Harris tells? No? They were constantly seeing this enormous coon, but always just as they almost got their hands on him, he disappeared. One night the boys came running in to say that the wonderful coon was up in a persimmon tree in the middle of a ten-acre lot; so they got the dogs and the lanterns and guns and ran out, and sure enough they saw the wonderful big coon up in a fork of the tree. It was a bright moonlight night, but to make doubly sure they cut down the tree and the dogs ran in--the coon wasn't there.

"Well, but, Uncle Remus," said the little boy, "I thought you said you saw the coon there."

" So we did, Honey," said the old man, "so we did; but it's very easy to see what ain't there when you're looking for it."

Another method of increasing fertility at increased expense deserves notice. The vacant public lands are for the most part desert-like, and their utilization can come about only through irrigation.

This land can be made to produce the finest crops in the world; and the tremendous volumes of water that flow from the mountains to the sea, once harnessed and piped or ditched to this land, will transform it into beautiful gardens and farms.

With the work being done by the United States Government, and that of the various states, we may look forward in the not distant future to this land being made habitable to man.

It is well known that with the dry, even climate and with an abundance of water applied as vegetation needs, this now arid waste is far more productive than the Eastern states, where the crops are at the mercy of the elements, sometimes having too much moisture and at other times not having enough.

"Irrigation offers control of conditions such as is found nowhere except in greenhouse culture. The farmer in the humid country cannot control the amount of starch in potatoes, sugar in beets, protein in corn, gluten in wheat, except by planting varieties which are especially adapted to the production of the desired quality. The irrigation farmer, on the other hand, can produce this or that desirable quality by the control of the moisture supply to the plant. He can hasten or retard maturity of the plant, produce early truck or late truck on the same soil, grow wheat or grow rice as he deems advisable."

"On the irrigated fields of the Vosges, Vaucluse, etc., in France, six tons of dry hay becomes the rule, even upon ungrateful soil; and this means considerably more than the annual food of one milch cow (which can be taken as a little less than five tons) grown on each acre."

"The irrigated meadows round Milan are another well known example. Nearly

22,000 acres are irrigated there with water derived from the sewers of the city, and they yield crops of from eight to ten tons of hay as a rule; occasionally some separate meadows will yield the fabulous amount--fabulous to-day but no longer fabulous to-morrow--of eighteen tons of hay per acre; that is, the food of nearly four cows to the acre, and nine times the yield of good meadows in this country." ("Fields, Factories, and Workshops," pages 116-117.)

" If irrigation pays "--and no one now questions that--"the whole Western country of rich soil, which asks but a drink now and then, will be turned into a Garden of Eden." (Maxwell's Talisman.)

Agriculture may be revolutionized with the advent of irrigation.

A new method of disposing of sewage and at the same time irrigating the soil, has come into use recently, and will be found valuable to those who are situated so that they can make use of it.

The sewage from buildings is drained into a large tank where the heavier matter can settle to the bottom. When the water rises nearly to the top of the tank it is siphoned into another tank, and from there it is piped about the field.

The piping is very simple--ordinary drain tile conveys the water. Beginning at the highest point of the field to be irrigated, a six-inch (or larger) line of tile should be laid along the highest ground with a fall of not over one inch to each ten feet. From this main trunk should be branch lines of "laterals," laid from eight to twelve feet apart, as they would be laid for draining a field. These branch lines may be laid at an angle to the main trunk as may be most convenient; all the joints must be covered so as to keep out the flirt. The whole system should be laid deep enough in the ground to be secure from frost; but to be most effective it should not be over fourteen to sixteen inches below the surface, hence sub-irrigation cannot be used very successfully in the Northern states. In a sandy loam soil with a clay subsoil it works best at sixteen to twenty-four inches.

This is substantially Colonel Waring's method of sewage disposal. To get the best use of it for plants, the water should be assembled and kept in the sun for ten to twelve days, then turned into the pipes until the ground is well soaked, and then shut off and not allowed in the pipes again for ten to fifteen days, according to the weather and condition of moisture in the soil. The crop should be cultivated between each watering.

However, as Bailey says, "Evidently in all regions in which crops will yield abundantly without irrigation, as in the East, the main reliance is to be placed on good tillage."

"Most vegetable gardeners in the East do not find it profitable to irrigate. Now and then a man who has push and the ability to handle a fine crop to advantage, finds it a very profitable undertaking." ("Principles of Vegetable Gardening," page 174.) Bailey, however, was not thinking of "overhead irrigation."

The late J. M. Smith, Green Bay, Wisconsin, was one of the expert market gardeners of his region. "The longer I live," wrote Mr. Smith, then in the midst of a serious drought, "the more firmly am I convinced that plenty of manure and then the most complete system of cultivation make an almost complete protection against ordinary droughts." (Same, page 330.)

If the soil is cultivated carefully and intensively, it will hold water within itself and carry a storage reservoir underneath the growing crop. Finely pulverizing and packing the seed bed, makes it retain the greatest possible percentage of the moisture that falls, just as a tumbler full of fine sponge or of birdshot will retain many times the amount of water that a tumbler full of buckshot will. The atmosphere quickly drinks up the moisture from the soil unless we Prevent it. This we do by means of a soil "blanket," called a "mulch" This finely pulverized surface largely prevents the moisture below from evaporating, and at the same time keeps the surface in such condition that it readily absorbs the dew and the showers. Water moves in the soil as it does in a lamp wick, by capillary attraction; the more deeply and densely the soil is saturated with moisture, the more easily the water moves upward, just as oil "climbs up" a wet wick faster than it does a dry one. One can illustrate the effect of this fine soil "mulch" in preventing evaporation by placing some powdered sugar on a lump of loaf sugar and putting the lump sugar in water. The powdered sugar will remain dry even when the lump has become so thoroughly saturated that it crumbles to pieces.

"We have no useless American acres," said Secretary Wilson. "We shall make them all productive. We have agricultural explorers in every far corner of the world; and they are finding crops which have become so acclimated to dry conditions, similar to our own West, that we shall in time have plants thriving upon our so-called arid lands. We shall cover this arid area with plants of various sorts which will yield hundreds of millions of tons of additional forage and grains for Western flocks and herds. Our farmers will grow these upon land now considered practically worthless."

In this way it has been estimated that in the neighborhood of one hundred million acres of the American desert can be reclaimed to the most intensive agriculture. (See a study of the possible additions to available land in Prof. W. S. Thompson's "Population, a Study of Malthusianism": Col. U, 1915.) Frederick V. Coville, the chief botanist of the Department of Agriculture, does not hesitate to say that in the strictly arid regions there are many millions of acres, now considered worthless for agriculture, which are as certain to be settled in small farms as were the lands of Illinois.

Land that was thought to be absolute desert has been made to yield heavy crops of grain and forage by this method without irrigation.

Macaroni wheat will grow with ten inches of rainfall, and yield fifteen bushels to the acre. This however is less than the average wheat yield in the United States.

Much can be done by dry farming; that is, by plowing the soil very deep and cultivating six or eight times a season, thus retaining all the moisture for the crops and reducing evaporation to a minimum.

There are thousands of acres in different sections of Montana that grow good crops without irrigation. In Fergus County, for instance, the wonderful yield of 45 bushels of wheat per acre is grown without irrigation. Heavy crops of grain and vegetables are grown in the vicinity of Great Falls by the dry farming system.

The money and time spent in spraying is also well invested. The New York Agricultural Experiment Station began a ten-year experiment in potato-spraying to determine how much the yield can be increased by spraying with Pyrox or with Bordeaux mixture.

In 1904 the gain due to spraying was larger than ever before. Five sprayings with Bordeaux increased the yield 233 bushels per acre, while three sprayings increased it 191 bushels. The gain was due chiefly to the prolongation of growth through the prevention of late blight. The sprayed potatoes contained one ninth more starch and were of better quality.

The average increase of profit per acre from spraying potatoes was figured to be about $22 on each acre. The result was arrived at from experiment, two thirds of which was by independent farmers. (Particulars will be found In Bulletin No. 264, issued by the Department.)

In fourteen farmers' business experiments, including 18 acres of potatoes, the average gain due to spraying was 62-1/2 bushels per acre, the average total cost of spraying 93 cents per acre; and the average net profit, based on the market price of potatoes at digging time, $24.86 per acre.

"One class of gardeners," Burnet Landreth explains, "may be termed experimental farmers, men tired of the humdrum rotation of farm processes and small profits, men looking for a paying diversification of their agricultural interests. Their expenses for appliances are not great, as they have already on hand the usual stock of farm tools, requiring only one or two seed drills, a small addition to their cultivating implements, and a few tons of fertilizers. Their laborers and teams are always on hand for the working of moderate areas. In addition to the usual expense of the farm, they would not need to have a cash capital of beyond 20 to 25 dollars per acre for the area in truck."

"Other men, purchasing or renting land, especially for market gardening, taking only improved land of suitable aspect, soil, and situation, and counting in cost of building, appliances, and labor, would require a capital of $80 to $100 per acre. For example, a beginner in market gardening in South Jersey, on a five-acre patch, would need $500 to set up the business, and run it until his shipments began to return him money. With the purpose of securing information on this interesting point, the writer asked for estimates from market gardeners in different localities, and the result has been that from Florida the reports of the necessary capital per acre, in land or its rental (not of labor), fertilizers, tools, implements, seed and all the appliances, average $95, from Texas $45, from Illinois $70, from the Norfolk district of Virginia the reports vary from $75 to $125, according to location, and from Long Island, New York, the average of estimates at the east end is $75, and at the west end $150."

I have before me now one of the roseate advertisements, which we so often see in the newspapers, telling how fortunes can be made by investing a few dollars in a tropical plantation in Mexico.

It gives what are supposed to be startling yields per acre, and yet the returns, which must necessarily be taken with considerable allowance, are only from $580 to $1087 per acre on various plantations.

There are market gardeners and nurserymen near New York City who are making their acres produce better returns than this. It is not necessary to go off into the tropical wilderness seeking a fortune which is usually a gold brick that some fellow is trying to sell you, when as good results can be secured right at home.

Market gardeners in and near Philadelphia pay $25 to $50 an acre and upwards rent for land, and work from five to forty acres. This is as much as similar land in many parts of the country could be bought for. But it is not a high rent when they are right at the market--one man makes the round trip in two and one half hours--manure costs them nothing--for years they have been using the excavations from the old style privy wells, which has been hauled to their farm and deposited where they wished it, free. They have modern facilities, such as trolley and telephone, and are as much city men as any clerk in an office. They clear far higher profits from an acre than the average farmer, raising never less than two, and often three crops in a season. They employ several men to the acre, and at certain times many more, working the men in gangs. Only the difficulty of getting good help at their prices prevents them from using twice the number.

However, the possibilities of putting capital into land at a profit are still infinite.

What chiefly attracts the gardener to the great cities is stable manure; this is not wanted so much for increasing the richness of the soil--one ninth part of the manure used by the French gardeners would do for that purpose--but for keeping the soil at a certain temperature. Early vegetables pay best, and in order to obtain early produce, not only the air, but the soil as well, must be warmed; that is done by putting great quantities of properly mixed manure into the soil; its fermentation heats it. But with the present development of industrial skill, heating the soil could be done more economically and more easily by hot-water pipes. Consequently, the French gardeners begin more and more to make use of portable pipes, or thermosiphons, provisionally established in the cool frames.

Competition that stands in with the railroads can be met only by being near the market or having water transportation. Indeed, the erect of water transportation in getting manure, and in delivering the produce from the railroads, appears in the early history of trucking. The railroads often crush out boat competition by absorbing docks and standing in with the commission men. This could be met by such cooperative selling agencies as the flower growers already have.

"One of the earliest centers for the development of truck farming in its present sense was along the shores of Chesapeake Bay, where fast sailing oyster boats were employed for sending the produce to the neighboring markets of Baltimore and Philadelphia. In a similar way the gardeners about New York early began pushing out along Long Island, using the waters of the Sound for transporting their produce. The trucking region on the eastern shore of Lake Michigan is another sample of the effect of convenient water transportation in causing an early development of this industry. The building of the Illinois Central railroad opened up a region in southern Illinois that was supposed to be particularly adapted to fruit growing." (" Development of the Trucking Interests," by F. S. Earle, page 439.)

If one goes into the trucking business on so large a scale as to be able to make deals with the railroads, such as The Standard Oil Company has made, of course additional prices could be gotten, owing to the possibility of putting competitors at a disadvantage. That business is a large one.

In doing business on this scale, much will depend on your ability as a merchant.

"It is useless to grow good crops unless they can be sold at a profit; yet it is safe to say that ten men grow good truck crops for one who markets them to the best advantage."

Three Acres and Liberty: Ch. XI-XV

CHAPTER XI
HOTBEDS AND GREENHOUSES

Whether to get an early start on the garden or for raising plants for field crops, a hotbed is all but indispensable. In making a hotbed what we seek to do is to imitate Nature at her best, so get the best soil and the sunniest spot you can find.

In all hotbeds the underlying principle is the same: They are right-angled boxes covered with glass panes set in movable frames and placed over heated excavations. The bed may be of any size or shape, but the standard one is six feet wide, since the stock glass frames are usually six feet long by three feet wide. You can have any length needed to supply your requirements. "Tomato Culture," by A. J. Root, tells us that the cheapest plan is to get some old planks, broken brickbats or stone, and piece together a box-like affair in proper shape: to provide drainage, the front should be at least ten inches above the ground and the rear fourteen inches. A hotbed knocked together in this way is all right to start with, if you cannot do any better, but will last only two or three seasons. For a permanent bed, probably the best way is to make cement walls extending to the bottom of the manure. The bed ought to face south or southeast and be well protected on the north. It should be banked all around with earth or straw to keep out the cold, and mats or shutters should be provided for extra cold weather. The best material for heating the bed and the most easily obtained, is fresh horse manure in which there is a quantity of straw or litter. This will give out a slow, moist heat and will not burn out before the crops or the plants mature. Get all the manure you need at one time. Pile it in a dry place and let it ferment; every few days work the pile over thoroughly with a dung fork; sometimes two turnings of the manure are enough, but it is better to let it stand and heat three or four times.

"You can make a hotbed also on top of the ground without any excavation. Spread a layer of manure evenly one foot in depth and large enough to extend around the frame three feet each way. Pack this down well, especially around the edge, put on a second and third layer until you have a well-trodden and compact bed of manure at least two and one half feet in depth. Place the frame in the center of this bed and press it down well." A two-inch layer of decayed leaves, cut straw, or corn fodder, spread over the manure in the frame and well packed down, will help to retain the heat. Ventilate the bed every day to allow steam and ammonia fumes to pass off.

"The soil inside should be equal parts of garden loam and well-rotted barnyard manure. Tramp well the first layer of three inches. To make it entirely safe for the plant seeds in the hotbed, add another layer of the same depth. Use no water with garden loam and manure if you can possibly help it."

"Before sowing any seeds put a thermometer in the bed three inches deep in the soil. If it runs over 80 degrees Fahrenheit, do not sow. If below 55 degrees it is too cold; you will have to fork it over and add more manure. If the bed gets too hot, you can ventilate it with a sharp stick by thrusting it down into the soil."

Another way that the old gardeners have to make a hot bed is with fire. On a large scale this is cheaper, though more complicated than the fermentation of manure. In making this kind choose your location and build the frames as before. "Cut a trench with a slight taper from the east end of the plot to the end of the hotbed, and on under the ground to about four feet beyond the end of the bed. This taper to the outlet will create a draught and so keep a better fire. Arch this over with vitrified tile. The furnace end where the fire is should be about six feet away from the bed. When the trenches are completed, cover over with the dirt that was taken out of them. Two such trenches under the frames will make a good hotbed. Anyone can do this sort of work."

A hotbed can also be heated by running steam pipes through the ground, but unless you happen to be where exhaust steam could be used, this method is not economical except for big houses. The care and expense of a separate steam plant would be too great to pay, unless for growing winter vegetables for market or flower culture. If you go into that on a scale large enough to pay, new problems at once demand solution.

Vegetables under glass have kept pace with other crops. Within fifteen miles of Boston are millions of square feet of glass devoted to vegetables, chiefly lettuce. There are more than five million feet in the United States used for other crops. Ordinarily, under favorable conditions, glass devoted to this work will yield an average of fifty cents per year per square foot.

About the lowest estimate of cost per sash is five dollars; this amount includes the cost of one fourth of the frame and covers. There are usually four sashes to one frame. A well-made mortised plank frame costs four to six dollars. A sash, unglazed, costs from one to two dollars. Glazing costs seventy-five cents. Mats and shutters cost from fifty cents to two dollars per sash, depending upon the material used. Double thick glass pays better in the end as being less liable to breakage. These prices vary greatly, however.

The following sample estimate by a gardener is for a market garden of one acre, in which it is desired to grow a general line of vegetables. It supposes that half of the acre is to be set with plants from hotbeds.

One eighth acre to early cauliflower and cabbage, about 2000 plants, if transplanted, would require two 6 X 12 frames, from two hundred to two hundred and fifty plants being grown under each sash.

These frames may be used again for tomato plants for the same area, using about 450 plants. This will allow a sash for every 55 plants.

One frame should be in use at the same time for eggplants and peppers, two sashes of each, growing fifty transplanted plants under each sash.

Two frames will be required for cucumbers, melons, and early squashes; for extra early lettuce, an estimate of sixty to seventy heads should be made to a sash. It is assumed that celery and late cabbages are to be started in seed beds in the open.

In the fashionable suburbs of Boston "one hotbed 3 X 6 feet was used in which to start the seeds of early vegetables. Plantings were made in the open ground as soon as the weather permitted, and were continued at intervals throughout the season whenever there was a vacant spot in the garden. The following varieties of vegetables, mostly five-and ten-cent packets, were planted: Pole and wax beans, beets, kale, cabbage, carrots, cauliflower, celery, corn, cucumbers, corn salad, endive, eggplant, kohlrabi, lettuce, muskmelon, onions, peppers, peas, salsify, radish, spinach, squash, tomatoes, turnips, rutabagas, escarole, chives, shallot, parsley, sweet and

Irish potatoes, and nearly a dozen different kinds of sweet herbs."

"In the larger garden, tomatoes followed peas, turnips the wax beans, early lettuce for fall use took the place of Refugee beans. Corn salad succeeded lettuce."

"The spinach was followed by cabbage, while turnips, beets, carrots, celery, and spinach gave a second crop in the plot occupied by Gardus peas and Emperor William beans."

" Winter radishes came after telephone peas, Paris Golden celery was planted in between the hills of Stowell's blanching. The plot of early corn was sown to turnips. The hotbed was used during the late fall and winter to store some of the hardy vegetables, and the latter part of October there was placed in it some endive, escarole, celeriac, and the remaining space was filled up by transplanting leeks, chives, and parsley." (Bailey, "Principles of Vegetable Gardening," page 38.)

"If spinach is grown in frames, the sash used for one of the late crops above may be used through the following winter.

"This, like the last case, makes a total of five frames, the cost, depending on make and material, from one to five dollars; twenty sash and covers, at, say, $2.75, $55; manure at market price, calculating at least three or four loads per frame. This is a liberal estimate of space, and should allow for all ordinary loss of plants, and for discarding the weak and inferior ones. It supposes that most or all of the plants are to be transplanted once or more in the frames. Many gardeners have less equipment of glass." (Same, pages 49-50)

Growing vegetables under glass gives smaller returns than flowers; as, for instance, a head of lettuce brings much less than a plant of carnations, and suffers more from the competition of southern crops. Nevertheless, the greenhouse-grown vegetables have come into prominence lately because they can be raised in houses that are not good enough for flowers. Lettuce and tomatoes are the principal crops; some growers raise thousands of dollars' worth each year. The greenhouse is also used for forcing plants which are afterwards transplanted to the open air. This develops them at a time when they could not grow outdoors and gives them such a start that they are very early on the market, thereby realizing the highest prices.

"Nearness to market is the most important feature in a greenhouse. In large cities, manure, which is the chief fertilizer, can be had in most cases for the hauling. The short haul is an important item, and, most important of all, the gardener who is near the market can take advantage of high prices, if the grower is near enough to the city to make two or three trips; in such a fluctuating market as New York, it is to his advantage."

Some kind of a greenhouse is necessary, but one large enough to produce a living would cost a very large sum. Vegetable raising under glass has been made profitable in special localities where nearly the whole community gives its time to building up the industry, but complete success can be attained only by having absolute control of all the conditions entering into production, and giving assiduous and undivided attention to detail.

Leonard Barron, in the **Garden Magazine,** says: "The best type of greenhouse for all-round purposes is unquestionably what is known as the even span--that is, a house in which the roof is in the form of an inverted V, so as to be exposed as much as possible to sunlight, and having the ridge-pole in the center. All other types of houses are modifications from the simplest form, and are designed in some way or other to fit some special requirements. These requirements may be: the cultural necessities for some particular crop; a desire to have the atmospheric conditions inside more or less abnormal at given seasons (as in a forcing house); or an adaptation to some peculiarity of the situation, as when a greenhouse is built as an adjunct to other buildings."

"It is plain common sense that the ideal greenhouse is one in which the light is most nearly that which exists outside, and in which the heat is as evenly distributed. It is practical experience that a structure with as few angles and turns m it as possible and with a minimum of woodwork in its superstructure, best answers these conditions.... Greenhouse building has developed into a special industry, and the modern American greenhouse is the highest type of construction. It is built with as careful calculation to its situation and its requirements as is the country dwelling-house. Such a thing naturally is not cheap."

"The low-priced 'cheap greenhouse' is a makeshift of some sort. Perhaps its roof is constructed of hotbed sash, a perfectly feasible method of construction, which for ordinary, commonplace gardening will answer admirably. Or, its foundation is merely the plain earth. Such a building does admirably in the summer time, and even in the late spring and early autumn; but woe betide the enthusiastic amateur in winter, who, being possessed of one of these light greenhouse structures, has indulged in a few costly, exotic plants. They will be frozen, to a certainty! It is economy to pay a fair price in the beginning to secure a properly built greenhouse that will withstand the trials of winter."

" If iron frame is used instead of wood there is greater durability, and the structure being more slender, will admit more light, but the cost will be increased."

" It makes very little difference in cost what shape of house is to be erected. The cost per lineal foot for an even span is practically the same as for a lean-to of the same length and width. In the lean-to, in order to get the sufficient bench and walk space inside, it is necessary to carry the roof to a point much higher than in the even span. The extra framework and material for the roof cost a good deal, yet add practically nothing to the efficiency of the house."

"Heating of greenhouses is best done by hot water, and in a small house the pipes may well be connected with the heating system used for the dwelling, if the greenhouse and the home are within any sort of reasonable distance from each other. For large houses, or ranges of several houses together, the independent heating plant is necessary. Steam is used for heating by commercial florists, but it is economical only on a large scale."

"As a uniform temperature must be maintained in the house, the fires, where steam is used, need watching continuously during cold weather, for the moment the water ceases to boil, the pipes cool off and a considerable time is consumed in starting the heat running again. With hot water there is much more latitude in attention, for though the fires dwindle' the water which fills the pipes will carry heat for a long time, and it will circulate until the last degree is radiated. But a hot-water system costs in the installation about one fourth more than steam. Very small houses may be successfully heated by kerosene stoves, which may be placed inside the house. A much better way would be to use oil heaters for an inside water circulation, carrying off all products of combustion by means of a flue. Coal stoves should never be installed inside the house. It has been done successfully by some amateurs, but the danger of coal gas being driven back into the house by a down draft in the chimney is too great a risk. Coal gas and illuminating gas are two virulent poisons to plants."

It is obvious that the amateur must proceed with great caution in undertaking intensive cultivation under glass. Build at first the simplest and least expensive kind of hotbeds or greenhouses. It takes three to five seasons to train even an experienced farmer along these special lines. Separate crops require special treatment. Do not experiment, but follow well-tried procedure. It is comparatively easy to farm an acre under glass, but it should be worked up to, each step being taken only after a solid foundation is ready to build on. Learn by your mistakes. Don't get discouraged by failure. By not making the same mistake twice, you will soon learn by experience just what is essential to production. The more you learn about the way nature does things, the more likely you will be to succeed when you seek to imitate her.

CHAPTER XII
OTHER USES OF LAND

We had intended to write an interesting chapter on the use of a few acres of land for poultry, and another on raising a vast drove of rabbits, both from practical men, but a good average man, just such as this book is written for, sent the following:

"I am very sorry that I cannot comply with your request to write a chapter on poultry for your new book. It is true that I am physically and mentally capable of performing that feat, and it would be possible for me to prepare an essay that might entertain the reader, and even make him believe that there is money in commercial poultry. I prefer, however, to leave that sort of romancing to the poultry journals who, by much practice, are adepts in the art. The fact is, I did not make poultry raising pay, and had I remained on my chicken ranch, I would have gone broke. I do not mean to say, however, that there is no money in poultry, but merely that I could not get it out. Perhaps others who are better equipped for the work can make a success of such an undertaking, but I could not. The numerous poultry journals are filled with instructions how to do it and with letters from people who assert that they have done well with poultry; but, really, during the four years that I was in the business I cannot recall a single case of success, and, on the other hand, I learned of failures without end. I had the reputation of having the best planned and most completely equipped in this part of Washington, and perhaps in the entire state. My stock was thoroughbred and healthy, and they seemed to attend to business strictly. I devoted about all my waking hours to them, did everything that seemed necessary that was suggested by my own success, and yet I could not make it go, am glad I am clear of it, and have no desire to try it again. I am perfectly willing to admit my possible unfitness for the business, but I am also compelled to admit that I could not succeed and that no advice of mine could help others."

Although many, either under exceptional circumstances or because of exceptional ability, have made a success of wholesale poultry raising, it seems on reflection that Mr. Wolf's ideas are in the main correct.

The price of chickens is fixed, like all other prices, by supply and demand, and toward the supply every farmer contributes his chickens and their eggs which cost him practically nothing; at least he counts that they cost him nothing.

Now it is clear that if you considerably increase the supply at any place, the price will fall, and the farmer, whose chickens and eggs cost him almost nothing in money, will sell them low enough to command a market and will continue to raise them, however little he gets for them.

So you are against inexhaustible competitors who can neither be driven out nor combined with. It is worse than competing with bankrupt dealers. To make much money you must have at least some monopoly, and even a little bit of the earth that is well suited to your purpose where there is no unreasonable and unreasoning competition, will give you a chance.

But while it is true that the farmer's subsidized hens have a very disastrous effect at times upon the market, the fact is that, notwithstanding the tariff, we import millions of dozens of eggs laid each year by the pauper hens of Canada and often of Denmark.

Another fact to be considered is, that it is when eggs are most plentiful that the farmers depress the market. With their ways of handling their poultry, their hens lay only when conditions are most favorable, and in the winter when eggs are as high as fifty cents a dozen in cities, they have no eggs to market. Like the market gardener, to be timely in market is to succeed. A week may mean an annihilation of profits.

It is a different proposition to raise a few chickens as a side line as the farmers do.

A workman at the Connecticut place of one of the experts who has revised this book had a bit of land not more than 100 X 200 feet, and for several years cleared $100 a year by raising eggs and broilers, doing the work together with that of a little garden of small fruits before and after working hours The chickens fed largely on green food in summer.

In selling your surplus at a profit, the same principles apply as in raising a surplus to sell at a profit.

While poultry and egg raising does not require that you must be first, it does require that you market your produce at a time when the prices are highest.

You must hatch at a time which will allow the young hens to begin laying as winter approaches; the food must keep up animal heat and the house must be warm enough to make the hens comfortable, and the conditions must be such as to keep them laying.

As an experiment, we once raised six pullets. They were hatched in May, and in December they began laying. All during the winter they laid never less than four and some times six eggs a day, and kept this up until spring.

They were fed on wheat and corn and plenty of meat scraps and green food. They were kept in what was practically a glass house, receiving the benefit of the sun during the day, and were protected from the winds. The effect was to bring as near as possible the condition of the warm months; these paid very well.

Ducks are less frequently raised than chickens and often realize good returns.

The popular fallacy that ducks require a stream or pond is gradually passing away. There was a time when nearly all ducks were raised in this way, feeding on fish as the principal diet, but experience has proved that ducks raised without a stream or pond tend to put on flesh instead of feathers, and they have not the oily, fishy flavor of those raised on the water. Nearly all of the successful duck raisers now use this method.

This is bringing the duck more into prominence as an article of food; as James Rankin says in "Duck Culture," "People do not care to eat fish and flesh combined. They would rather eat them separate."

The white pekins are the popular birds, because they are larger, have white meat, and are splendid layers. They lay from 100 to 165 eggs in a season and are the easiest to raise. They can do entirely without water; and Rankin tells of selling a flock to a wealthy man, who afterwards wrote asking him to take them back, because he had bought them for an artificial lake in front of his house, so that his wife and children could watch them disporting in the water. He complained that they would not go into the water unless he drove them in and would remain only so long as he stood over them.

Ducks are easier to raise than any other fowl and are freer from disease. They are ready for market when eight weeks old.

The industry is assuming large proportions, and ranches are now raising ducks by the tens of thousands and are finding better markets each year.

In starting any poultry business, it is better to begin with twenty-five fowls and master details with those, then double the number as fast as they have been made to return profits.

The Atlantic Squab Company, of Hammonton, N. J., says "it is a simple matter for the beginner to figure out on paper net profits of four or five dollars per year from each pair of breeders, but we doubt if it can be made. It is, however, 'pigeon nature' to lay ten or eleven times a year, but hardly natural to presume that each and every egg will ultimately mean a Jumbo squab in the commission man's hands.

"A loft [that is, a pair] of high-class Homers, properly mated, should average six pair of squabs per year. For one year our squabs averaged us a fraction over 60 cent per pair; say $3.60 has been the returns from each pair of breeders. It has cost us 90 cent per pair to feed for twelve months; remember, we buy in large quantities; it would cost the small breeder $1 a year per pair to feed. It would be well to allow 60 cent a pair for labor and supplies, such as grit, charcoal, tobacco stems, etc., although the bird manure, which we find ready sale for at 55 cent. per bushel, has covered these incidental expenses for us. The inexperienced beginner, with good management and close attention to details, should clear $2 a year from each pair of birds, provided he starts with well-mated pure Homer stock." Pigeons are particular about their mates, and will rather go single than take a disagreeable partner.

Raising Belgian hares at one time promised to be a most profitable industry. The Belgian hare is a distant relation of the ordinary rabbit. Its flesh is white, close-grained, and tender, resembling the legs of the frog, and has a very savory flavor. It is considered by many superior to poultry, and the rapidity with which they breed gave promise of fortunes. The doe brings forth a litter of about eleven every sixty days, and with prices ranging from $1.50 to $2.50, as they were about the year 1900, with the cost of raising from thirty to forty cents, the reason for this promise is evident. In Southern California thousands turned their attention to it, and some firms entered the business with equipment to the value of fifty thousand dollars.

Besides the ordinary market prices realized for the hares, some went extensively into breeding fancy stock, and realized from $50 to $250 apiece for them.

This industry had indications of becoming extensive and enduring, but by 1900 so many went into the business that the markets became glutted and prices fell with disastrous effect.

Whether it will pay you depends largely on the attitude of your customers toward the hare as a food product.

Bee-keeping offers an interesting and remunerative field of employment. More than the average living awaits those only who will make a careful and intelligent study of bees and their habits and will give them the proper care and attention.

One need not be a practical bee-keeper to enter this field. He can purchase even one hive and, while increasing from this, he can gain an experience that he could get in no other way.

How shall one start bee-keeping?

Get one hive or a few hives. If you have no room in the yard, put them upon the roof. One man in Cincinnati, Ohio, makes his living from bees kept on the roof of his house.

Wm. A. Selzer, a large dealer in bee-keepers' supplies, in Philadelphia, established many colonies on the roof of his place right in the heart of the business district, where it would seem impossible for bees to find a living.

Very little space is required for bee-keeping; hives can be set two feet apart in rows, and the rows six to ten feet apart. No pasture need be provided for them. There are always fields of flowers to supply the nectar.

White clover produces a large yield of nectar of very fine flavor. The basswood or linden tree blossom produces a fine nectar which some consider better than white clover. Buckwheat also gives a good yield of nectar, but it is dark in color and brings a lower price for that reason. There are other plants which yield large quantities of nectar, and it would be necessary to know the locality to say what would be the best plants; but as white clover is found almost everywhere in the northern states, it is safe to say this will be the best producer in the spring, and goldenrod, where found, the best for the fall supply.

Frank Benton, in United States Department of Agriculture Bulletin 59, says: "It may be safely said that any place where farming, gardening, or fruit raising can be successfully followed is adapted to the profitable keeping of bees."

There is always a farmer here and there who keeps a few hives of bees. These often can be purchased at a very reasonable price, but unless they are Italian bees and are in improved hives, it would be better to purchase from some dealer. He may sell you a very weak colony, but after the first year these ought to be as strong as any. Start in the spring; when you have your bees, read good literature on the subject. A. I. Root's "A B C of Bee Culture" is good for beginners; subscribe for the ***American Bee Journal,*** of Chicago, or ***Gleanings in Bee Culture,*** Medina, Ohio. They are full of the latest ideas on the subject.

A yield of fifty pounds of honey in a season can be obtained from one hive of bees in almost any locality. In fact, this is often done where bees are kept in built up cities. One hundred pounds would be considered a very small yield by many apiarists, and twice this amount is often gathered in favored localities where up-to-date methods are followed.

One man can take care of two hundred hives or colonies, as they are termed, if he is working for comb honey, and perhaps twice that number if for extracted honey.

Comb honey is stored usually in one-pound boxes set in a super or small box over the main hive body, which is itself a box about seventeen inches long, eleven inches wide, and ten inches deep into which frames of comb are slid side by side. These combs are accessible and can be lifted out, exposing to view the inner workings of the hive. It is in these combs that the queen lays as many as three thousand eggs some days, and in which the young bees are hatched. They are also used for storing honey for winter use.

The extractor has been invented to remove this honey without damaging the comb. The economy of this can readily be seen, as ten pounds of honey can be stored while one pound of comb is being built.

This leaves the bees free to gather honey instead of using a portion of their force to build comb, as is necessary when comb honey is desired.

The extractor is a round tin can on a central pivot with a revolving mechanism. Into this the full combs of honey are placed and are whirled around, throwing the honey out into the can by centrifugal force. It is then run out at the bottom into bottles or barrels, and the empty combs are replaced in the hive for the bees to fill again.

Twice as many pounds of honey can be produced by this method; but the price of extracted honey is much less than that of comb honey. Adulteration of extracted honey with glucose is becoming so prevalent that it threatens to ruin this branch of the industry. But there will always be a good market for honey sold direct by the producer to residents, or even through storekeepers, in medium size towns, where customers can be sure that the honey is pure.

The average wholesale prices of honey are about fifteen cents a pound for extracted and twenty cents for fancy comb, so if the apiarist with two hundred hives produces the small average of fifty pounds of comb honey and sells it at fifteen cents a pound, he will receive $1500 for his season's work. If he goes in for extracted honey and produces one hundred pounds per hive, he will receive even more. Of course, expenses will have to come out of this.

That this has been done over and over again is proved by men who started in with only a few hives and have accumulated considerable property from the business.

But no one need expect to do this unless he is willing to give the bees the attention which they will require. To neglect them once means often a total loss. Most of the work will have to be done during the swarming season in May, June, and July. There has been so much written on the subject and so many inventions and improvements made in the hives that bee-keeping more than any other branch of similar employment has been reduced to a science, and any one can thoroughly master it in two or three years. It is because its possibilities are not generally recognized that so few are now engaged in it.

The fear of stings will always deter many from entering this business and so check competition from forcing prices down.

The price of honey makes it a luxury, and there will be an unlimited opportunity in the crop as long as the price does not get near the cost of producing, which is far below the present prices.

To use land directly is to open almost infinite opportunities. Department of Agriculture, Farmers' Bulletin 204, says: "In the United States the term 'mushroom' refers commercially to but a single species (Agaricus Campestris) of the fleshly fungi, a plant common throughout most of the temperate regions of the world, and one everywhere recognized as edible."

It is unfortunate that the commercial use of the term "mushroom" restricts it to a single species. There are about twenty-five common varieties of edible fungi in the Northern states.

The successful cultivation of mushrooms in America has not been so general as in most European countries. It is in France and in England that the mushroom industry has been best developed. France is the home of the industry. Unusual interest has been shown in the United States in the growth of mushrooms within the past few years, and it is to be hoped and expected that within the next ten years the industry will develop to the fullest limit of the market demands. The demand will, of course, be stimulated by the increasing popular appreciation of this product. In some cities and towns there is already a good market for mushrooms, while in others they may be sold directly to special customers. This should be borne in mind by prospective growers.

While many American growers have been successful, a much larger number have failed. In most cases their failures have been due to one or more of the following causes:

(1) Poor spawn, or spawn which has been killed by improper storage.

(2) Spawning at a temperature injuriously high.

(3) Too much water either at the time of spawning or later.

(4) Unfavorable temperature during the growing period. It is therefore important to the prospective grower that careful attention be given to the general discussion of conditions which follow.

Mushrooms may be grown in any place where the conditions of temperature and moisture are favorable. A shed, cellar, cave, or vacant space in a greenhouse may be utilized to advantage for this purpose. The most essential factor, perhaps, is that of temperature. The proper temperature ranges from 53 degree to 60 degree F., with the best from 55 degree to 58 degree F. It is unsafe to attempt to grow mushrooms on a commercial basis, according to our present knowledge of the subject, in a temperature much less than 50 degree or greater than 63 degree F.

Any severe changes of temperature would entirely destroy the profits of the mushroom crop. From this it is evident that in many places mushrooms may not be grown as a summer crop. With artificial heat they may be grown almost anywhere throughout the winter. Moreover, it is very probable that in this country open-air culture must be limited to a few sections.

A second important factor is moisture. The place should not be very damp, or constantly dripping with water. Under such conditions successful commercial work is not possible. A place where it is possible to maintain a fairly moist condition of the atmosphere, and having such capability for ventilation as will cause at least a gradual evaporation, is necessary. With too rapid ventilation and the consequent necessity of repeated applications of water to the mushroom bed, no mushroom crop will attain the highest perfection.

Even a little iron rust in the soil is reported as fatal to the Campestris, the only fungus so far successfully propagated.

If other fungi than the Campestris come up wild, don't throw them away as worthless. Many are better eating than the one you seek, and you can avoid the risk of poisonous ones by learning to recognize the dangerous family--send for the Agricultural Department's Bulletin No. 204. Meanwhile, (1) all mushrooms with pink gills, (2) all coral-like fungi, (3) all that grow on wood, and (4) all puffballs, are good to eat if they are young and tender--only don't mistake an unspread Aminita for a puffball.

An ingenious person may find other sources of income in the country. A young hotel porter in Ulster County, New York, bought seventy acres of mountain woodland four miles from the railroad for two hundred and fifty dollars, and puts in his winters cutting barrel hoops, at which he makes two dollars a day. Meanwhile the land is maturing timber. That is hard work, but to gather wild mushrooms or to cut willows, or sweet pine needles to make cushions, or to catch young squirrels for sale, is lighter, if less steady employment.

And with all our uses of land, we must not forget a little corner for the hammock and the croquet hoops for the wife and the children. In the Province of Quebec, where the land is held in great tracts under the Seigniors, I have seen croquet grounds no bigger than a bed quilt in front of the little one-room cottages.

The Frenchman knows the importance of such things as that, has meals out of doors in fine weather, goes on little picnics, and keeps madame contented in the country.

A swing, or a seesaw, and a tether ball (a ball swinging from the top of a pole eight feet high) for the children will help to keep the family peace.

CHAPTER XIII
FRUITS

Fruit raising can succeed in either of two ways. Either planting the orchard in some one fruit and specializing thereon, or diversifying the operation to cover many varieties. In the first way it is usual to establish orchards in favorable localities without special regard to nearness to market; because in these days of refrigerator car lines the product of an orchard in any part of the country can be sent to market quickly enough to avoid loss. Where many varieties are grown, the best site is usually near a large city where the grower can market his own product on wagons and get the benefit of retail prices.

Remember that it is far more profitable to raise twenty baskets of fine, well-shaped, clean, handsome apples or peaches or any other hand-eaten fruit, than to raise a hundred barrels of stuff that is good only for the common drier or for the mill or hogpen.

Care and common sense are the jackscrews to use in raising fine fruit.

The apple is the great American fruit for extensive orcharding. The question is whether there is a profit in apple growing. The answer is, where the conditions are favorable and when the business is well conducted there is. Under average conditions, with poor business management, there is little or none.

As Professor S. T. Maynard in *Suburban Life* tells us, "In a suburban garden of one of our Eastern cities are seven Astrachan trees, about twenty years old, from which have been sold in a single season over one hundred dollars' worth of fruit. A friend near Boston put three thousand barrels of picked Baldwins into cold storage. None of the fancy apples sold for less than three dollars a barrel, and the others netted more than two dollars. They were the product of less than forty acres of trees which had been planted about twenty-five years. Another fruit grower showed me several returns of commission men of five, six, and even seven dollars a barrel for fancy Baldwins. At such prices, and under such conditions, there is a large profit in apple growing."

"The other side of the picture, however, is the more common one. A friend sent fifty barrels of fancy Baldwins to a commission house, to be shipped to European markets, the returns for which were just enough to pay for the barrels. The majority of apples grown in the United States are sold to buyers, one buyer in each section, for a dollar to two dollars for No. 1 quality, and a dollar for No. 2. With the cost of barrels at about forty cents, labor for picking, sorting, and packing, these prices leave little or nothing for the use of the land, cost of fertilizers, spraying, thinning, etc., all of which are necessary for growing fruit of the best quality."

Holmes further says, in substance, that we must make the trees grow vigorously, whether upon poor or good soil. Growth is the first requirement. To do this, we need a strong, deep, moist soil,--good grass land well underdrained makes the best. If this is on an elevation with a northern or western exposure, it will be better than a southern or an eastern one. While apple trees will grow on a thin soil, so much care and fertilizing is required that the crop will be of little or no profit upon such land. Lastly, we must protect our fruit from insect and fungous pests.

On land that is free from stones and not too steep, thorough and frequent cultivation will give the quickest and largest returns. On such land, hoed garden or farm crops may be profitable while the trees are small, but after five or six years it will generally be found best to cultivate it entirely for the growth of trees. Organic matter in the form of stable manure or cover crops will be needed, and must be applied in the fall or very early in the spring to keep up the supply of humus in the soil.

Stony land that cannot be plowed or cultivated except at a great cost may be made to grow good crops of fruit.

While the trees are young, the soil should be worked about them for the space of a few feet and then the moisture retained by a mulch system, making use of any waste organic matter like straw, leaves, meadow hay, brush, and weeds cut before they seed. Most of the first prize apples at the Pan-American Exposition at Buffalo were grown under the "turf-culture" system.

Unless you have trees already on your land, it is too long to wait six or seven years for a crop. We can graft good fruit on almost any tree, though the new dwarf trees will bear much sooner, and if we have trees we need not even wait for the harvest of our crop, since the windfalls will keep us in apple sauce, jellies, and pies, for no apple is too green for apple sauce, not even the ones that the boys can't bite.

The greatest difficulty in the profitable growth of the apple is the market. Much of the profit in apple growing, whether in the East or the West, will depend upon the extent of the business done, especially if one is a considerable distance from markets. The above are the essentials noted by this practical scientist. Next to the apple crop, perhaps the most important fruit crop for shipping is the peach. The locality is perhaps the most important consideration in a peach orchard. In the Eastern and Southern states, and in Connecticut, Delaware, New Jersey, Maryland, and Virginia, and, of late years, Georgia, peaches flourish and produce enormous crops. As a general rule, the nearer the orchard is to large bodies of water, the more likely one is to get a crop, as the temperature of the water prevents a too early budding out in the spring and delays killing autumn frosts.

Generally speaking, a sandy, porous soil is best for peaches, but they may be raised on clay lands if provided with plenty of humus.

Another fruit which is profitable in districts suited to its growth is the grape. Bulletin No. 153, Cornell Experiment Station, says: "Grapes are a dessert fruit. They are not used to a large extent in the kitchen (though they might be), so there are few incidental or secondary products; that is, they are not dried, canned, made into jellies, and the like, to any extent, that is, in the United States.

The grape is peculiarly a sectional product. Central New York has a large area devoted to it. In northern Ohio, a strip along Lake Erie, and some of its islands, are devoted almost exclusively to grape vineyards. In districts where grapes are intensively grown, a great part of the crop is used for wine, and American wine is extensively sold m our home markets, although it frequently has foreign labels.

Any one purchasing a farm should plant some grapevines for home use. Grape juice is easily made and kept and is a pleasing beverage. Grape jelly is excellent and could be readily marketed in any nearby town, since there is very little, comparatively, on sale. A grape arbor gives shade, needs little care, and can be planted near the house where it will not interfere with the crops. For you cannot cultivate all of your land; some grassy space must be left around the house if only for drying clothes. But if ground is scarce, vines or lima beans can be trained up the back porch or up the sunny side of the house; or a few climbing nasturtiums will give decorations without care, while the young leaves make a good salad.

Of home orchard fruits, the plum, pear, and quince are all profitable specialties, especially for intensive acre raising. In general, the same remark may be made of them as of the other fruits, that they need careful selection of land to get the best results. The cherry has recently come to be recognized as a good commercial specialty. Mr. George T. Powell, in *The American Agriculturist,* says: "The crop is a precarious one to market.... The risk and loss may be largely reduced by making a proper selection of site for the orchard. This should be on high ground where the air generally circulates freely. This is especially necessary for sweet varieties. The soil should be rich, with naturally good drainage."

He says: "I have had Rockport trees produce four hundred pounds each and the fruit net ten cents a pound for the entire crop. The English Morello trees may be grown fifteen feet apart each way, which will allow two hundred trees to the acre. The larger trees ought to be planted somewhat thinner.... Cherries are packed largely in eight-pound baskets and in strawberry quarts. Each basket is filled with carefully assorted fruit, every imperfect specimen being taken out, after which they are faced by placing the stems downward so that the cherry shows in regular rows upon the face. Girls and women do this work. The Eastern fruit grower must bear in mind that he has to meet in his market the competition of the Pacific coast growers, who excel in fine packing; and although our Eastern grown cherries are of a finer flavor, they are sent to the market in such a crude manner and in such unattractive condition that they sell for much less than the California fruit."

Regarding bush berries, he says, you will get a small crop the second year after planting and for the third and subsequent years a full crop. The important thing is to keep the dead canes well pruned out, as the cane borer is one of the worst insect pests. When they appear they can be stopped by cutting off the shoot several inches below the puncture as soon as it begins to droop, and burning the part cut off. Again, Mr. Powell says, "Currants require rich soil. A clay or heavy loam is better than a heavy dry soil. They should be planted in the fall. The average from ten thousand bushes should be about four quarts each. The cherry currant is perhaps the largest in size, but not so prolific as some others. Currants are shipped and sold in thirty-two quart crates and have to be carefully packed to get to market in good condition."

Gooseberries are raised by the acre. Mr. A. M. Brown, Kent County, Delaware, in *The American Agriculturist,* tells of a plantation in Central Delaware where over twenty four thousand pounds were gathered from a scant four acres. The product was sold to the Baltimore canners for six cents a pound, making $1440 in all. In addition to the gooseberries grown on six acres, a large crop each of apples and pears were grown on the same ground. Like currants, the gooseberry must be sprayed to destroy the worms, and cut back and burnt to destroy the cane borer.

There is little special knowledge required, however, in raising this fruit, and it is well adapted for growers with small acreage and little money.

In going into the cultivation of bush fruits, it is usually best to grow them in great variety near the market where they are to be sold. The bush fruits are then uniformly profitable. In *Suburban Life* Mr. E. C. Powell tells us that the spring is the best time for planting raspberries and blackberries, just as soon as the ground is dry enough to work. The first season the plots should be well tilled. It is possible to grow vegetables between the rows the first year before the berries begin to bear, but unless pressed for space, it probably doesn't pay.

Perhaps the best of small fruits, however, and most largely used is the strawberry. The strawberry can be planted by the acre. The ground must be rich loam and plenty of humus, well drained, with a southern exposure. Well-grown plants set out in the open will bear a small crop the first season, but will not become of maximum bearing till the second year. After the crop is taken off in the fall a mulch of straw or leaves should be placed over the plants to protect them during the winter. The strawberries are picked by boys and girls.

The strawberry is an exceedingly profitable crop if properly handled, and is one of the best small fruits for people with little capital. While the price in the general market varies from fifteen to thirty cents per quart, they sometimes run as high as fifty in the early spring; yet it is possible to grow strawberries worth six dollars a quart by intensive culture in greenhouses. Mr. S. W. Fletcher, in *Country Life in America,* says: "The forcing of strawberries is a specialized industry of the highest type. Everybody cannot make it pay everywhere.... Strawberries are forced in pots or in benches. The pot method is preferred by those who find a demand for the highest quality of fruit regardless of expense.... If fruit is desired for Christmas, the plants are not checked to any extent, but are kept in continuous growth. The conditions of springtime are simulated as far as possible. At Christmas time a quart box of forced Marshall strawberries sells at from one-fifty to eight dollars per quart, averaging about four dollars."

Our most valuable allies against the insect armies are toads, bats, wasps, dragon flies, and birds; they enjoy the battle.

There cannot be too many toads or bats. Toads will eat all sorts of flies, potato bugs, squash bugs, rose bugs, caterpillars, and almost anything that crawls.

If the wasps become a nuisance, it is easy to poison them; but the birds are often a nuisance--the robins eat the strawberries and cherries the instant they are ripe. They soon get used to scarecrows; and to cover the fruit with nets gives the insects a free hand. Some growers raise sweet cherries or other fruits specially to feed up the birds so that they will let the rest alone. Early rising and a plenty of cats is about the best remedy. A man, or even a woman, working on the land is the best scarecrow.

There are a few other fruits that grow wild in certain sections and are gathered and sent to market. Among these the cranberry is the most important. It grows in nearly inaccessible bogs, principally in New Jersey, and the usual custom is for owners of land on which there are cranberry bogs to let out the bog to pickers on a percentage basis. Cranberries can be cultivated, and there is a considerable profit in the business. The swampy nature of the ground needed, however, will deter all except the most persistent from this industry. Some cranberry bogs bring as high as a thousand dollars an acre.

The blueberry or huckleberry, or, as we call it in Ireland, the bilberry, or fro-hen, grows wild in the northerly states, and is much sought after in the market. Many efforts have been made to grow the blueberry commercially; but, as is well said by Mr. J. H. Hale in the ***Rural New Yorker,*** "The blueberry proved to be a good deal like Indians--it would not stand civilization, and was never satisfactory, although I monkeyed with it for a period of about ten years." Mr. Fred W. Card, of Rhode Island, in the same issue reports a similar experience. With our present knowledge of the blueberry, it is doubtful if it can be made a commercially culti-vated crop. Lately, however, it is claimed that it can be grown in very poor, non-nitrogenous soil.

A variety, however, called the Garden Blueberry, gives almost incredible yields, five bushels being reported from sixty plants. It keeps all winter *on the branches,* if stored in a cellar, and is of fine flavor and especially good for preserves. A little frost improves it.

But wild berries, crab apples, and elderberries and others, are good to preserve and find a ready sale if attractively put up; they also help out tile table greatly. Then think of the fun!

In recent years, certain varieties of nuts, like the English walnut, the pecan, and the hickory nuts have been grown commercially. In the South particularly, the pecan has been found a good crop to plant on cotton plantations which have been overworked. In the *Rural New Yorker,* Mr. H. E. Vandevan gives an account of an old cotton plantation of 2250 acres Iying on the west bank of the Mississippi River in Louisiana. The pecan tree was indigenous to the land, and the wooded portion of the plantation has thousands of giant pecan trees growing on it. The previous owners of this plantation had done all in their power to destroy these trees, but they flourished in spite of that. Mr. Vandevan, however, saw in the pecan a large profit, and he has planted ten thousand trees on six hundred acres, all in a solid block. The trees are set fifty feet apart both ways, except where a roadway is left. Between the pecan trees Mr. Vandevan has planted fig trees for early returns, with the intention of canning the fruit.

The English walnut is grown principally in California. Its value has been recognized only recently, as all of the nut crops take a good many years before the trees begin to bear. Nut growing on a small scale is not of much value to a man with a little bit of land, except as an additional source of income.

If you find a sweet chestnut tree or a shell-bark hickory or two in your wood lot, they will well repay protection and careful cultivation.

If you don't, why--there are great promises in quick maturing nut trees. There is now an English walnut which is claimed to bear the third or even the second year after setting out. My own small experience with these in New Jersey, however, has not been a success.

CHAPTER XIV
FLOWERS

Every city in the United States affords an opportunity for flower gardening and nurseries, but a study must be made of the market in order to know what is best to raise and where to raise it.

The choice of crops depends on the popular taste. The flowers which are now in greatest demand are the rose, carnation, violet, and chrysanthemum.

Near every large city there are hundreds of florists with glass houses, some covering twenty acres or more. There were over 2000 acres of flower land under glass reported at the last census. As almost all industries to-day are specialized, so is floriculture; in one place we see ten acres of glass given over to the rose, in another thousands of dollars devoted to the carnation or the violet, while one grower in Queens, Long Island, has 75,000 square feet of glass for carnations.

The specialist who devotes his thoughts and energies to raising one flower can produce better results than if he raised a variety. He has only one crop to market, and can do it more successfully than with a number of crops. If he raises enough to make himself a factor in the market, he can sell direct instead of sending his product to a commission man, thereby receiving better prices.

Little capital is required to start; intelligent effort is the road to success. Very few, indeed, who are now leaders in floriculture, started with more than $500 capital, and many with much less. One of the largest growers of roses in the United States, whose plant covers more than ten acres, did not have $500 when he started, and many others not so well known are making handsome livings and have accumulated thousands of dollars of property from a start of less than $500.

But practical knowledge is much more necessary than in raising vegetables, as small mistakes will have more serious results. Therefore, if you have some capital and wish to go into flower raising, it will pay you, if circumstances permit, to hire out to a florist, even at small wages, till you have learned the business--even though you have raised flowers successfully in a home garden.

Mr. Frank Hamilton, manager of C. W. Ward's of Queens, tells of at least a dozen men, who have been in their employ during his twenty-five years' experience, some of whom got only twenty dollars a month at first, and afterwards started in a small way for themselves, who are now making a substantial living.

Although the market depends largely on the wealthy class in the large cities, many florists devote considerable time and space to flowers which are bought by the poorer class of city dwellers who have no space or time to raise their own.

There are always good markets somewhere for the crop, and it is not an uncommon thing to ship flowers from New York to Chicago, Buffalo, Boston, Philadelphia, Baltimore, and Washington, or vice versa. The chances of success for a lover of flowers are better in this business than in any in which one with a like amount of capital can engage. If the business at first is not large enough to use all his time he will find no trouble in securing employment in his immediate vicinity. There are always some who want such a person to care for their lawns or to give some time to their conservatories.

In the last ten years the business has doubled, and while many have gone into it, the profit they are making indicates that supply has not kept pace with demand, and that it is not likely to be overdone the near future.

Professor B. T. Galloway, in an article in **The World's Work,** says, "An acre of soil under glass pays fifty times as much as an acre outdoors. There are annually sold in this country six to seven million dollars' worth of carnation flowers There are no less than eight to ten million square feet of glass in the United States devoted to this flower alone."

Although Mr. Rockefeller's place at Tarrytown is the largest competitor in the New York market for violets, there is no local monopoly in that, and the local producer with personal attention can do well.

In the **Country Gentleman** an account is given of a violet farm on the north shore of Illinois, where two women are supplying local florists.. One of them says: "We started our farm last spring in the face of most discouraging prophecies from our friends and the keenest competition of violet growers of New York. But we believed we could be successful. We had studied the best scientific methods of grow-ing the plants, had imported the best soil obtainable, and built a greenhouse fully adapted to our needs, so we just went ahead and we found it to be a paying proposi-tion.

"Our first experiment was in using cuttings from the violet farm of a lady at Lansing, Michigan, who has been a most successful grower. These did not thrive, and we next imported 3000 cuttings from the Tarrytown neighborhood, where vio-let culture has been most successful.

"The first rule is to keep the temperature of the greenhouse between forty-five and fifty degrees. Violets are spring flowers, and wither and droop if the tempera-ture is not at the right degree. Most people think the double violets have no fra-grance because most of those that we get lose their fragrance in transit.

"We supply 2000 flowers a week, and as they reach our patrons within two or three hours at the most from the time of cutting, they retain their fragrance. They are also larger and of a deeper color than the New York flowers. Next year we hope to go in on a much larger scale.

"While the work is not hard, it requires infinite care and vigilance when the little plants are growing. As a career for a woman, violet growing offers greater in-ducements than anything I can think of."

Then, surely, others can succeed in other flowers at other places. While there is little choice between the standard styles of greenhouses for violets, there should be abundant provision for supplying fresh air, either from the sides or top, which-ever is chosen. The system of ventilation should admit of operation either from the inside or the outside of the house, as fumigation with hydrocyanic acid gas is sometimes necessary, in the fumes of which it is impossible to enter, unless with a gas mask.

The arrangement of the house should secure the greatest possible supply of sunshine in December and January, and the least possible during the growing sea-son, when, as Miss Howard points out, it is necessary to secure as low a temperature as possible, so as to obtain good, vigorous, healthy-growing plants. The best site is a level piece of ground, or one sloping gently to the south.

Of the diseases to which cultivated violets are subject Mr. P. H. Dorsett, of the Department of Agriculture, names four as especially dangerous: Spot disease, producing whitish spots on the foliage; root rot, apt to attack young plants transplanted in hot, dry weather; wet rot, a fungus apt to appear in too moist air or where ventilation is insufficient; and yellowing, of the cause of which little is known. Any of these diseases is difficult to exterminate when it once gains a foothold. The best thing to do is to get strong, vigorous cuttings, and then to give careful attention to watering, cultivation, and ventilation, and the destruction of dead and dying leaves and all runners as fast as they appear.

Among insect enemies, the aphids, red spiders, eel worms, gall flies, and slugs may be mentioned. Most of these can be easiest controlled by hydrocyanic acid gas treatment.

Chrysanthemums, especially of preternatural size and bizarre colors--the college colors at football games, for instance--are in great demand. They are extremely decorative, and their remarkable lasting quality insures their permanent popularity. I have heard that the unexpanded bud can be cooked like cauliflower for the table; but we have not learned to use them in that way. In Japan and China the leaves of the chrysanthemum are esteemed as a salad. One attempt has been made by English gardeners to introduce this use of them into England, but it was unsuccessful.

The annual shows of chrysanthemums and of roses indicate the importance of the business.

It is not generally known, but the poppies are coming into favor for cut flowers in spite of the fact that they do not keep very well. Miss Edith Granger avoids this difficulty, as she explains in the **Garden Magazine,** "by picking off all blooms that have not already lost their petals in the evening, so that in the morning all the open flowers will be new ones. These are cut as early as possible, even while the dew is still upon them, and plunged immediately into deep water."

You need not be discouraged by the low prices at which flowers, especially violets and roses, are often offered in the streets. Those flowers are the discarded stock or delayed shipments of the swell florists. You will find that those flowers are fading, or revived with salt, and will not keep.

That they are so peddled, shows that everybody, at hotels, dinners, funerals, weddings, in the home, and the young men for the young women, want flowers, the loveliest things ever made without souls. We have only to supply such a want to find our place in life.

As a side line the common flowers will bring good prices; mignonette, bachelor buttons, cosmos, and even nasturtiums, which you can't keep from growing if you just stick the seed in the ground, or lilies of the valley, which you can hardly get rid of once they start, never go begging, if they are fresh.

A favorite flower with many is the sweet pea, which can be grown out of doors in the summer time where you have a good depth and quality of soil.

I have seen May blossoms and autumn leaves on the branch and even golden-rod brought into town and sold at good prices.

Enterprises often look attractive at a distance; for instance, raising orchids, especially as some of the flowers remain on the plants ready for market for weeks and bring high prices. But to ship flowers at a profit they must be in quantities, else the expenses eat up the returns, and they must be shipped with considerable regularity, else you lose your customers. To get such a supply of orchids would take a very large capital and involve so much labor that it is doubtful if more than good interest could be realized on it.

Many florists make money by keeping constantly on hand ferns, palms, and other plants like rubber trees, which they rent out for social functions, weddings, and other occasions. Most florists in the larger cities have also quite a thriving business in tree planting, which is everywhere on the increase. A highly specialized department of horticulture is that of raising young trees and plants to sell for improving grounds, planting orchards, or similar uses. The nursery business bears much the same relation to the commercial florist or orchardist as seed growing does to the market gardener.

Certain communities, through favorable soil or climate, are best adapted to the production of nursery stock. Consequently, one finds this industry most highly developed in scattered localities. It is true that people with small capital should not tackle a business so technical as this.

The business of bulb production is another highly specialized department. In certain sections of Holland large areas of the rich lowlands are given over to bulbs of various kinds of lilies, nearly all of which are propagated in that manner. To attain perfection, at least in the North, most bulbs require deep, rich, warm, and highly manured soils; and assiduous attention at every stage. In many plant specialties, the gardeners of Europe still far surpass our own, because conditions there have forced them to make use of every available means to increase production. The immense price that European gardeners have to pay for land has been a most potent factor in forcing them to seek out and apply the most ingenious forcing methods. The time is upon us here in America also when we must find out the highest use of land and apply it to that use.

As the aesthetic qualities of our people become more highly developed, the business of raising flowers must become of increasing importance, and will readily reward any one who goes into it conscientiously. Flower growing is peculiarly adapted to women, since the work is light There are few disagreeable features, unless it be the handling of the manure incidental to the best results.

Still, the enjoyments of agriculture depend upon individual tastes. I have seen "lady gardeners" picking strawberries with the footman holding up an umbrella to screen them from the sun.

Some women would like that, some not.

CHAPTER XV
DRUG PLANTS

A source of profit from land to which little attention has been given in the United States is collecting or raising plants, some part of which may be used for medicinal purposes. We condense from Farmers' Bulletin No. 188, United States Department of Agriculture:

Certain well-known weeds are sources of crude drugs at present obtained wholly or in part from abroad. Roots, leaves, and flowers of several of the species most detrimental in the United States are gathered, cured, and used in Europe, and supply much of the demands of foreign lands. Some of these plants are in many states subject to anti-weed laws, and farmers are required to take measures toward their extermination.

The prices paid for crude drugs from these sources save in war time are not great and would rarely tempt any one to this work as a business. Yet if in ridding the farm of weeds and thus raising the value of the land the farmer can at the same time make these pests the source of a small income instead of a dead loss, something is gained.

One rather alluring fact contained in an article by Dr. True, is that a shortage has become keenly felt in "Golden Seal," which the early American settlers learned from the Indians to use as a curative for sore and inflamed eyes, as well as for sore mouth. The plant grows in patches in high open woods, and was formerly found in great abundance in Ohio, Indiana, Kentucky, and West Virginia, but is now so rare that its price has risen from thirty-five cents wholesale in 1898 to over seventy-five cents a pound. Persons in different parts of the country have undertaken the production of Golden Seal on a commercial scale. More than six hundred dollars' worth can be grown on an acre: so a crop this year would be a fortune. The methods of raising it can be ascertained upon application to the Department of Agriculture.

Ginseng is one of the drug crops which paid handsome returns a few years ago, perhaps because it takes from five to seven years to grow from seeds; but so many went into that line that few men to-day make anything at it. Furthermore, the Chinese, who use a large part of it, will buy only the wild roots--and they know the difference. Those who control the trade have burned quantities in the effort to keep up the price.

There are some drug plants which might be raised with success by those who would specialize in one plant, but the lesson we learn from ginseng should act as a warning.

Raising drugs is one of those things that seems to be more profitable to teach others to do than to do yourself. A well known Professor said to me: "If I were twenty-five and knew what I know about drugs and the market for them, I should go into the drug-raising business. But I should expect to lose money for some years. If I were a small clerk, say, or an old man who wanted to get out of city life, and I had $500 I really wanted to venture in drug raising, I should divide it in half--half I should put in the bank and the other half I should throw into the Hudson River. Then I should be sure of $250 instead of being drawn on to spend it all."

"Most of the people who have been in the business, notably the Shakers, who used to do the most of it, are gradually getting out of it. The few men who make money raising drugs keep it to themselves."

In many cases when weeds have been dug the work of handling and curing them is not excessive and can readily be done by women and children.

Too much emphasis cannot be placed upon the importance of carefully and thoroughly drying all crude drugs, whether roots, herbs, leaves, barks, flowers, or seeds, and putting them under cover at nightfall. If poorly dried, they will heat and become moldy in shipping, and the collector will find his goods rejected by the dealer and have all his trouble for nothing. Leaves, herbs, and flowers should never be washed.

It is important also to collect in proper season only, as drugs collected out of season are unmarketable on account of inferior medicinal qualities, and there will also be a greater shrinkage in a root dug during the growing season than when it is collected after growth has ceased.

The roots of annual plants should be dug in the autumn of the first year just before the flowering period, and those of biennial and perennial plants in the fall of the second or third year, after the tops have dried.

After the roots have been dug the soil should be well shaken from them, and all foreign particles, such as dirt, roots, and parts of other plants, should be removed. If the roots cannot be sufficiently cleared of soil by shaking, they should be thoroughly washed in clean water. Drugs must look wholesome at least. It does not pay to be careless in this matter. The soil increases the weight of the roots, but the purchaser is not willing to pay by weight for dirt, and grades the uncleaned or mixed drugs accordingly. It is the bright, natural looking root, leaf, or plant that will bring a good price.

After washing, the roots should be carefully dried by exposing them to light and air, on racks or shelves, or on clean well-ventilated barn floors, or lofts. They should be spread out thinly and turned occasionally from day to day until completely cured. When this point is reached, in perhaps three to six weeks, the roots will snap readily when bent. If dried out of doors they should be placed under shelter at night and upon the approach of rain.

Some roots require slicing and removing fibrous rootless. In general, large roots should be split or sliced when green in order to facilitate drying.

Barks of trees should be gathered in spring, when the sap begins to flow, but may also be peeled in winter. In the case of the coarser barks (as elm, hemlock, poplar, oak, pine, and wild cherry) the outer layer is shaved off before the bark is removed from the tree, which process is known as "rossing." Only the inner bark of these trees is used medicinally. Barks may also be cured by exposure to sunlight, but moisture must be avoided.

Leaves and herbs should be collected when the plants are in full flower. The whole plant may be cut and the leaves may be stripped from it, rejecting the coarse and large stems as much as possible, and keeping only the flowering tops and more tender stems and leaves.

Both leaves and herbs should be spread out in thin layers on clean floors, racks, or shelves, in the shade, but where there is free circulation of air, and turned frequently until thoroughly dry. Moisture will darken them.

Flowers are collected when they first open or immediately after, not when they are beginning to fade. Seeds should be gathered just as they are ripening, before the seed pods open, and should be winnowed in order to remove fragments of stems, leaves, and shriveled specimens.

The collector should be sure that the plant is the right one. Many plants closely resemble one another, and some "yarbs," contrary to the popular impression, are deadly poison--nightshade (belladonna) and the wild variety of parsnips, for instance. Therefore, where any doubt exists, send a specimen of the entire plant, including leaves, flowers, and fruits, to a drug dealer or to the nearest state experiment station for identification.

Samples representative of the lot of drugs to be sold should be sent to the nearest commission merchant, or drug store, for inspection and for quotation on the amount of drug that can be furnished, or for information as to where to send the article.

In writing to the different dealers for information and for prices, which vary greatly, it should be stated how much of a particular drug can be furnished and how soon this can be supplied, and postage should always be inclosed for reply. The collector should bear in mind that freight is an important item, and it is best, therefore, to address the dealers accessible to the place of production. The package containing the sample should be plainly marked with contents and the name and address of the sender. When ready for shipment crude drugs may be tightly packed in burlap or gunny sacks, or in dry, clean barrels.

Burdock root brings from three to eight cents per pound, and seed five to ten cents. About fifty thousand pounds of the root is imported annually, and the best has come from Belgium. Of dock roots, about 125,000 pounds are imported annually, at from two to eight cents.

The field for the sale of dandelion root is large.

Of couch grass, the roots of which cause much profanity in this country, there are some 250,000 pounds annually imported at from three to seven cents per pound.

A common weed with which there is a considerable trouble is the pokeweed, the root of which brings from two to five cents per pound and the dried berries five cents per pound.

Forty to sixty thousand pounds of foxglove are imported from Europe. Analysis has shown that the leaves of the wild American foxglove are as good as the European article, the price of which per pound ranges from six to eight cents.

Of mullein flowers about five thousand pounds used to be imported, chiefly from Germany. The leaves are also imported.

Dried leaves and tops of lobelia bring from three to eight cents per pound, while the seed commands fifteen to twenty cents per pound.

Of tansy about thirty-five thousand pounds have been imported annually at a price rallying from three to six cents.

The flowering tops and leaves of the gum plant are used as drug. They bring from five to twelve cents per pound.

Boneset leaves and tops bring from two to eight cents per pound. Catnip tops and leaves two to eight cents per pound.

Of horehound about 125,000 pounds are imported annually, prices being three to eight cents per pound.

Blessed thistle is cultivated in Germany, and it is imported to a limited extent.

Yarrow is a weed common from the New England states to Missouri. It is imported in small quantities, and brings from two to five cents per pound.

Canada fleabane brings from six to eight cents per pound. Of jimsonweed, leaves are imported, from 100,000 to 150,000 pounds annually, and 10,000 pounds of seed. Leaves bring two and one half to eight cents per pound, and seeds from three to seven cents per pound.

Of poison hemlock, seeds are imported from ten to twenty thousand pounds annually. Price for the seed is three cents per pound, for the leaves about four cents. The flowers are also used.

The American wormseed has been naturalized from tropical America to New England; the seed commands from six to eight cents per pound; the oil distilled from this seed brings one dollar and a half per pound.

Black mustard, which is a troublesome weed in almost every state in the Union, is nevertheless imported in enormous quantities, the total imports of the seeds of the black and white mustard amounting annually to over five million pounds, the prices being from three to six cents per pound. All these prices and quantities were before the war and may greatly change after it.

In studying the wild drug plants, one may learn the immense variety of field salads and greens. On a visit to the Spirit Fruit Society at Ingleside, Illinois, one of the girls took me out to gather wild vegetables for dinner. We pulled up about a dozen varieties out of the corners of a field; two or three of the nice looking ones that I gathered the young lady threw out, saying she did not know them; but it seemed to me that she took almost anything that was not too tough. The following are commonly used as salads: Dandelion, yellow racket, purslane (pusley), watercress, nasturtium; and the following as greens for cooking: narrow or sour dock, stinging nettle, pokeweed, pigweed or lamb's quarters, black mustard. Young milkweed is better than spinach, and also makes an excellent salad. Probably all the salad leaves could be cooked to advantage. Rhubarb leaves and horseradish tops are garden greens usually neglected most unfairly

Osage Orange (maclura aurantiaca) s generally supposed to be poison, and is described in Webster's dictionary as "a hard and inedible fruit," but I have found one kind, at least, superior to quinces.

Capsicum or red pepper, licorice (the imports of which have all been in the hands of one person), camphor, belladonna, henbane, and stramonium are possible fields for culture; but they are all experiments.

If you are growing poppies for the flowers it might be worth while to gather some opium, especially if the new process succeeds in separating morphine directly from the plant.

Caraway seeds, anise, coreander, and sage are common garden plants that may be sold as drugs.

CHAPTER XVI
NOVEL LIVE STOCK

Occasionally we hear stories of the wealth which is being made on a frog farm here or there. But as a rule little commercial success has attended attempts in this direction.

The difficulty lies in feeding them. A single frog can be fed by dangling a piece of meat before it, but it would be impossible to feed thousands this way. There are so many enemies that few tadpoles become adult frogs; besides, the frog is a cannibal and will eat not only the larvae or eggs, but the tadpoles and young frogs as well.

Frog culture is successful in some places where ponds are large enough to be partitioned, separating the tadpoles and young frogs from the old ones, and where insects are abundant enough to supply food naturally for them. Near San Francisco there are a number of frog ranches. Even in 1903, according to Mary Heard in *Out West,* one ranch sold to San Francisco markets 2600 dozen frogs' legs, netting $1800. This was considered poor. Frogs' legs are sold to hotels and restaurants, and bring in New York, according to size and season, from fifty cents to a dollar a pound.

Tons of frogs come to New York markets each year from Canada, Michigan, and from the South and West. Few people outside of the cities eat them. The United States Fish Commissioners reported the product in one year: Arkansas, 58,800 lb., valued at $4162; Indiana, 24,000 lb., valued at $5026; Ohio, 14,000 lb., valued at $2340; Vermont, 5500 lb., valued at $825, etc.--a total of $22,953.

The enormous and increasing prices of large diamond backed turtles, and the cheapness of little ones shows that maturing, at least, if not actually breeding them, would be well worth investigation. Many wealthy New Yorkers send direct to Maryland for their supplies. Where turtle meat is bottled or canned, the snapping turtle and the common box tortoise are sometimes used as "substitutes." Both are capital eating.

The carp is one of the most excellent fresh water fish, and is of great value on account of the facility of culture and the enormous extent to which this is carried on. "In Europe some artificial ponds comprise an area of no less than 20,000 acres, and the proceeds amount to about 500,000 pounds of carp per annum." (Hessel, in "Carp and Its Culture.")

It attains the weight of three to four pounds in three years without artificial feeding, and much more under more favorable conditions. It lives to a great age and continues to grow all the while.

"In Europe it is common to see carp weighing from thirty to forty pounds and more, measuring nearly three and one half feet in length and two and three quarters feet in circumference."

It lives on vegetable food, insects, larvae, and worms, and will not attack other fishes or their spawn. It is easy to raise, and, provided certain general rules are followed, success will attend its culture.

The localities best adapted to a carp pond are those in which there is sufficient water at hand for the summer as well as the winter. A mud or loam soil is best adapted for such a pond. A rocky, gravelly ground is not suited for carp; the water should be the same depth all the year, as variation has an injurious effect on the fish.

Carp spawn in the spring. In stocking a pond three females are calculated to two males. The females lay a great number of eggs, but only a small number are impregnated. The most liberal estimate will not exceed from 800 to 1000 to one spawner, the aggregate per acre amounting to from 4000 to 5000.

The large cities containing large numbers of Europeans furnish the principal markets for carp. The Jewish people will not, as a rule, buy carp unless they are alive, so it is not an uncommon thing to see fish dealers in the Hebrew quarters pushing through the streets carts constructed as tanks and peddling the carp alive.

Some years ago carp ponds were quite a fad among farmers of the Central West. Americans have been slow to adopt the German carp as a food fish.

Trout, of course, can be raised, and the high prices which they bring, both in market and for fishing privileges, make them very attractive; but the cold running water needed makes opportunity for breeding them with access to a good market generally unavailable to owners of five acres.

There is another fish, famous for its eating qualities, which well repays effort put upon its production. I refer to the black bass. It is indigenous to the waters of the Eastern states, where it is usually found in creeks or rivers. It can be successfully bred in properly constructed ponds.

Mr. Dwight Lyell, in Forest and Stream, has this to say about a breeding place for the small-mouthed black bass. "The pond should be six feet deep in the center and two feet around the edge; the bottom should be of natural sand; water plants should be growing in profusion, particularly such aquatic plants as the Daphnia, Bosmina, and the Corix, to furnish food for the young bass. A good size for a breeding pond is 100 X 100 feet." For spawning, artificial nest frames are built in rectangular form. They are made two feet square without bottoms. On two adjoining sides these frames are four inches high and on the other two adjoining sides sixteen inches high. These frames are made because the bass needs a barrier behind which the spawning may be done and which will protect the nest when made. For raising the fish to a size large enough for food, ponds can be of any convenient size. In order to keep the water in healthful condition the pond must be fed by a flowing brook with some provision to prevent the water being disturbed by freshets. This can usually be arranged by a sluice to carry off the surplus water during heavy rains. Black bass raised in shallow ponds will take the fly all summer, so that considerable may be made from fishing privileges.

In the absence of minnows, which are the food of the bass, they must be fed on fresh liver cut in threads like an angle worm to tempt the fish. Even then the liver diet must be varied by feeding minnows from September until the bass goes into winter quarters. In no other way can fertile eggs be assured for the spring hatching. Minnows left in the pond all winter will breed and so furnish fry on which the young bass can feed tile next summer."

What has been said refers particularly to the small-mouthed black bass. The conditions are substantially the same for the large-mouthed bass (which grows to a much larger size), except that the bottom may be made of Spanish moss imbedded in cement.

There is a growing market for the young bass or fingerlings to stock streams and ponds. The relation between the producer of stock fish and those who expect to raise bass of a marketable size is about the same as exists between the professional seed grower and the market gardener. It is much better for the small farmer who has or can make an artificial pond to buy his fingerlings from the professional breeder, who has facilities which are too elaborate to be duplicated on a small scale.

Fish culture, except under government auspices, is little known in the United States.

American Homes and Gardens has an account of the breeding of pheasants, which is of interest. That it is possible to breed pheasants, even around an ordinary suburban home, is shown by Mr. Homer Davenport, the famous cartoonist, who succeeded in breeding and raising some of the choicest pheasants on his place at Morris Plains, New Jersey.

A great variety of species are commonly bred, but all of them came from China or India. The pheasant can be tamed by careful handling, but cats and dogs and other small animals must be kept away. The pheasantry should be placed on high, well-drained ground with a southern exposure, where the soil is good enough to raise clover, oats, and barley. The quarters for pheasants and the management are very much like those for fancy chickens. The yard should be inclosed by wire netting both on sides and top to keep the birds from wandering away; and there should be houses for roosting and breeding with nesting quarters attached.

In Central Park, New York, the running space allotted to three or four birds is not more than ten by twenty feet, and Mr. George Ethelbert Walsh tells of a case where sixty pheasants were kept in excellent condition in a house ten by fifty feet, with five yards attached, averaging 10 X 25 feet. However, with pheasants, as with all the bird family, especially turkeys, the more ground they have for ranging the less liable they will be to disease. The chief difficulty in breeding game birds like the pheasant is to secure the insects, such as flies, maggots, and ant eggs, which are the natural food of the young. Sufficient green food like lettuce, turnip tops, cabbage, etc., must also be provided. There is always a market at fancy prices for more of the matured birds than can possibly be supplied.

Some people make money in breeding or training fancy birds like canaries, mocking birds, finches, parrots, and so on; but this industry can be carried on almost as well in rooms in the city as in the country. Specializing on any kind of animal rearing must be gone into with extreme caution, because in the breeding of animals there are many factors to be dealt with which do not confront the breeder of plants. Make haste slowly, and before branching out be sure that you master each step in its turn.

An industry which is practically unknown in this country, but which flourishes in Burgundy, France, is the raising of snails for food. Those who are shocked by this will he surprised to learn that snail culture was practiced by the Romans at the time of the Civil War between Caesar and Pompey, as Jacques Boyer says in **American Homes and Gardens.** The snail lays from fifty to sixty eggs annually. They are deposited in a smooth hole prepared for them in the ground and hatched within twenty days. So rapidly do they grow that they are ready for market six or eight weeks after hatching. The snail park is made by inclosing a plot of damp, limy soil with smooth boards coated with tar to prevent the snails climbing out, and held in place by outside stakes strong enough to withstand the wind. The boards must penetrate the soil to the depth of eight inches at least, and at a level with the ground they must have a sort of shelf to prevent the snails from burrowing under them. When the snail encounters an obstacle in its path, it lays its eggs, sensible beast. Ten thousand snails can be raised on a plot of land one hundred by two hundred feet. The ground is plowed deeply in the spring, the snails are placed on it and covered with from two to four inches of moss or straw which is kept damp. They must be fed daily with lettuce, cabbage, vine leaves, or grass; as they eat at night, they are fed shortly before sunset. Aromatic herbs, like mint, parsley, etc., are planted in the inclosure to improve the flavor of the snails.

In October, the snails having become fat through the summer, retire into their shells, the mouths of which they close with a thin gelatinous covering. They are now ready for picking, and are put on screens or trays which are piled together in storehouses, where they remain several months without food. When the fast has been sufficiently prolonged, the shells are brushed up and the snails cooked in salt water in a great pot holding about ten thousand. When cooked, they are immediately sent to the consumer in wooden boxes holding from fifty to two hundred. The business is a very profitable one, as the snail is considered a great delicacy by epicures.

Perhaps the silkworm is not exactly in place in a chapter on Novel Live Stock.

It is at present not much more than an interesting experiment, but there will be money in silkworm culture as soon as a market for the product is developed. The main difficulty is lack of food, as the worm thrives best on the leaf of the white mulberry tree. Until a substitute is found, it will be necessary therefore to set out young trees, which in two years will bear enough leaves to supply food. The labor of silkworm rearing all comes in one month. It can be carried on in any large, airy room The eggs are hatched by the summer heat, and the worm does not become a heavy eater until the last two weeks. It sheds its skin four times, and after the final moult it climbs into loose brush prepared for it and spins the cocoon. These are then dried and shipped.

At the South, where the climate is well suited for silk culture, an obstacle has been found in the unadaptability of the cheap labor, particularly colored labor, to the delicate handling, and especially winding of the silk from the cocoons.

Many people make money by breeding dogs. Not much land is required and very little capital, as kennels can be multiplied as demand increases. There is always a profitable market for dogs, and some of the lap species, like the King Charles spaniel, bring fabulous prices. Hunting dogs, such as setters, pointers, retrievers, really require a game country and a practical hunter who can train the puppies, to make much of a success of it; with these, if properly handled, the business is a safe one, as there is little other technical skill required beyond ordinary care, such as is given to domestic animals.

Cats are a better venture than dogs because they are sold to women who will pay any price for what strikes their fancy. Fashions in cats change about as fast as fashions in coats, but cats breed faster than coats wear out, so it is quick business.

Just now, coon cats, tortoise-shell cats, and bizarre colors of Persian cats are mostly in vogue, but the tailless Manx cat, and even freaks like the six-toed cat and Iynx cats always find a ready market.

Of course, these can be raised in the city, but if it is done in a large enough way to make a living out of it, the Board of Health and the neighbors will raise-- something else.

Fishing and hunting are primitive industries of which we think only in connection with wild land. But every bay and pond and wood will supply at least some subsistence or profit to the intelligent seeker.

Oysters, clams, crabs, mussels, frogs, and common fish are found in abundance in many places, and help out with table expenses. Even English sparrows are delicious.

Almost any wild animal is much more wholesome to eat than pork. Squirrels and even weasels are cleaner feeders than pigs, and the Indians eat them with great relish, while everybody knows the keenness of the darkies for "coon." Most snakes are better eating than eels and not near so repulsive--when you get used to them.

The woodchuck is a nuisance to the farmer, covering his field with loads of subsoil from the burrow and then eating the tender sprouts; and the farmer does not know enough to eat his tender corpse, but he is good to eat. If a rabbit and a chicken could have young, it would taste like a woodchuck

Muskrats, mink, raccoons, and gray and fox squirrels are easily trapped; and the skins of those killed in that way find a steady market. Skins of poisoned animals do not sell so well, as they are rough and dry.

In order to be profitable, these do not need to pay very well in proportion to the time they take, since they are hunted as recreation and at odd times.

But there is a larger field in raising wild animals, which our Western people have not been slow to avail themselves of, and we hear of men being prosecuted for breeding wolves, coyotes, and bobcats, a kind of lynx, to get the government bounty for the snouts or scalps.

In a legitimate way profit may be had from such animals.

Ernest Thompson Seton has an article in *Country Life in America,* on raising fur-bearing animals for profit; this offers a good chance for small capital and large intelligence. He suggests the beaver, mink, otter, skunk, and marten, and says that whoever would begin fur farming is better off with five acres than with five hundred. He describes two fox ranches at Dover, Maine. They raise twenty to forty silver foxes a year, on a little more than half an acre of land. The silver fox's fur is one of the most valuable on the market and sells at an average of $150 a pelt, that is, $3000 to $6000 gross for the year's work. Foxes are not expensive to breed, their food consisting chiefly of sour milk and cornmeal or flour made into a cake, and a little meat about once a week.

The capital required is small. A fence for the inclosure should be of one and a half inch mesh No. 16 galvanized wire, ten feet high, with an overhang of eighteen inches to keep the foxes from escaping, and is about the only outlay except for purchase of stock.

Stakes should be driven close to the fence to keep them from burrowing out.

They are naturally clean animals, and with careful attention are free from disease. Mr. Stevens reports that in his two years' experience he has had twenty to thirty foxes and lost none by disease, while Mr. Norton, with five years' experience, carrying thirty to forty, reports that one to two die each year.

They breed as well in captivity as in their wild state, usually bringing forth a litter of six or seven in the spring. These breed the following spring and their fur is ready for market the following December. And now breeders sell fine stock to other breeders who are entering the industry, sometimes getting three to four hundred dollars per pair. Mr. Seton remarks, "I am satisfied that any man who has made a success of hens can make a success of foxes, with this advantage for the latter a fox requires no more space or care than a hen, but is worth twenty times as much, and so gives a chance for returns twenty times as large."

This is an infant industry, but if others can get the same results, it will pay handsomely. To get the best furs, however, requires a district where the winters are cold and long.

There are a few skunk farms in the West. It is said that the scent gland can be taken out, though that is not necessary, and that the farms do well. Their oil is also said to be valuable. But while skunks are so common there cannot be much in breeding them.

If your fancy goes to "critters" rather than crops it is much better to raise game birds. Wild turkeys raised under a hen or in an incubator and made pretty tame (if too tame they do not thrive so well in a small area), "wild" ducks, grouse, partridges, quails, even wood ducks which build their nests in trees are no longer experiments.

All the common enemies you have to contend against are foxes, dogs, cats, rats, mink, skunks, hawks, owls, crows, frogs, turtles, snakes, poachers, game legislators, and disease.

It has been calculated that one pair of quails and its progeny would produce five or six million birds in eight years if there were no losses. But so would chickens; and probably you will not get that many.

All about these game birds is set forth in an advertising booklet called, "Game Farming" of the Hercules Powder Co., which has offices in a dozen cities, so we need not enlarge.

CHAPTER XVII
WHERE TO GO

Intensive cultivation, raising a big crop on little land, can be carried on most profitably near areas of dense population; for perishable products, like fruits and vegetables, can be best marketed near the consumer. The limit for delivery by auto is about fifteen to twenty miles, and then only if roads are good; if the land selected lies on the line of a railroad which gives equal terms to way freight and to through freight, you will fare nearly as well. Railroads control agricultural development. Sparsely settled regions always practice extensive cultivation, raising light crops on big farms, because only such crops can be grown as can be raised on large areas by machinery, and are not perishable. Staples like corn, wheat, pork, and beef are transported at low prices for long distances by the railroads. This forces the settlers in newly opened portions of the country to sell in a market created by the railroads, in competition with what is produced within the areas of intensive cultivation, that is, with access to adjacent markets.

So we find the bonanza wheat farms of California, the Dakotas, and the Canadian Northwest, the pampas of the Argentine, the Steppes of Russia, and the Indian uplands devoted to wheat raising; in the United States corn belt, fields of from five to twenty thousand acres are still not uncommon. Conversely, intensive cultivation is most advanced in China, where a dense population forced the people long ago to bring into use every foot of tillable soil that is left open to them.

Near the towns of the United States a few market gardeners supply such vegetables as the people do not raise for themselves. The states along the Atlantic seaboard have all the facilities for successful intensive cultivation--a dense population and idle, cultivable land. In choosing a location, the home crofter should well consider his experience, and try to enter a community where he can engage in analogous pursuits. Dairy regions never have enough men who understand cattle and horses; fruit-growing districts always need experienced pickers; market garden regions need men who understand rotating crops and making hotbeds, transplanting, etc.

If you have a little money, you can probably do best by buying and draining some swamp land, which is the most productive of all, as it contains the washings of the upland for centuries. Swamp land can usually be cleared and drained for from thirty to forty dollars per acre. It can be bought very cheap and when ready to cultivate will have increased many times in value.

The next best is the "abandoned" or worn-out farm. Proper methods of cultivation will bring it back to more than its original fertility. The Eastern states from Maine to Virginia abound with them at from five to twenty-five dollars per acre. In many cases the buildings are worth more than the whole price asked.

The nearest land easily available in the East is in the state of New York. The writer believes it is true that "there are twenty thousand farms for sale in this state, and nearly, all at such low prices and upon such favorable terms as to make them available for any one desiring to engage in agriculture or have a farm home. The soil of these farms is not exhausted, but on the contrary is, with proper cultivation, very productive. Nearly all have good buildings and fences, are supplied with good water and plenty of wood for farm purposes, and in nearly all cases have apple and other fruit trees upon them." (List of Farms, occupied and unoccupied, for sale in New York State. Bureau of Information and Statistics, Bulletin, State of New York, Department of Agriculture.)

These farms are distributed all over the state, some in nearly every county. In Sullivan County, for example, there are farms for sale ranging in price from ten to one hundred dollars per acre. These can, almost without exception, be bought by small payments, balance on long mortgages, and it is wonderful how cheap they are. In Ulster County thirty farms, some of which I have seen, are offered for sale at trifling prices.

Of course, many of these farms have been sold since the first editions of this book, and the prices have advanced, perhaps on the average doubled; but cheap automobiles have improved roads and have made others available that were useless ten years ago. The development of the Southern states, with eradication of the cattle tick (the cause of "Texas Fever") and irrigation and rotation of crops, has opened up new countries. N. O. Nelson writes he has bought many Louisiana farms for his cooperative enterprise for about what the improvements are worth.

Cut over woodlands which we have learned to make produce incomes of about five dollars each year per acre by intelligent forestry, as well as swamp lands which we now know how to make healthful by drainage and by the extinction of mosquitoes, can still be had at low prices in New York and other states. Numerous others are in the market from five dollars per acre up, and so it goes through the state, from Wyoming County in the extreme western end, where farms ranging from thirty to three hundred acres are in the market at from thirty to forty dollars per acre, to St. Lawrence County in the north, where land can be bought as low as fifteen dollars per acre.

When it is considered that these lands are within easy access to established markets with transportation and mail facilities, rural delivery, and telephone a proper idea may be formed of their value in opportunity. The authority quoted further states that "probably fifty thousand agricultural laborers can find employment on the farms of New York at good wages. Families particularly are wanted to rent houses and work farms on shares." Wages for new hands run from twenty to thirty dollars and upwards per month with board. Men who know how to milk are especially in demand throughout the dairy regions. These conditions make it possible for experienced farmers, although entirely without money, to get to the soil.

Over three hundred thousand aliens annually settled in the cities of New York State during some years in the last decade. These people could be got out of the cities, where in normal times they are little needed, into adjacent country districts where they are much needed.

In the *Real Estate Record and Guide,* Mr. A. L. Langdon says: "It is most remarkable that there are on Long Island, within from thirty-five to seventy miles of New York, thousands of acres of land which have never been cultivated, which have for years produced nothing but cordwood, and which the owners allow to be overrun with fire almost every year. A large part of this land has soil two or three feet deep underlaid with gravel. The best water in the world is abundant and the climate is more equable than on the mainland, and in each locality where any reasonable effort has been made to cultivate the soil, it has produced plentifully of all fruits and vegetables which can be grown in this latitude."

Long Island should produce all the fruit, vegetables, poultry, eggs, and milk needed by its own residents, with a large surplus for the city markets, instead of getting, as it does, a large part of its supply of these things from the city.

When it is considered that about a quarter of a million acres of this land so close to the city is now scrub oak and uncultivated waste, and that there are about a million adult workers in the city, the importance of the experiment is obvious; especially as we learn from the United States census that over ten thousand of these workers are already in agricultural pursuits within the city limits.

"Here midway on Long Island, and just beyond the limits for a man to locate who expects to earn his living by daily work in the city, is a territory about forty miles long and ten miles wide which by intensive farming would yield a good living for more than two hundred thousand inhabitants. In this agricultural section, a man of small means who expects to live on the land the year round, should purchase a plot not too small to produce enough to support himself and family and a surplus to sell, not less than six acres. Probably all men have more or less land hunger a desire to own land and it is a worthy object to encourage to the extent of inducing a man to purchase what he can pay for and be satisfied with, but it is a shameful thing to induce a poor man, who has to earn his living in New York, to buy on the installment plan a small lot so far from his place of employment that he cannot live on it and travel to and from his work every day, and where there is the strongest probability that he will never make more than two or three payments, and will consequently lose what he does pay." The writer hears of one plot which was sold nineteen times and the contracts defaulted on after payments, before any one took title.

If the seeker is not satisfied with the opportunities which the state of New York offers, he may turn to New Jersey, equally accessible and equally rich in chances.

New Jersey Year-Book: "There are in the southern part of the State large tracts of land which are still uncleared, or covered with brushwood, and which are adapted to tillage and capable of producing large crops of small fruits and market garden vegetables. The wood on them is mainly scrub oak, with some dwarfed pitch pine and yellow pine, and hence they are called oak lands to distinguish them from the more sandy lands and tracts on which the pitch pine grows almost exclusively. The latter are known as pine lands. The total area of cleared (farm) lands in the southern division of the State, southeast of the marl belt, is about 450,000 acres. The pineland belts have an aggregate area of 486,000 acres, making at least 800,000 acres accessible by railways from the large cities and also near to tidewater navigation. The maps of the Geological Survey show the location and the extent of these lands, their railway lines, and their relation to the settlements already made and to the cities.

"The soils of these tracts are sandy and not naturally so rich and fertile as the more heavy clay soils of the limestone, the red shale, and the marl districts of the State, but they are not so sandy and so coarse-grained as to be non-productive, like some of the pineland areas. The latter are often deficient in plant food and are deservedly characterized as pine barrens, being too poor for farm purposes. The growth of oak and pine, as well as chemical analyses, shows that the oak-land soils contain the elements of plant production. They are not so well suited to pasturage or to continuous cropping as naturally rich virgin soils; they are better fitted for raising vegetables, melons, sweet potatoes, small fruits, peaches, and pears than wheat, Indian corn, hay, and other staples. The eminent superiority of this kind of farming in New Jersey over the old routine of wheat, corn, hay, and potatoes is well known. These South Jersey soils are easily cleared of brushwood or standing timber, and of stumps, with a hand or horse-power puller which is a cheap affair, and the wood is salable in all this part of the State at remunerative prices, often bringing more than the original cost of the land. The long working season and the short and mild winter favor the arrangement of work, so that all is done with the least outlay for help. They also favor the mosquitoes.

"The success of Hammonton, Egg Harbor City, Vineland, and other places is notable, and equally good results are to be had at a hundred or more places as well situated as they are. These lands are sold at low figures, and the settler saves in capital and interest account. Only the difficulty of getting money to help in building interferes with rapid settlement.

"The West Jersey Railway, the Pennsylvania, and the Philadelphia and Reading's Atlantic City Railroad, the Philadelphia and Seashore Railway, the New Jersey Southern Railroad, and other branch roads afford excellent facilities for access to New York, Philadelphia, and the cities of the State. The Cohansey, Maurice, and Mullica rivers head well up near the northwest limits of these lands, and their navigable reaches run for miles across them. The waters of the Delaware Bay and the ocean are within a few miles of a large part of this oak-land domain.

"The advantages of an old settled and Eastern State, within easy reach of these large markets, of land which is easily tilled and generous and quick in its response to feeding, and at low prices, make them equal to, if not better than, the rich prairie soils of a new West, or the low prices and cheap lands of the abandoned hillsides of New England."

Wages for unskilled farm labor are about the same as for New York--twenty to twenty-five dollars per month. The canning and fruit industries make room for a large number of people in the late summer and fall, who may thus, by taking a temporary place, kind some permanent location where they may improve their health and fortunes.

"Delaware also offers unequalled opportunities to immigrants. It is ideally situated on the Atlantic Ocean and the Delaware Bay, and is penetrated by numerous creeks and rivers.

"The railroad, steam, and electric facilities of the State are developing steadily year by year, while every section of the State possesses easily navigable streams, with vessels for carrying freight and passengers.

"Over fifteen millions of people live within a radius of three hundred miles; the large majority reside in cities and towns and furnish the finest markets in the world. Within five hundred miles are more than one third of the people of all North America.

"Wilmington is a city of seventy-five thousand people, is growing rapidly, and is becoming a great manufacturing place.

"These people may be reached in one day by the luscious fruits that grow in Delaware, and every one of them is perfectly happy when he gets a Delaware peach. Many other Delaware products are as good as the peaches.

"As cattle and wheat raising developed in the great West, Delaware people thought that they were ruined. They did not change at once, but slowly discovered that the light lands are wonderfully productive of fruits and vegetables, and that they pay much better than cattle and grain ever could. But these new methods have not been adopted in all parts of the State, so that land neglected and unprofitable is for sale. The tides of immigration have swept westward and left Delaware untouched. Men, money, and enterprise are needed.

" There are few unoccupied or 'abandoned' farms in Delaware." The land is mostly held by descendants of the early settlers, who form a species of landed aristocracy. Lately, owing to the younger members of these families having become established in the newer states and on account of the death or incapacity of the older members left in possession, there has been a marked tendency to sell off these farms. However, "a large proportion of the farms in Delaware are not for sale at any price. Some of them have been in the same family for generations, and if put on the market would sell for from one to two hundred dollars per acre."

The soil is all the way from a heavy white oak clay, which is too stiff and too sticky for most crops, to very light sand.

The heaviest clay is made lighter and more porous, and the lightest sand is readily made retentive of moisture and extremely productive, by plowing in different kinds of crops as green manure, such as cow peas, soy beans, the vetches, etc.; crimson clover, winter oats, rye, turnips, and numerous other crops may be sown in August or later, and produce a fine crop for turning under early in the spring. Crimson clover grows nearly all winter. Pure cold water is reached at from twenty to fifty feet by dug or driven wells.

The climate is good; there are no cyclones. There is some damp weather in winter, but there are no malignant fevers, and there is little or no malaria, except in a few marshy places. There are some mosquitoes and flies, but they are not especially troublesome, and there are no poisonous reptiles.

The population is mostly native, five sixths white, one sixth colored. The white population is almost entirely of Anglo Saxon descent.

"Perfect titles may be secured, but all titles everywhere should always be searched by a competent lawyer, the usual fee for which is ten to twenty dollars.

"Farm hands receive from twenty to twenty-five dollars per month and board, for a season of nine or ten months, sometimes for the whole year. Day hands receive from seventy-five cents to two dollars per day and board themselves."

Those who are tempted by the advertisements for fruitpickers should beware. Delaware, like some other states, allows fees to constables and to the "squires"-- Justices of the Peace they would be elsewhere--for arrests, and it is a common practice to advertise for fruit pickers, then arrest them as tramps when they come, and the next day release them on condition that they will leave the county at once--and leave the trap open for the next comer.

Delaware peaches have made fortunes for many, but will make still greater fortunes in the future for the owners of the land.

Pears, plums, grapes, watermelons, and cantaloupes thrive, and find an ideal home, and small fruits all flourish. Sweet potatoes yield bountifully and are of the finest quality. Asparagus and early white potatoes pay handsome profits. Tomatoes, the great canning crop, are grown by the thousands of acres.

"The grasses and clovers grow in luxuriance, and hence dairying and beef production are profitable. Poultry pays as well as anywhere else; chickens often run on green clover all through the open winter.

"The game consists of various species of ducks, quails, reed birds, hares, marsh rabbits, and other small creatures. Shad, trout, herring, crocus, black bass, pike, white fish, rock fish, oysters, clams, crabs, and terrapin are abundant in Delaware waters."

The tax in the rural counties is generally sixty cents on the hundred dollars. Besides this there are taxes on business and a very light school tax. There is no state tax, yet the state makes large appropriations for the support of the public schools, which are free to everybody.

Maryland has established a State Bureau of Immigration in Baltimore to give information to home seekers, and advise them as to choice of location, opportunities for getting started in agricultural production, and aid them in any way consistent with a State Bureau. Most of these facts are taken from such reports.

Southern Maryland and the eastern shore are especially adapted to gardening and trucking, as well as fruit growing. Land is cheap and can be purchased in tracts of any size from an acre upwards, at from ten to fifty dollars per acre. Farms from twenty acres to seven hundred acres and up are for sale in nearly every county in the state. The removal of a large part of the negro population from the country to the cities has resulted in the partition of the large estates into smaller farms, thus affording an opportunity for home seekers who are seeking cheap land amid congenial surroundings. Nearly all of these farms have buildings, some in need of repair, others in very good condition.

For those who wish to avoid the hard work of breaking woodlands, the eastern and western shores offer abundant well-cultivated lands with buildings, orchards, and woods, in the immediate vicinity of navigable rivers and railways, on good roads at from twenty dollars per acre upwards. That seems cheap.

For settlers who are accustomed to mountainous regions, western Maryland has land for sale at even cheaper rates.

"There are many large tidal marshes in Maryland, as might be expected in a territory watered like this state. They are of the richest soil to be found, because the Chesapeake Bay is a great river valley, receiving the drainage of a vast area of fertile land, comprising nearly one third of New York and nearly all of the great agricultural states of Pennsylvania, Maryland, and Virginia. Every year this drainage brings down a black sediment, called oyster mud, which is deposited on the marshlands and enriches the soil, making it, with proper cultivation, of productivity like that of the rice and wheat fields of Egypt. These unreclaimed lands are used chiefly for grain."

Proper drainage of small tracts of this land would bring unsurpassed and absolutely untouched fertility.

The Chesapeake River valley is not so large as that of the Nile or Ganges, but is of enough consequence to play an important part in human affairs and to support in comfort and prosperity a population as large as that of many famous states.

"The eastern shore is uniformly level, with good roads. The proximity of the ocean and the bay greatly modifies the temperature. It has a great trunk railway, with connections along its entire length, called the Delaware Division of the Pennsylvania railroad, which furnishes direct transportation to Philadelphia, New York, and other northern cities."

"On the eastern shore there are many thousand acres of land devoted to garden truck, and the strawberry crop has of late years become of importance. Over one hundred carloads of strawberries are shipped daily during the season to the Baltimore, Philadelphia, New York, and Boston markets."

Land properly cultivated will yield four thousand quarts of strawberries to an acre.

The canning of various fruits and vegetables has grown to be larger than that of any other state and is one of the most profitable of the industries of Maryland. The principal articles canned are peaches, peas, and tomatoes.

The tomato crop is also profitable to the grower. The young plants are set out in the spring; many do this with a machine, but two persons can easily plant seven acres in a day by hand.

An acre will produce from six to eighteen tons of tomatoes, according to the quality of the soil. All such products bring better prices now in Maryland markets than they did before canning was resorted to. The Maryland tin can is known wherever civilization reaches.

Tobacco is extensively produced only in southern Maryland, although it can be raised in any section of the state.

In the neighborhood of the larger cities trucking and fruit growing are profitable, combined with poultry raising, often on farms of not more than five or ten acres.

Many farmers devote part of their time successfully to bees, and there is nowhere a better climate for flowrs than that of Maryland. Two English florists who have settled in Baltimore County, ten and thirteen miles northeast of the city, daily send to all parts of the United States and even to Canada many large boxes of beautiful roses, carnations, violets, and other choice flowers. Both of these men began on a small scale and have prospered.

The farmer who has a couple of thousand dollars to pay cash for a small farm in Maryland is assured of a good living. But also a less favored settler, if he has only from four to eight hundred dollars, can have a good start in Maryland, and probably as good a chance for independence and prosperity as anywhere.

Families of immigrants when traveling to the Western, Northwestern, and Southern states of America have to spend from one hundred and fifty to two hundred dollars for railroad tickets from New York to their destination; by going to these adjoining states they can save all that money, and invest it in land.

The Virginia Department of Agriculture and Immigration also publishes information for the home seeker.

To most people the name Virginia carries with it limitless vistas of tobacco fields covered with darkies plying the hoe, or picking off the ubiquitous worm. Before the War this picture would have been a true one; but since the awakening of the younger generation to a better understanding of her resources, together with the withdrawal of large numbers of the colored people into industrial occupations, no state offers more attractive inducements to the homecrofter than Virginia. In climate, diversity of soils, fruits, forests, water supply, mineral deposits, including mountain and valley, she offers unsurpassed advantages. Truly did Captain John Smith, the adventurous father of Virginia, suggest that "Heaven and earth never agreed better to frame a place for man's habitation."

Virginia lies between the extremes of heat and cold, removed alike from the sultry, protracted summers of the more southern states, and the longer winters and devastating storm and cyclones of the North and Northwest. Its limits north and south correspond to California and southern Europe.

The climate is mild and healthful. The winters are less severe than in the Northern and Northwestern states, or even the western localities of the same latitude, while the occasional periods of extreme heat in the summer are not more oppressive than in many portions of the North.

Tidewater Virginia, or the Coastal Plain, as it is sometimes called, receives the name from the fact that the streams that penetrate it feel the ebb and flow of the tides from the ocean up to the head of navigation. It consists chiefly of broad and level plains, while a considerable portion, nearest to the bay, has shallow bays and estuaries, and marshes that are in most instances reached only by the ocean tides. These marshes abound with wild duck and sora. Tidewater is mainly an alluvial country. The soil is chiefly light, sandy loam, underlaid with clay. Its principal productions are fruits and early vegetables, which are raised in extensive "market gardens," and shipped in large quantities to Northern cities. The fertilizing minerals--gypsum, marl, and greensand--abound, and their judicious use readily restores the lands when exhausted by improvident cultivation.

Middle Virginia is a wide, undulating plain, crossed by many rivers that have cut their channels to a considerable depth and are bordered by alluvial bottom lands that are very productive. The soil consists of clays with a subsoil of disintegrated sandstone rocks, and varies according to the nature of the rock from which it is formed.

The principal productions of middle Virginia are corn, wheat, oats, and tobacco. The tobacco raised in this section and in Piedmont, known as the "Virginia Leaf," is the best grown and the best known in the United States. In this section, as in Tidewater, the low bottom lands formed by the sediment of the waters are exceptionally productive.

The Piedmont section is diversified and surpassingly picturesque. The soil is heavier than that of middle Virginia, the subsoil being of stiff and dark red clay. On the slopes of the Blue Ridge grapes of delicious flavor grow luxuriantly. These produce excellent wines, and the clarets have a wide fame. The pippin apples of this section are of unrivaled excellence.

The "Great Valley," as it is descriptively called, is in the general configuration one continuous valley, included between the two mountain chains that extend throughout the state; it is one of the most abundantly watered regions on the face of the globe. Deep limestone beds form the floor of the Great Valley, and from these beds the soil derives an exceeding fertility, peculiarly adapted to the growth of grasses and grain, and it bears the name of the "garden spot" of the state.

Five trunk lines of railroads penetrate and intersect the state. The lines of steamboats that ply the navigable streams of eastern Virginia afford commercial communication for large sections of the state with the markets of this country and of Europe. Norfolk and Newport News maintain communication with the European markets by steamers and vessels, while from these ports is also kept up an extensive commerce along the Atlantic seaboard. The seaports are nearer than is New York to the great centers of population, and areas of production, of the West and Northwest.

Market garden crops of every description can be grown. The following result was obtained on a four-acre patch near Norfolk:

"The owner stated that in September he sowed spinach on four acres. Between Christmas and the first of March following he cut and sold the spinach at the rate of one hundred barrels to the acre, at a price ranging from two to seven dollars per barrel--an average of $4.50 per barrel. Early in March the four acres were set out to lettuce, setting the plants in the open air with no protection whatever, 175,000 plants on the four acres. He shipped 450 half-barrel baskets of lettuce to the acre, at a price ranging from $2 to $2.75 per basket.

"Early in April, just before the lettuce was ready to ship, he planted snap beans between the lettuce rows; and today, June 2d, these are the finest beans we have seen this season.

"The last week in May he planted cantaloupes between the bean rows, which, when marketed in July, will make four crops from the same land in one year's time.

The cantaloupes will be good for 250 crates to the acre, and the price will run from $1 to $1.50 per crate. A careful investigation of these 'facts, figures, and features' will show that his gross sales will easily reach $2000 per acre; his net profits depend largely upon the man and the management; but they surely should not be less than $1000 clear, clean profit to the acre."

"This is for farming done all out of doors. No hothouse or hotbed work--not a bit of it, with no extra expense for hotbeds, cold frames, or hothouses."

"Intensive," thorough tillage and care of the soil will probably pay as well here as at any point in the United States.

Apples are the principal fruit crop of the state. There is a yearly increasing number of trees. In one of the valley counties a seventeen-year-old orchard of 1150 trees produced an apple crop as far back as 1905 which brought the owner $10,000, another of fifty twenty-year-old trees brought $700. Mr. H. E. Vandeman, one of the best-known horticulturists in the country, says that there is not in all North America a better place to plant orchards than in Virginia; on account of its "rich apple soil, good flavor and keeping qualities of the fruit, and nearness to the great markets of the East and Europe."

The trees attain a fine size and live to a good old age, and produce abundantly. In Patrick County there is a tree nine feet five inches around which has borne 110 bushels of apples at a single crop; other trees have borne even more. One farmer in Albemarle County has received more than $15,000 for a single crop of Albemarle Pippins grown on twenty acres of land. This pippin is considered the most delicious apple in the world.

The fig, pomegranate, and other delicate fruits flourish in the Tidewater region.

New England, from Maine to Rhode Island, is suffering from one disease--lack of intelligent labor. Thirty years ago the sons and daughters who, in the natural course of events, would have stayed to cultivate the home acres, left to form a part of the westward throng making for the level, untouched prairies of Illinois and Iowa.

The old folks have died or become incapacitated. New interests chain their children to adopted homes. Result,--unoccupied lands by the hundred thousand acres, awaiting energy, skill, and faith.

Ten dollars an acre is a common price for the rocky hills of New England. The choice river bottoms, and land near the larger cities is as high priced as similar land anywhere else. Intending settlers can buy small areas for little money; usually the smallest farms have good buildings worth in many cases more than the price asked for the whole farm. Climatic conditions are not favorable to single cropping. In the old days general farming, grain, beef, sheep, and hogs were the rule; nowadays, special crops, dairying, fruit growing, etc.

Tobacco is the great staple in the rich Connecticut River bottoms, and even on the uplands, if properly manured, it pays from one to three hundred dollars per acre. Tobacco can be raised on small areas far from the railroad, as, when properly cured and packed for shipment, it is not perishable. To many the worst feature of New England is the climate--long, cold winters and short summers. Maine being farthest north suffers most in this respect, but that does not prevent her producing hundreds of thousands of tons of sweet corn for canning and vast quantities of eggs and butter. Fruit does well on the lower coast; a small orchard of peaches or plums will in three or four years from planting make a comfortable living. Bush fruits grow in abundance and give never-failing crops.

Poultry is peculiarly successful on the rocky hills, because they are nearly always dry or well drained. Dairying can be made to pay if near a creamery, or where milk can be sold at retail. The prospective settler here should bear in mind that wherever he goes, the first year will produce little more than a kitchen garden; the second enable him barely to pull through, and the third give him a start at a permanent income. In farming, as in all other businesses, only those will succeed who know what they want and how to get it; who have selected with care the locality best suited to the special crops they intend to raise; and after having once made a selection, stick until they have compelled success.

The lure of the vast West and of the new South is not forgotten; but the time has passed when the young man could go West to take a farm of Uncle Sam's. Desirable land is too expensive for the pioneer, and the constant toil and comparative isolation of the prairie farm offers but a poor sort of liberty, though it still affords a living.

But close to the growing towns in those states small plots of land can still be had to work with the same bright prospects that are offered near the great metropolis.

In nearly all the sections within the area of intensive cultivation, timber is still plentiful enough to make it the cheapest building material; and persons who really want to get to the land can contrive a sufficient shelter, like a pioneer's, for from two to five hundred dollars.

CHAPTER XVIII
CLEARING THE LAND

It is pretty good fun to hack at bushes and to chop trees down and then to chop them up. If there is only a small part of the land to be cleared, a man can easily learn skill with the ax and do it at odd times, but he was a wise old man of whom his little girl said, "When grandpa wants anything, that moment he wants it." It is now that we need the land; but even if it is covered with trees, there is no cause for discouragement. Lumber is so high that the local or portable sawmill men will buy the timber by the acre. They will cut the trees and haul the logs.

If you decide to cut a tree yourself, a little inquiry will show for what purpose it will bring the highest price. Locust sticks, for example, four to six inches thick, will bring in New York ten or fifteen cents a running foot for insulator pinions. If a maple proves to be either "curly" or "bird'seye" (this depending not on the variety, but on the accidental undulations of the fiber), it will be in demand for the manufacture of furniture.

Sugar maples ten or fifteen feet high can be transplanted or sold. Nut and fruit trees will nearly always be worth keeping.

Cedar sticks fourteen feet long will bring twenty cents in most places for hop and bean poles. See what can be sold instead of burned, and don't cut down recklessly; an unsalable tree may be valuable as a windbreak or as shade for your house. The wrong tree for shade is the dense foliaged, low-branched tree which forms a solid dome from the ground up. The right tree, in the opinion of Henry Hicks (in Country Life in America), is the American elm, which ought to be called the umbrella tree. Pliny speaks of the plane tree, our sycamore or buttonwood, as excellent, because of the horizontal branches which, like window blinds, allow free passage of the breezes while intercepting the heat of the sun.

The ideal shade tree is a canopy like a parasol over the house, with high, leafy branches that do not shut off light and air from the windows. This cools a house by keeping the sun off and cools the air by the rapid evaporation from its leaves, and will make it ten to fifteen degrees cooler in summer. It will be cheaper and more effective than a combination of awnings, piazza, and eaves. Woodman, spare that tree.

Stumps may be burned out To get a good draught, bore a hole in a slanting direction far down among the roots. The smoke goes through the hole first and then the flame, boring the body to the roots deep enough to plow. Land can also be cleared by dynamite. We condense from Edith Loring Fullerton in *Farming,* on what has been done.

To go into the desolate, uncultivated, burned over "waste lands" near a great city and put ten acres under cultivation in the shortest possible space of time was our problem. We undertook it at short notice in an uncertain season--the autumn--with the determination to get at least a portion of the land seeded down to winter rye before cold weather prohibited further work.

United to this problem was that of working a small farm to its utmost capacity rather than half cultivation of a large one, which is difficult to handle from lack of time and labor and an unwise proposition for the East under the most favorable circumstances.

Ten acres of scraggy-looking woodland was purchased, sixty-eight miles from New York City on the north shore of Long Island. The plot had a few second and third growth oak and chestnut trees and "sprouts" along the borders. All else had been burned, and the center of the acreage exhibited the mangled and blackened remains of a once thrifty woodland.

We proceeded to choose as our helpers native Long Islanders whom we were desirous of allowing to work. We succeeded by strenuous efforts in getting together a "gang" of both colored and white men to the stupendous number of eight. They fell to work with a right good will, at first cutting down here and trimming up there as directed. However, after giving them a fair trial, we decided that they must be replaced by Italians. The question of housing the eighteen Italians soon came up. Tents might be adopted or even the unsanitary "dugout" be allowed to mar the landscape. A shanty was entirely too ugly to suit our tastes, and also expensive, and useless when the men were through with it. Tents were too airy, as we knew the work would continue until freezing weather, and perhaps well into the winter. We "passed" on the "dugout." The ideal was something that would be of use after the work of clearing was completed, and for that purpose we decided upon "condemned freight cars." They cost but ten dollars each, the railroad being glad to get rid of them. We bought two, ultimately using one for a chicken house and the other as a barn. In the meantime it was decided to remove the stumps by dynamite, as trying to yank them out by stump pullers or by mattock and plow was both slow and brutal. The ordinary custom of allowing nature to work six years at the stumps and gradually eliminate them by decay was not to be thought of.

Dynamiter Kissam, a Long Island expert, arrived and set to work, using fuses for small stumps up to two feet in diameter.

With the advent of the Italians work began in earnest; they cleared out every useless tree, cutting cord wood where any could be obtained and burning the branches and charred trees as they went. They also cleared out all underbrush thoroughly.

The dynamiter with his helper followed them up. This is the most exciting and interesting part of clearing land by modern methods.

The dynamite is put up in half-pound sticks. They are a little larger than an ordinary candle and are wrapped in heavy yellow paraffined paper. One folded end of this paper is opened up and a hole made by a wooden skewer into the dynamite stick, which is plastic and resembles graham bread in color and consistency.

For magneto-battery work where several charges are required, a copper cap in which is a minute quantity of fulminate of mercury, and which is exploded by a spark, is attached to fine electric wires and sealed by sulphur. This cap is placed in holes in the sticks of dynamite, and then securely tied by drawing string tightly around the paper which is raised to admit the cap.

In preparing a charge for fuse ignition, the cap is crimped to the end of a piece of mining fuse and this is inserted in the dynamite stick and securely fastened as previously described.

These prepared charges are placed in a basket and carried very tenderly to the stumps which have been prepared by the dynamiter's assistant. All the work is handled very carefully, for while there is not much danger of an accident unless fire is placed near the explosive, nevertheless extreme caution is used at all times. It requires a nature serene, calm, and deliberate.

Deep oblique holes were then made with a round crowbar under the stump singled out for execution. This hole should be as nearly horizontal as possible and directly under the stump so that all the explosive force may be expended on the wood and not on the earth between the dynamite and the stump. The earth acts as a cushion and the natural tendency of dynamite to exert force downward is counteracted.

As soon as a small strip was blown, the Italians, gathering up all the stumps, roots, and fragments, removing any pieces that were loosened but not completely torn out, and piling them at intervals, immediately burned them. This cannot be done when stumps are removed by any other method, for by the digging process the earth must be picked and scraped from them and ultimately the stump hacked in pieces before it will burn.

By our method the stump is burned and the finest kind of unleached wood ashes--containing lime to "sweeten" and potash and phosphoric acid to furnish plant food--are spread upon the ground a few hours after the stumps are blown out. These ashes would under other circumstances have to be purchased at a cost of perhaps two dollars a barrel, and as five barrels at least to the acre are required for good fertilization, these ashes gave us the first credit upon the books.

Following the burners came the manure spreaders; five carloads of manure had been purchased and was delivered before it was needed. When the manure was spread upon the land (one half carload to the acre), the plow started its work smoothly and with none of the strain and jerk on man and beast usual in new land. The soil was turned over with the greatest ease, for the explosions had shivered and torn out even the smallest roots, so the plow ran through the ground much more easily than in sod land.

Our friable, sandy loam, with a light admixture of clay, pulverized and aerated by the explosions, was in market garden condition at once and without the year's loss of crops assured by old methods.

A tooth harrow was next run over the plowed section, and gleaners followed the harrow, picking up the fine roots as they were brought to the surface. As piles of these fine roots grew, they were burned and the ashes immediately spread upon the land. The tooth harrow was run again across the rows, the disk harrow following chopped and pulverized the earth into the finest possible condition. Thirty five and one half working days after Larry and his gang arrived, rye was drilled into three and one half acres.

The condemned freight cars were placed upon skids and drawn to the desired position over soaped planks. They were raised from the ground to give good under ventilation. The north and east sides are filled or banked up with sand which came out of the well. This keeps out the cold winds, and, in the case of the chicken-house car, allows the fowls a shaded shelter on hot summer days.

The chicken-house car was placed facing the southeast. The western end has a large glazed sash placed on it, and two in the southern side. One half the car was partitioned off for roosting quarters, while the other half serves as a laying and scratching house. This farm keeps only a few chickens for family use.

The artesian well was started in October. The well was, naturally, a necessity, but there was much to be considered in regard to the method of pumping. Under ordinary circumstances a windmill would do, and is generally a good auxiliary; a ten-foot iron tower and a ten-foot fan wheel cost about fifty dollars, but our farm is not to be allowed to be a failure for lack of water in a dry season. In case of drought (and every summer brings one of greater or less duration) water must be on hand, and as a drought usually is accompanied by windless weather, the windmill could not be depended upon. An engine was obviously necessary. Both gasoline and kerosene engines were closely investigated, with the result that a kerosene oil engine was decided upon. (The new style of heavy oil engine is better and cheaper to run. Ed.) An advantage of the engine over a windmill is that it will furnish power for cutting wood, grinding grain, or lighting the buildings, a two and one half horsepower engine running twenty-five 16 c.p. lights easily.

The rye was turned under green in the spring to furnish humus, the greatest and only vital need of this particular spot of virgin soil.

Since that was written an excellent and cheap stump puller has been introduced, but the account of work is still typical. Dynamiting is still the modern way to clear land as well as to break up a stiff subsoil or hardpan, so as to loosen the earth to let deep roots like trees or alfalfa go down and to secure drainage.

Primitive American man regarded trees as "lumber" instead of as timber and still destroys countless millions in valuable wood as he "clears the ground."

After it is cleared, it is vital to keep it cleared of weeds, which worse garroters of crops than trees. To do that we don't need to bow to the Earth, nor to hammer her with a hand hoe.

"The Man with the Hoe" began to be a back number when Arkwright invented the ark or the mule or whatever he did invent. The man with the wheel hoe is the man that is "It." A wheel hoe costs from $6 to $12, and will do the work of several men without breaking the heart or even the back of one of them. It has as many attachments as a summer girl and is equally versatile. It must be run between the rows as soon as the ground is dry after every rain, so as to slay the weeds before they are born. If you don't they will slay your profits, if not yourself.

Crops grown on that experimental farm are: Asparagus, berries, beans, beets, cabbage, cauliflower, celery, carrots, cucumbers, corn, eggplant, endive, fruit trees, kale, kohlrabi, lettuce, limes, melons, martynias, onions, okra, parsley, parsnips, peas, potatoes (sweet and white), pumpkins, radishes, rhubarb, salsify, squash, tomatoes, etc. Marketed strictly choice radishes May 18, peas June 10, lettuce June 21, beans June 29, beets July 8, carrots July 10, cabbage July 11. Surely a rapid result.

Hemp is hardly worth your growing for itself under ordinary circumstances; the returns per acre are not sufficient. But Charles Richard Dodge, in one of the United States Yearbooks of the Department of Agriculture, says that as a weed killer it has practically no equal.

In proof of this, a North River farmer stated that thistles heretofore had mastered him in a certain field, but after sowing it with hemp not a thistle survived; and while ridding the land of this pest, the hemp yielded him nearly sixty dollars an acre, where previously nothing valuable could be produced.

As it grows from Minnesota to the Mississippi Delta, its value for this purpose is considerable.

But there is a way easier and cheaper of clearing land than by blasting, if we can afford to wait a little; and Mr. George Fayette Thompson, in Bulletin No. 27, Bureau of Animal Industry, tells us how, giving some interesting facts about Angora goats, of which the following is a condensation:

To people taking up raw land, particularly where there is a heavy undergrowth to be cleared away, goats of some kind are an invaluable aid. In its browsing qualities the common goat is as good as any, but, aside from the clearing of the land, the profit in his keep is very little, though some demand is growing up for goat's milk for infants and for some fancy cheeses. A much better animal from the standpoint of profit, while in use as a scavenger, is the Angora goat. Their long, silky hair has been used for centuries in making blankets, lap robes, rugs, carpets, and particularly the "cashmere" shawls, formerly a great luxury in this country. Much of the camel's hair dress goods is in reality made from the hair of the Angora goat, or mohair, as it is called. Angora goats thrive best in high altitudes with dry climates. They exist in greatest number in the United States in California, New Mexico, and Texas. They have been used successfully in the Willamette Valley of Oregon to eat the underbrush off the land, doing for nothing that for which the farmers pay Chinese laborers twenty-five to forty dollars per acre. The cost of Angora goats is about ten to thirty dollars each for does, with bucks at fifty to two hundred dollars, so that even with a small area of land to clear it would pay to buy a little flock for that purpose. Dr. Shandley, of Iowa, says that two to three goats to the acre is sufficient for cleaning up land, and that in two years the goats will eat all of the underbrush from woodland, such as briers, thistles, scrub oak, sumac, and, in fact, any shrub undergrowth. They need no other food than what they can secure from the woods themselves. Consequently, the income from the sale of mohair is nearly net.

The more nearly thoroughbred the goats are, the better the mohair and the higher the price. The meat of the Angora goat is superior to mutton, although if sold in the market under the name of goat meat, it commands only half the price of mutton.

As an example of the Angora's utility in cleaning up land, the Country Gentleman says: "Mr. Landrum exhibited ten head at the Oregon State Fair. In order to demonstrate their effectiveness as substitutes for grubbing, he left them on three acres of brush. At the end of the second year the land was mellow and ready for the plow."

It might be possible to build up a business in clearing lands for others by means of a herd of Angoras.

CHAPTER XIX
HOW TO BUILD

If you find an "abandoned farm" on which the buildings are worth more than the whole price asked, as frequently happens, you are all right. Even if the buildings are somewhat dilapidated, you can fix them up for a few dollars. But in buying small plots of ground, larger farms have to be broken up. If you buy from the resident owner, he may sell you five acres off his larger tract, and keep his house to live in. Certain it is that if a farm of 100 acres is subdivided into twenty five-acre farms, at least nineteen new houses must be built, although sometimes an old barn can be made into a fair residence.

If you can do no better, it is possible to start by tenting. An outfit large enough for a family of six would be about as follows:

1 wall tent with fly, 10 X 14, for sleeping 1 wall tent with fly, 10 X 14, for dining

1 old cook stove (to be erected outdoors), 2 floors, 10 X 14, at $5 each

Brown tents, at least for the sleeping rooms, are best; they last longer, are cooler, and do not attract the flies; though indeed we need not have house flies if we keep the horse manure covered up--they are all bred in that. If the tents are in the shade, the cost of the cover or fly can be saved in the dining tent; but it is necessary in the living tent, because wet canvas will leak when touched on the inside. To make the tent warm for the winter, we must bank up to the edges of the platform with earth and cover the whole with another tent of the same shape, but a foot larger in every dimension. These are commonly used in Montana.

It is to be presumed that no one would attempt moving in without household utensils, which may be as simple or elaborate as you please. If there is a sawmill in the vicinity, a temporary shack for winter, say 22 X 30 feet, could be built for from

$400 to $600, depending on the interior finish. Partitions can be made very cheap by erecting panels covered with canvas, burlap, old carpet, etc. Such a building does not need to be plastered, but can be made warm enough by an inside covering of burlap, heavy builders' paper, or composition board. Tar paper laid over solid sheeting makes a roof that will last for two or three years. For such a shack draw the plans yourself. All you really need is a living room, bedroom, and kitchen.

A cheap and effective water supply can be gotten from a driven well, which in most places costs about one dollar per foot. Have it where the kitchen is to be, so that the water can be pumped into a barrel or other tank over the stove. With a good range you can have as good a supply of hot and cold water as you had in the city.

If so fortunate as to find a piece of land with a good spring on it, you can lay pipes and draw the water from that. If you can get twelve or fifteen feet fall from the spring to the kitchen, you don't need a pump at all.

For a toilet closet, build a shed four feet wide, six feet long, and eight feet high. Use a movable pail or box. Lime slaked or unslaked or dry dust or ashes must be scattered every time the closet is used. Always clean before it shows signs of becoming offensive: keep it covered fly tight and mix the contents with earth or litter, and scatter on the garden.

A shack can be built of logs which will do for comfort and will look dignified.

Horace L. Pike, in ***Country Life in America,*** says: "The lot on which we meant to build our log house stood thirty-five feet above the lake. The problem was how to build a cabin roomy, picturesque, inexpensive, and all on the ground.

"The ground dimensions are thirty-two by thirty feet outside. This gives a living room sixteen by fourteen; bedrooms twelve by twelve, twelve by ten, and nine by seven; kitchen eleven by nine; a five-by four-foot corner for a pantry and refrigerator; closet four by six, front porch sixteen by six feet six inches, and rear porch five by five--705 square feet of inside floor space and 130 square feet of porch.

"A dozen pine trees stand on the lot, and maneuvering was required to set a cottage among them without the crime of cutting one. The front received the salutes of a leaning oak, the life of which was saved by the sacrifice of six inches from the porch eaves, the trunk forming a newel post for the step railing.

"We closed the contract immediately for 120 Norway or red pine logs, thirty feet long and eight by ten inches diameter at butts. The price was low--one or two dollars their like should have brought. We used, however, only eighty-one logs; forty thirty-foot, fourteen eighteen-foot, thirteen sixteen-foot, and fourteen fourteen-foot.

"Work was begun on April 22. Two days sufficed for the owner and one man to clear and level the ground, dig post holes, set posts, and square the foundation. The soil was light sand with a clay hardpan three feet down.

"Twenty-seven days each were put in by two men from start to finish, with assistance rendered by the owner. There were seven days by the mason, eight by carpenters, and four teen and one half by other labor. On June 4 the cabin was ready for occupancy, and the family moved in. The prices, as in most cases cited, are higher to-day. Cheaper transportation or lower tariff may reduce them again.

"Making allowances for increased cost of logs and differences in any of the material cost, this cabin can be duplicated for less than $700 by any one who has the ground, a few tools, and some building ability. It is compact, convenient, and more roomy than a superficial glance reveals, and it can be occupied (slight care is required) from April to November with only the kitchen stove and the fireplace supplying the heat. The same plan can be used for an all-frame structure, perhaps at less cost. It could be sheathed and slab covered in a locality where slabs, edged to six or eight inches wide, could be had; or slabs could be used perpendicularly in the gable ends and on the outside of the rear extension."

We must not overlook the differences in cost of lumber and labor in different places, sometimes more than doubling nor the fact that different contractors will vary often twenty-five per cent in their bids.

A mere cabin, like a wooden tent, 12 X 10 with a platform adjoining, will accommodate one or even two persons and can be built by a contractor even at war prices for about fifty to one hundred dollars. This will serve for tool house or store-room when a more convenient residence can be afforded. A number of such can be seen at "Free Acres," New Jersey, an hour from New York City on the D. L. & W. Railroad.

Thoughtful provision and planning will go far to reduce costs. A stove pipe which should run up inside the house, not outside, so as to conserve heat and fuel, serves as chimney and fireplace. A Franklin stove, practically an open fireplace set out entirely inside the house, is a practical device, though it costs from $18 to $30. It gives a cheerful open fire to burn wood or coal and has a flat top to keep things hot, a clutch oven of sheet iron, and a bob can be attached to the front of the grate.

But remember that though you may have trees or fallen wood for the cutting it takes a lot of time to cut it. A cylindrical self-feeding coal burner is most economical for heating and a lined sheet iron cooking stove for the kitchen.

A fireless cooker, which retains the heat all day by means of soapstone or insulation and slowly cooks the food without losing the juices, is an economical device. It can be made at home by copying what you see in the stores or by getting directions from the U. S. Department of Agriculture.

Don't forget double windows at least toward the north; and on all windows have heavy holland shades which make an air space between the cold window-panes and the atmosphere of the room.

Portable houses sound attractive, but they do not pay unless you will need to move them. Manifestly it costs more to make a house like a trunk than like a shed. The houses shipped ready made of the "Aladdin" type, with all the parts ready marked to be nailed together by unskilled labor are a much better investment and are not shaky.

It is true that living is expensive in the train suburbs, when almost all that is eaten comes from the city, with freight and monopoly rates added. But one can raise most of what the family eats, and save besides in car fares and doctor's bills.

The rent, perhaps a quarter of the income, that was paid for a place so small that the cat had to jump on a chair when the baby sat down, will be a clear gain.

Mrs. Warrington's cottage at Rose Valley, Pennsylvania, forms a very interesting subject, and is built from designs of well-known architects of Philadelphia, who have taken up building small, inexpensive modern houses in a practical manner. The house is built with a stone foundation and a wooden superstructure with exterior walls covered with metal lath and cement stucco which is stained a cream color. The trimmings are stained a soft brown and the sashes are painted white. The roof is covered with shingles, and is left to weather finish. The front porch, from which a vestibule leads into the house, has a hooded cover formed by the main roof sweeping down sufficiently to form a protect tion. The vestibule forms an entrance to both the living room and the kitchen; the kitchen is at the front of the house, allowing the main rooms and a private porch to be at the south side. The interior throughout is trimmed with cypress and stained a soft brown. The second floor joists are exposed to view and are stained in a similar manner, while the ceiling space between the joists is plastered. A broad archway separates the living and the dining rooms, and while it forms a separation, it does not preclude the possibility, when desired, of throwing the two rooms into one large apartment. The large, open fireplace is built of clinker brick, and its facings extend from the floor to the ceiling; it has a wooden shelf supported on corbeled brackets. A semi-boxed stairway rises out of the living room to the second floor. There are three bedrooms with good-sized closets, and a bathroom on the second floor. A cellar, under the entire house, has a cemented bottom, and contains a laun dry. This house costs about $2000 complete.

Houses built of cement blocks are growing in favor. Cement blocks can be made anywhere by unskilled labor. All that is needed is a competent foreman to direct the making and seasoning of the blocks and laying them in the walls.

The cost of concrete compared to frame or brick structures is, if anything, all things considered, in favor of concrete. Houses built of wood are likely to become increasingly expensive because of the deforesting which is going on in all parts of the United States.

There are abundant books of plans and costs published, showing what may be built, and several responsible publishers recklessly offer to refund the cost of the plans if the expense of building the house exceeds their estimates.

There are also a number of manufacturers of ready-made portable houses, running in cost from about three hundred dollars for four rooms, upward. Some of these are adapted to all-the-year-round use and may be used where land is taken experimentally.

CHAPTER XX
BACK TO THE LAND

L ife, to the average man, means hard, anxious work, with disappointment at the end, whereas it ought to mean plenty of time for books and talk. There is something wrong about a system which condemns ninety-nine hundredths of the race to an existence as bare of intellectual activity and enjoyment as that of a horse, and with the added anxiety concerning the next month's rent. Is there no escape? Through years of hard toil I suspected that there might be such an escape. Now, having escaped, I am sure of it, so long as oatmeal is less expensive than Hour, so long as the fish and the cabbage grows, I shall keep out of the slavery of modern city existence, and live in God's sunshine." (Hubert, "Liberty and a Living.")

The wealthy class are taking up farming as a healthy and beautifying diversion, and we may expect others to follow, as it certainly promotes happiness and adds to the attractions of those who adopt it. With the aids which science has given, a farmer can now make good profits with less labor than was formerly necessary to get a bare living. The amount that a single well-managed, well-tilled acre will produce in a season is simply incredible. This accounts for the increased demand for farming lands wherever they are to be had on reasonable terms. The wage earners are learning this, and it is only a question of a little time when manufacturing plants will have to be convenient to lands where the families of the hands can have a small tract of land to cultivate. This requires good transportation facilities from the homes to the factories.

Corporate operation has been a great aid to human progress. Organization is man's orderly way of following the Divine Plan for his economic salvation vet the far mer has profited less by organization than trades unions. Where farmers have organized to aid each other to buy and sell, they have gained wonderfully, but a beginning in this direction has but served to show how much more is needed.

To the individual farmer with large area and small means, the improvements in machinery that cheapen his production are not at present available. The discoveries in methods of fertilization of the soil only make it more difficult for him to earn a living in competition with those whose ample capital increases production by its use. Improvements in fruits and vegetation, by hybridization and various methods that add wealth to those of means, only add to the troubles of our present small farmers.

Hitherto corporate operation has been mainly for the benefit of stockholders. The cases where those whose labor creates dividends get more than wages have been rare. "A living wage" has been the ambition of labor itself: all profit beyond this is supposed to be the right of capital. There is with some persons an unconscious reluctance to share profits with labor lest the laborers become independent, and thus reduce their number to an extent to raise the labor market, so that it is difficult to get fair consideration of any business proposition that promises better conditions for the producer or independence for the laborer. This is undoubtedly short sighted, as the higher intelligence of the people who have land increases production and gives enlarged opportunities for the profitable employment of money. However, if capitalists persist in this narrow view, the money of the people when they learn and think, can be applied to this purpose instead of being deposited in savings banks, where much of it is used in increasing the wealth of those who already have abundance.

The idea of "helping others to help themselves" finds a responsive chord in the hearts of many wealthy people. But the question is, how can all be helped? No business method by which this can be accomplished has, as yet, been practically demonstrated.

In no field does corporate operation promise more for the betterment of human conditions, for a higher standard of morals and of education, or great certainty of profit for capital, than by systematically aiding men to obtain farms.

Progress proceeds on the line of returns for expenditure. When a man's economic condition permits, his first thought is to give his children an education and a better chance in life than he had. Those who extol the simple life as the ideal condition of happiness do not mean that want and deprivation of necessities is the ideal condition. If they did, they would put their children in that condition to make them happy. Both extremes of wealth and of poverty are burdens and retard mental and moral progress. The ideal condition is to be found on a farm where the land is paid for and ample means are at hand to supply the necessities for physical demands, with leisure to learn and enjoy those pleasures of the mind which come with knowledge of Nature's laws, and wisdom to live in harmony with them, and in a measure comprehend the purposes of creation.

Mr. G. W. Smith, founder of the Hundred Year Club, suggests that there is an opening in intensive farming for the benevolent but canny wealthy who are interested in the soil and want to combine philanthropy and percentage.

His plan is to get capital to secure land and all the necessary means, give to each approved applicant perpetual leases of land for a small farm and a lot in a village site convenient thereto, with a house merely sufficient for shelter, requiring as a first payment sufficient to secure capital against loss in case the farmer forfeits his contract, say $100. Let the company provide scientific supervision and conduct the operation mainly as though the farmers were employees, all the necessaries to be charged to each with only sufficient profit to pay the expense and a fair interest on the capital employed. Through a purchasing and sales department all products should be sold in the best market and each farmer credited with the net result of his productions until the agreed sale price is received, when title should pass in fee to the farmer, who, during the time, has become scientific so far as that piece of land is concerned, and in future can operate it with the advantages which progress has made. A public building would be necessary for a storehouse, in which rooms for meetings of various kinds should be provided, also such shelter as might be necessary for assembling and storage of products for shipment.

The expense of public buildings and other utilities could be paid for out of the increased value that they bring to the land. The company should have a nursery to provide fruit tree, etc., the growth of which, with the increase of population would make the farms, when paid for, worth far more than their cost. Such opportunities as this, opened to all, would do away with the tramps who are now able to live on the charitable, only because of the known difficulties of finding work.

The farmers should be utilized as far as possible in the purchasing and sales department, and should divide into committees to try various experiments connected with their business, that through their reports all may be benefited by the knowledge gained. Dairying and large orchards on land suitable and not of use in the general farming plan could be conducted by the community, each farmer being a stockholder. The labor performed on these cooperative undertakings should be paid for and charged to cost of production, each one who performs a share of the labor participating in the profits as near as may be. As money is received by the company from products, it can be used in similar operations. When the farms are paid for, the farmers can continue the cooperative features that experience has proved useful and extend the business principle to other fields, such as heating, light, and power by electricity, machinery for preparing products for market, drying, canning, etc., as well as for the cultivation of the soil.

Where the land is level the farms can be laid out on a general plan that will admit of the use of steam plows to reduce the cost of plowing, save hard labor, and reduce the number of work animals.

Among the multitude of advantages the individual would have in these communities, social, educational, and economic, health and physical development appear as not the least.

The farm, as it is, still furnishes a horde of recruits for insane asylums; its isolation and monotony of everyday life, with its lack of social intercourse and educational advantages, nearly counterbalance the strain and poverty of the cities.

But the greatest difficulty is the growing inability of the farmers' sons to secure land and the means to cultivate it when they arrive at a marriageable age. Those who have seen for threescore years the ever-increasing flow of boys and girls from the farms to the cities, greater in proportion to the rural population than in any other age, realize the necessity for aid in this direction. While it is true that the farm has contributed largely to the numbers of our successful city men, the fact remains that the mass of boys who come to the cities as well as the city born, lack the faculty to grab or save, and fail, while the healthy girls swell the ranks of prostitution, where an average of eight years lands them in a pauper's grave.

Our soldiers, as well as those of other countries, are not up to former physical standards. Degeneracy, disintegration is apparent in every direction.

The power of a nation depends on the physical and mental condition of the great mass of people, and to leave the people in ignorance that they may be controlled by the intelligent few who understand their needs and may have their welfare at heart, is a mistake that other nations than Russia have made. The law of the survival of the fittest has wiped out races and nations who have ignored this fundamental law, that all men must progress together.

A race or civilization with such a basis of farmers as this plan would create would be enduring.

The nation or race, like the individual, must have intelligent organization and live in harmony with the laws of nature in order to survive. Opposition to them means destruction Cooperation is constructive.

If we are to profit by this lesson, it is necessary that we improve the conditions surrounding our lower classes. That this is recognized by a large number of leading minds is proved by the efforts of the many who are engaged in educational and other social movements, most of which result in little net good to the wage-earners.

Obstacles to small farming near large cities are that farms of three to ten acres with buildings are not plentiful, and that mortgage loans are hard to get in the East and loans to help in building are hardly to be had at all.

Land is either held intact as large farms or is sold entire to speculators who hold it until it can be divided into city lots. Here, it would seem, is an opportunity for those who are interested in bettering the condition of their fellow men by wholesale, and can invest large capital, but little time, in the work.

Let them buy up land in large acreages and cut it up into small plots of from one to ten acres, charging enough advance to return interest on the money invested and to meet the necessary expenses in such operation. Then make liberal building loans to buyers. Inquiries among real estate men show that they always have a larger demand for small acreage than they can meet, so an immediate market with large profits would await those who are first in this field.

There is no use in blaming people for not leaving the cities to go to the farms; they don't know enough to go, they don't know enough to make a living if they do go, and they don't know enough to enjoy it. Besides this, they have not the capital. We must teach them and help them.

George H. Maxwell's Homecrofters' Guild at Watertown, Mass., where boys are taught what to do with the earth and how to do it, is worth whole shelves of books on "The Exodus to the Cities" or the "Prosperity of the Settler."

It is reported that the state of Texas offered six million acres of land for sale to settlers, at one dollar per acre. It has been suggested that it would be better that the states should rent out the land at four per cent of the sale price. This would leave more money in the hands of settlers and enable many to get farms who cannot pay the price and have enough left to raise a crop. In reality it would be better for the state to help farmers get a start rather than to tax them one dollar per acre to begin with. However, under our system of government, we permit only those who have money to have land.

There can be no doubt that the state of Texas and her people would be better off if the land were leased than to have it sold. Probably a tax on the value of the land instead of a rent would be the best for all the people, especially as it would check speculation.

CHAPTER XXI
THE COMING PROFESSION FOR BOYS

In order that as little as possible may seem to be taken for granted or as mere expressions of the opinions of the author, we cite the views of specialists as to the possibilities of this field, so new in this country, of intensive agriculture. These will show that the conviction has become general that, as workers, as teachers, and as discoverers, there is no career more inviting or more lucrative or more dignified than that of the skillful foster-father of plants.

"Children brought up in city tenements tend to become vicious and sickly, but if transported to country homes they may grow up strong and self-respecting men and women.

"There are hundreds of applicants for every position in the cities, and competition forces the pay down to the lowest level. Living expenses are heavier. The risk to health from sedentary occupations, long hours in ill-ventilated offices, stores, and workshops is serious.

"There are few inducements to out-door exercise. Even if he lives at home, the boy who is forced to the street or into the factory before he has the strength or education to do good work remains an unskilled worker all his life.

"Manufacturing is upon a larger and larger scale. The division of labor is greater and greater. Not only does the gulf between capitalist and laborer widen, but with it the gulf between skilled and unskilled labor." ("What Shall Our Boys Do for a Living?" Charles F. Wingate.)

It is the city that breeds or attracts most of the pauperism and crime. The country has its own healthy life.

Every one is born with some natural gift, and it is a good thing to discover early in life what one's natural gifts are so that each may be educated in the direction suited to natural capacity.

How are you to treat a lad who has naturally an inclination for the work on the farm? In the first place do not provide him with any spending money unless he earns it. The prime thing necessary is to give the boy a personal interest in what is going on upon the farm. Give him a plot of land as his own, let him understand that anything he may grow upon this land shall belong to him, but do not give him this plot and say, "There, take that; do as you like with it," he will wonder what to do with it. He will need somebody to help him by teaching him what he is to do. Enter into a partnership with him at the start, give him some instruction as to what it is best for him to do with his plot. Find out his inclinations; give him sympathy and help. Bring out his natural aptitude for farming life, teach him method in his work; teach him to think his way out; and, best of all, teach him to work for definite results; that is what is wanted in any line of life, especially in farm life.

Let the work of the boy have a meaning and a purpose. Let him understand that certain results cannot be accomplished in any other way, and give him chances to go outside and see what other people are doing. Let him see good scientific agriculture and be encouraged to pursue such methods.

Provide for him the very best reading that can be found in agricultural journals and books. Let him have three or four years at an agricultural college. All the influences there point to agriculture as the best calling for a young man who is fit for it, whereas in other colleges the influences are all in the opposite direction. At our agricultural colleges a youth has all the necessary advantages of general education, and also an education in the lines fitting him especially for the calling he has selected. (United States Department of Agriculture, Bulletin 138, condensed.)

"Among farmers and gardeners not enough thought is given to the whys and wherefores, or cause and effect; as a rule, they go on year after year without profiting by the personal opportunity afforded them of observation, or by the results of experiments at scientific stations.

"With rare exceptions the young farmer and gardener takes up his work, not from the scientific side, but strictly from the labor side; and he begins at the bottom, meeting the same difficulties as did his father and too often not acquiring information beyond what his father possessed.

"This should not be; agriculture should be taught in all our public schools in country districts, as it has been taught for years in Germany and Austria. It should be elevated as an art; in its higher estate it is already an art. No pursuit possesses a greater scope for development; the field is almost unoccupied by leaders, scientific and practical." (Burnett Landreth, in ***999 Queries and Answers.***)

In accordance with these ideas, the Baron de Hirsch Agricultural School at Woodbine, New Jersey, is giving practical courses in agriculture to Jewish boys, on the principle of individual plots--all free where necessary.

The trustees of the State Agricultural College of New Jersey, at New Brunswick, have established winter courses in agriculture, open to all residents of New Jersey over sixteen years of age. Courses will be for twelve weeks, and only a small entrance fee is required; few books will be needed.

Other states are doing likewise; all will need many teachers and experimenters. At present all who know anything about intensive agriculture are snapped up by the numerous government experiment stations at good salaries. The land like that of the Rockefellers, the Paynes, the Cuttings, on which farming is carried on by unnecessarily expensive methods, needs the services of trained agriculturists and professional foresters. The Division of Forestry at the start employed eleven persons, but now it has in the field as many hundreds of employees, including a lot of trained foresters.

The railroads also see the profit in teaching farming, and are devoting more and more money to experiments and lectures to show the farmers that they can get more and better crops with the same effort by intelligent selection of seeds.

The Chicago, Burlington, and Quincy Railway Company ran its first Seed and Soil Special over the entire system in the winter of 1904-1905, and has lectured to hundreds of thousands of farmers since.

They report to us that "there is no doubt that the lectures did a great deal of good, and necessarily the larger increase of crops which followed is due to the scientific methods of farming expounded by the various professors." The late President James J. Hill wrote much about the small farms' large yields.

The hundreds of thousands of "war gardens" unskillfully conducted and glutting the local markets with crops all matured at about the same local time will unreasonably disgust many with intensive cultivation, especially those who work but do not think. The remedy is more instruction. The effect the agricultural colleges and experiment stations is plain to the eye in the better appearance of farms as we near the centers of instruction.

Some years ago a clergyman published a book upon the Adirondacks; it was full of poetry, and he sent men up there who afterwards became known as "Murray's Fools." They knew nothing about the life and had no suitability and little preparation for it. We do not wish to bring out a crop of "Three Acres and Liberty Fools." We are telling what has been done and what can be done again. It does not follow that every man can or will do it, much less teach it or advance the art, but the field is a large one and holds out great promise to those who persevere and excel in it.

If any one thinks that the profit of the earth will come to the cultivator without very intelligent and steady work, he is mistaken. No owner of land, unless others require it to live upon, can make money by neglecting it.

Says *Maxwell's Talisman:* "The greatest good that can be done to the American farmer to-day is to teach him to make the greatest possible profit from the smallest tract of land from which a family can be supported in comfort. A great influence operating to-day against keeping the boys in the country is that the boy does not have money enough to buy a farm. It is unfortunately true that in some places there is a trend in the direction of absorbing farms into still larger farms with a consequent diminution of population, as in Iowa and other sections. The remedy for this is to demonstrate that if the value is in the boy rather than in the farm, and the boy is taught intensive, diversified, scientific farming, a good living with a surplus profit that will provide amply for old age, may be made from a comparatively small tract of land. The tract may be, say, ten acres, with ample cultivation, irrigation, and fertilization, or even without irrigation because a hoe and a cultivator in the hands of a scientific farmer may bring as good and better results in providing moisture for growing plants as can be had from a ditch and unlimited water in the hands of an ignorant farmer."

The field of discovery is always limitless, and it is to those boys or girls who devote their attention to this that the greatest return will come. "What a fine thing it would be to find even one plant free from rust in the midst of a rusted field. It would mean a rust-resistant plant. Its off-spring would probably be also rust resistant. If you should ever find such a plant, be sure to save its seed and plant in a plot by itself. The next year again save seed from those plants least rusted. Possibly you can develop a rust proof race of wheat! Keep your eyes open." ("Agriculture for Beginners," by Burkett, Stevens, and Hill, pages 76-78.) So you may pluck gain out of loss.

If you want to do experiments, the influence of ether on plants is one new and wonderful field. It seems to induce artificial rest, so that lilacs, for instance, can be made to bloom twice by a treatment, the last time near Christmas.

E. V. Wilcox says in *Farming* that in 1899 a small quantity of durum or macaroni wheat was introduced into this country for trial. It was found profitable in localities where there was too little rain for ordinary wheat. Six years later, 20,000,000 bushels per year of the wheat was grown in the United States. Its production has increased greatly every season and has added materially to the total of the wheat crop.. Thorough fall cultivation has been found to increase the yield, and in some parts of the wheat belt one in five of tile farmers has already adopted the practice. In certain states where manuring has been thought unnecessary, experiments have demonstrated that the yield may be be increased 60 per cent by this simple practice. The wheat production of Nebraska was increased more than 10,000,000 bushels by the introduction of a hardy strain of Turkey red wheat. Swedish select oats in Wisconsin have greatly augmented the oat yield of the state. In 1899 six pounds of the seed was brought to the state and from this small beginning a crop of 9,000,000 bushels was harvested five years later.

"Mr. Gideon, of Minnesota, planted many apple seeds, and from them all raised one tree that was very fruitful, finely flavored, and able to withstand the cold Minnesota winter. This tree he multiplied by grafts and named it the Wealthy apple. It is said that in this one apple he benefited the world to the value of more than one million dollars. You must not let any valuable bud or seed variant be lost." ("Agriculture for Beginners," page 61.)

"This fact ought to be very helpful to us next year when planting corn. We should plant seed secured only from stalks that produced the most corn. If we follow this plan year by year, each acre of land will be made to produce more kernels and hence a larger crop of corn, and yet no more expense will be required to raise the crop." (Same, page 71.)

The World's Work tells how the country got a new industry.

Mr. George Gibbs, of Clearbrook, Wash., has made his "stake" by growing tulip and hyacinth bulbs. He had a little place on Orcas Island, in Puget Sound. He did not know anything about growing flowers, but he did know that certain varieties of bulbs brought good prices in the East. He was observant enough to see that the moist, warm, climate and rich soil of the Puget Sound country were peculiarly favorable to flowers.

He had bad luck with his bulbs; that only meant that he still had something to learn. He kept his nerve even when he went bankrupt. His friends told him he was wasting time, but they could not shake his faith.

In twelve years he found that he was right. His wonderful gardens were making him rich. Other men have gone into the business, but he was first and has kept his lead. He has made the Puget Sound country the greatest rival of Holland in the sale of flowering bulbs.

Quantities of wild herbs, fruits, and roots that no one eats are good; the Jesuits had a list of over two hundred kinds that the Indians ate, but it was lost. Some one can do a great service by making it up again by research and experiment. Thousands more of the wild things must be good for dyes, fabrics, and fodder.

Fame like Burbank's and fortune awaits the one who is a good self-advertiser and can find the use of the poetic daisies, goldenrod, and thistle, the all-pervading "pusley," and such other vegetable vermin.

An interesting experiment is conducted in growing tea with colored child labor, at Tea, South Carolina, by the aid of education and machinery and the cooperation of the Agricultural Department at Washington, who will furnish particulars. Whatever may be its outcome, this will give an opening to some intelligent cultivators, and it points the way to other fields.

Those who are first in raising new or improved plants find a waiting market for them.

The Market Growers Gazette, of London, England, reports that Mr. A. Findlay, Mairsland, Auchtermuchty, Scotland, sold one season to five leading growers whose names are given five seed potatoes at L 20 each (which would be, perhaps, $500 a peck). He says enthusiastically: "It is as perfectly round-shaped a potato as can be imagined. There is a slight dash of pink on the outer rim of the eye. My stock of it is very small, only 126 lb. and I do not care to sell any. If next year's crop yields as well as this year's, we shall have twenty times that quantity." Mr. Findlay has other seed potatoes, just as high priced, for which he wants $125 per lb., which, he says, "means that I do not want to sell any."

This shows what progressive people think of the real value of good seed.

It is worth mentioning that "The land on which these are grown is not highly manured; the only artificial manure that it has received is about 200 lb. of potash per acre. It has the drawback of being rather stony."

Of course this is "a fad"; it is doubtful if it will pay any one to give such prices for seed except to sell to some bigger fool than himself. Of course, also, the market for a particular fancy thing may soon be overstocked, but it seems to be a nice thing for the Findlays meanwhile, and it does good in teaching people to appreciate good things.

Yet the average potato patcher prudently saves his small potatoes for next year's seed, which is just as if a breeder were to keep the colts that were too poor to sell, to be the parents of his herd.

In the dark ages of farming--to wit, in 1881, for this is a true story--a minister of the Gospel came into possession, by inheritance, of a fifteen-acre farm a short way from Philadelphia. He found the soil a reddish, somewhat gravelly clay, and so worn out from years of cropping that it did not support two cows and a horse. City born and bred, he was encumbered with no knowledge of agriculture which had to be unlearned. He began a careful and systematic study of the agricultural literature, and ultimately developed a novel system of dairy farming to which he adhered religiously.

The farm lying near the city is high-priced land; for this reason, and because of the limited acreage, the cows were kept in the barn the year round. For six years his bill for veterinary services was $1.50, while the income from the milk of his seventeen cows was about $2400 a year. In addition, from four to six head of young cattle were sold annually, netting about $500 a year. As the stock on the farm was stall fed every particle of plant food contained in the stable manure, liquid as well as solid, was utilized. No fertilizer was ever purchased. Yet all of the "roughage" for thirty head of stock was raised on the thirteen acres of available soil. Only $625 a year was expended for concentrated feeding stuffs. The net earnings of the farm for the period averaged more than $1000 a year. And this was during the early days of his experience; later he made more.

Professor W. J. Spillman, of the Agricultural Department, visited him in 1903, and studied the methods employed. Then, he says, the rush to see the farm became so great that the owner had to give it up.

Few people who know nothing about it, and won't learn, can take even three acres and make anything off it. To get the phenomenal yields takes capital--sometimes large capital, wisely spent. Sometimes we read of immense products "per acre"; this often means the product of a single rod of ground, this gives at the rate of so much "per acre," or might, if extended.

But any one can take a little bit of ground and use it thoroughly and increase his borders and his knowledge as he goes on. He will find plenty to pay him for doing or teaching whatever he has learned to do that no one else has done "If a man make but a mousetrap better than his fellows, though he makes his tent in the wilderness, the world will beat a path to his door."

The mission of this book is accomplished if it interests you to consider the possibilities of making a living on a few acres and leads you to investigate. It is not written as a textbook, for, as has been shown, there are authorities enough cited to supply all the technical information needed

Its sole object is to show what has been done and what can be done on small areas and to show that life in the country need not be so laborious if the same methods are used which make successes of business in other lines.

If it does this and is the means of checking in any degree the reckless trend of people from the country to the cities, the author will feel that his efforts have been well repaid.

CHAPTER XXII
THE WOOD LOT

If you have a bit of woods on your little farm, take care of it. By intelligent thinning you can make an average income of five dollars per acre from ordinary second growth wild woods. The cord wood, barrel hoops, fence posts, and so on will decrease your expenses, while the timber will increase in value. That lot is the place to start your boy as a forester.

Instructions how to treat the trees can be obtained from your State Forestry Department or from the National Forest Service at Washington: the care of growing timber is a big subject and requires study, but don't sell your standing timber without their advice. Forestry can hardly be made to pay on a small lot with hired labor or hired teams, and you must not pay much for your wood lot, else interest and taxes will eat up the returns.

To be of high quality, timber must be, to a considerable proportion of its height, free of limbs, which are the cause of knots; it must be tall; and it must not decrease rapidly in diameter from the butt to the top of the last log. In a dense stand of timber there is very great competition for sunlight among the individual trees, with the result that height growth is increased. Trees in crowded stands are taller than those in uncrowded stands of the same age. When the trees are crowded so that sunlight does not reach the lower branches, these soon die and become brittle they then fall off or are broken off by the wind, snow, or other agencies. By this process trunks are formed which are free from limbs, and hence of high quality.

It is evident, therefore, that trees in the wood lot should be so crowded that the crown or top of each individual tree may be in contact with those of its nearest neighbors. A crowded stand of trees produces not only a larger number but also a greater proportion of high quality sawlogs than an uncrowded stand. So vital a matter is their forest shade that it does not do to set out young trees which have grown in the forest. Ordinarily, the exposure to the sunlight stunts them and often kills them. Nursery trees are best; the next best are trees that have grown at the edge of the woods.

The actual value of woodland as pasture is small. One dollar per acre per year is probably a liberal estimate of the value of its forage. Thrifty fully stocked stands of timber will grow at the rate of 250 or more board feet of lumber per year. Adopting only 250 board feet as the growth and assuming the value of the standing timber to be from $5 to $8 per 1000 feet board measure, the value of the timber growth is from $1.25 to $2 per acre per year.

If the timber is given good care, moreover, the growth should be as much as 500 board feet per acre per year. The larger value of the wood lot for growing timber, as compared to the value of its forage only, is therefore apparent.

It must not be thought possible to secure this growth of timber and utilize the wood lot for pasture at the same time, because the stock eat the seedlings and damage the trees.

If shade, however, rather than forage is the wood lot's chief value to stock, it can doubtless be provided by allowing the stock to range in only a portion of the lot. The remainder can more profitably be devoted to the production of wood

Owners are doubtless in some instances indifferent about fires in their wood lots, because they do not realize that these may do great harm without giving striking evidence of the fact. They burn the fallen leaves and accumulated litter of several years, thus destroying the material with which trees enrich their own soil. The soil becomes exposed, evaporation is greater, and more of the rain and melted snow runs off the surface. The roots may also be exposed and burned. The vitality of the trees is weakened and their rate of growth decreased. Don't burn leaves or waste growth: it is dangerous and they are valuable for mulch and for manure.

It has been found in the prairie region that through the protection afforded by the most efficient grove windbreaks, the yield in farm crops is increased to the extent of a crop as large as could be grown on a strip three times as wide as the height of the trees.

At present the following states maintain nurseries and distribute young trees either free or practically at cost to planters within the state: Maine, New Hampshire, Vermont, New York, Maryland, Pennsylvania, Ohio, Michigan, North Dakota, and Kansas.

The names of nurseries which handle stock of certain trees and their quoted prices for all the more important species can be secured from the Forest Service, Washington, D. C.

Whether your wood lot pays a profit or not, like the profit from the rest of your land, depends largely on how it is taxed. The higher it is taxed the harder it is to make it pay. In most states timberland is assessed on the basis of its value, timber and land together. Woodland assessed on this basis is overtaxed as compared with land assessed on the basis of what it produces each year. The value of plowland for farm purposes is established by what it will earn. If the owner can make $10 an acre a year over all expenses by growing say wheat, corn, cotton or alfalfa on it, his land will have a value of perhaps $150 an acre. If it took two years to grow a crop, the land would be worth only half as much. Its owner in that case would kick vigorously if he could not get his assessment lowered. He would kick still more vigorously if he had to pay a tax also on the value of the standing crop, after having to pay too much on the land. "The Lord loveth a cheerful kicker."

With woodland the case is still worse. Each year the owner may have to pay a tax on the merchantable crops of many past years. It is as though the owner of plowland had to pay a tax on the value of his field crops twice a week throughout the growing season. When a full-grown tree is cut down or burned up in a forest fire, it may have been taxed 40 or 50 times over. Each year the land on which it grew has been valued not on the basis of its earning power, but on the basis of what it would bring if sold, timber and all. A tax levied on the income-earning value of the land would be much more equitable.

Certain states have applied this principle by legislation under which land to be used for growing timber can be classified so that the timber can be taxed separately from the land. The land there is taxed annually on its value, without timber. The tax on the timber is not paid until the crop is harvested. It is therefore a tax on the yield. In New York this yield tax is 5 per cent of the value of the crop harvested; Michigan 5 per cent of it; Massachusetts 6 per cent; and Vermont, Connecticut, and Pennsylvania 10 per cent, with different provisions for forests already established.

Such a method is much better than that adopted by a number of states which exempt, under certain conditions, reforested or reforesting lands for a term of years, or allow rebates or bounties on such lands.

The profit of a growing forest crop will depend largely on relief from excessive taxation. It is unthrifty public policy to discourage putting waste land to work. ("The Farm Woodlot Problem," by Herbert A. Smith, Editor Forest Service--from Yearbook of Department of Agriculture for 1914.)

CHAPTER XXIII
SOME PRACTICAL EXPERIMENTS

The Department of Agriculture at Washington, also Cornell University and various other schools publish special studies and monographs of different branches. For some a small charge is made, but they are mostly distributed free. Many of them are very valuable. The United States Department's pamphlet on the Diseases of the Violet is a notable example. The average person does not know how these can be obtained or even that they exist.

The Department's Year Books are most interesting reading, and both its Professors and the state colleges will answer particular questions of citizens.

These and the various United States and State Experiment Station publications will serve instead of most books (except this one), if properly filed, indexed, and crossindexed so that you can readily turn to all the information on a given subject--on bugs, for instance, before the insects have harvested your crop.

I am trying only to suggest things, not to advise, nor to induce my readers to try to do anything that they don't like or have no capacity for. It is difficult to make people understand that.

One reader of this book, a dear creature, wrote her experience for a Crafts magazine. She got the acres, built her house, and raised one fine crop of--swans? nuts grafted on wild trees? partridge berries? No--three tons of hay!

She called it " Three Acres and Starving"; I called it "Three Acres and Stupidity." She didn't eat the hay, and the Editor wouldn't publish my reply.

Everybody raises hay and potatoes; so don't you raise any unless for your own use.

Potatoes are a laborious crop, requiring constant care, manuring, cutting the seed eyes (on which there is much uncertain lore), hilling up or down according to drainage and rainfall, spraying with Pyrox or dusting with Paris green, and, neither least nor last, bug hunting.

The seed is expensive, but for your own use you may plant from whatever seed, otherwise wasted, may grow on the potato vine, on the tops of the plants. The crop will be small potatoes and all kinds of varieties, which won't sell in the market but which make each dinner a surprise party. You may strike a new and improved strain, though there are over a thousand varieties of potato listed already. New creations of merit bring good returns, and 'tis the enterprising experimenter that reaps the honor and the harvest, and he is worthy of his reward.

To select the most productive plants and breed again from these is, however, a more promising profit plan. Even then don't plant the tubers unless you will take the pains to soak the seed potatoes in scab preventer. If you won't, likely you will raise mostly scab, and the spores thereof will spoil your ground for potatoes for years.

It costs little in money to make it--half a pint of formalin to fifteen gallons of water. Not guessed but measured gallons. Then soak for an hour and a half by the Ingersoll. Don't reckon that one little hour or a few will do just as well. With one hour they will be under-done and spotty, with three over-done and weakly.

There is lots to be discovered yet about "the spuds." Sawdust is an excellent mulch for them, as for small fruits. When you store any seeds to plant, put carbolic moth balls with them. it checks insects and mice and helps to protect the planted seeds from birds.

In a general way, with potatoes and with other things that you want good and plenty, get specific directions and follow them. Most people won't read directions; more can't follow them. Those people have their knives out for "book farmers and professors," but you can't improve on experience and experiment by the light of laziness or of nature.

A delicate jelly is made out of the red outer pulp of rose berries. It would be romantic to develop a Rose fruit from those seed pods, as the peach was developed from the almond. We have invented stranger fruits than that, such as the Loganberry and the pomato.

But there is better chance for profit in doing the old things better, especially when the experiment costs little or nothing

You can have a strawberry garden on your roof or even on a balcony. This need not be costly. Clinch all the nails on the inside of a stout barrel. Bore half a dozen two-inch holes in the bottom, or put in a layer of stones, for drainage. Bore a row of eight holes about eight inches from the bottom of the barrel and about eight inches apart. Eight inches above this bore a second row of holes "staggered," and a third eight inches above those. Pile several old tomato cans with perforated bottoms one on the other in the center of the barrel: these should be the height of the barrel and placed upright in its middle. This is the conductor down which water should be poured at intervals before the soil gets quite dry. Fill the barrel with soil made of one half loam and one half well-rotted manure. Be sure the manure is not fresh. A little bone meal is a good addition.

Now plant the first row of strawberry plants ("ever-bearing" are best, though they don't ever-bear). Put each plant inside, spread the roots, and pull the leaves of each out through one of the holes. Press the soil down firmly around each root. Repeat the process for the other two rows; fill the barrel and set say six plants on the top. That will give you thirty plants, which should grow ten to twentyfive quarts of fine berries, or more. The illustration makes the holes twelve inches apart--for big leafy plants.

If there are any more, those will be you. Anyhow, you will know a lot about strawberries at the end of the season. Other things can be grown in the same way.

Better than growing vegetables, or where dry land can't be obtained, is to raise some crop like water cress that usually comes from a distance.

Often an otherwise poor season will help a specialty. One year wet weather jumped the price of mint and it sold at double prices. Hot, dry weather is required to make it produce its best.

Most of the mint produced in this country for peppermint oil is grown in Michigan. More than 4000 acres are reported from a single county. Mint oil is worth about $3.50 a pound and costs about a dollar to produce. Nice bright dried leaves sell for about 15 cent a pound.

The production of mint is sometimes as high as fifty pounds of oil to the acre. The bulk of it is grown on marshlands, which a few years ago were nowhere worth more than a few dollars an acre. The mint is sent to the manufacturers, where it is purified and made into flavoring extract or used in chewing gum, etc.

Why should we, with our infinite variety of climates, soils, and labor, import from England the coarser varieties of seeds of the cabbage family, savoy, Brussels sprouts, kohlrabi, or kale? We owe England enough already for the seed of Liberty we got from her. California now supplies some seed for onions, carrots, parsnips, and a few others. The finest cauliflower comes mostly from Denmark now.

Turnip seed, too, mangel-wurzel and swedes, onion, pea, bean, carrot, parsnip, radish, and beet seeds could be grown here by the same skill, care, and training as they are grown abroad.

An interesting method of forcing plants by the use of hot water baths is described in *La Nature* (Paris), by Henri Coupin. The process is much simpler than others now in use and may be employed by any one who has a small greenhouse, no expert treatment being necessary. Says Mr. Coupin:

"Most trees in our countries undergo a period of rest, during which all growth appears to be suspended. Branches do not enlarge and the buds on them remain as they are. They do not arouse from their torpor until spring, first, because they then find the conditions necessary for their development, and again, because, during the period of rest, chemical changes have taken place in them. These are indispensable, because if they did not occur, the trees, even in the most favorable conditions, would not open their buds. For example, plant branches that have quite recently dropped their leaves, in a warm greenhouse. They will not bud; but make the same experiment at the end of several months and the buds will appear.

"There are several ways of shortening this period of rest, some of which are rather odd. The best known is the process of etherification, which has been so much discussed recently, and which consists in placing the plants to be forced in the vapor of ether or chloroform for twenty-four to forty-eight hours. Afterwards when placed in a hothouse, the branches begin to develop almost immediately.

"A very ingenious botanist, Hans Molisch, professor in the University of Prague, has devised a method of forcing, simpler still and quite as effective. It consists in plunging the branches into warm water during a time that varies with the species. The best method is to plunge the plants in a reservoir of warm water, head downward, without moistening the roots, which would injure them. After a certain time, the plants are withdrawn, turned right side up with care, and placed in a greenhouse, where they develop at once.

"The duration of the warm bath should be nine to twelve hours at most. The best temperature is 30 degree to 35 degree [86 degree to 95 degree F] . . . That is to say, in the majority of cases, one may simply employ the water available in hothouses, which is just at the proper temperature. The process is thus at the disposal of all gardeners.

"It should be said that the good effects of the hot baths are confined to the parts actually immersed and do not extend to the whole plant. Thus, on the same stem we may see developing only the branches that have been treated with the bath, while the others remain torpid. This is easy to verify with the lilac or the willow.

"If Lobner is to be believed, we may substitute for the water bath one of steam. He has obtained good results with the lily of the valley. The thing is possible, but the method used by Molisch is more practical.

"How shall we explain the good effect of warm water on branches in a resting state? We are absolutely ignorant of its mechanism, as we are also in the case of etherification. But if we knew everything, science would be no longer amusing!"-- Condensed, from *THE LITERARY DIGEST.*

There are many new uses for water: It will not be long before every truck and every commercial flower garden will have overhead irrigation. This is merely gas pipes ("seconds" rejected for blow holes or porosity are usually used) supported on posts say six feet above the ground. They are usually placed parallel about fifty feet apart, which will make four to the acre square, and have a single row of holes and a handle on each pipe, so that the spray can be turned in either direction; with a high-water pressure, often supplied by gravity, they may be farther apart with larger holes.

These not only have saved us from fear of drought, but they supply the moisture in the natural manner and at the right time and increase fertility to an astonishing degree.

When you take a shower bath yourself, that is overhead irrigation.

The gasoline, kerosene, or heavy oil one man farm tractor, so made that it can be used to plow, to climb a side hill, to run a saw or a pump, is the coming factor in garden and farm advance. Huge fortune awaits the first manufacturer who will standardize it, cheapen it, and specialize on it. The horse is the greatest care and the greatest risk on the little farm. He costs more than a tractor would, he is eating his head off half the time, he can't he worked overtime without injury, not even as much as a man can be; all too soon he dies, more missed than any member of the family.

When this is popularized the "Three Acres" can well be extended to five.

CHAPTER XXIV
SOME EXPERIMENTAL FOODS

FIFTY-EIGHT years ago Abraham Lincoln said "Population must increase rapidly, more rapidly than in former times, and ere long the most valuable of all arts will be the art of deriving subsistence from the smallest area of soil. No community whose every member possesses this art can ever be the victim of oppression in any of its forms. Such community will alike be independent of crowned kings, money kings, and land kings."

The future, it seems, has many strange dishes in store for the American stomach. Whether you are rich or one of the plain people that have to work, whether the idea of new fantastic food appeals to your palate or to your pocketbook, you will be attracted by the array of foreign viands with curious names which have already been successfully introduced and are now beginning to be marketed in this country. Mr. William N. Taft, in the Technical World Magazine, presents the following wild menu for the dinner table:

Jujube Soup Brisket of Antelope Boiled Petsai Dasheen au Gratin Creamed Udo Soy Bean and Lichee Nut Salad Yang Taw Pie Mangoes Kaki Sake.

This, he assures us, is not the bill of fare of a Chinese eating house, nor yet of a Japanese restaurant, it is the daily meal of an American family two decades hence, if the Department of Agriculture succeeds in its attempt to introduce a large number of new foods to this country for the dual purpose of supplying new dainties and reducing the cost of living. Uncle Sam has determined to decrease the price of food as much as possible, and, for this purpose, delegated Dr. David S. Fairchild, Agricultural Explorer in charge of the Foreign Plant Section of the Bureau of Plant Industry, in particular, to see what can be done about it.

More than 30,000 fruits and vegetables have been tested by Uncle Sam's experts and, according to Dr. Fairchild, a goodly portion of the foodstuffs which have been regarded as staples since the days of the first settler are doomed. Consider for example "Jujube Soup!" Mention that to the average person and he will answer:

"But I thought the jujube was a fruit, like an apple. How can you make soup of it?" The average person is right. The jujube is a fruit--but a most remarkable one.

"It is about the size and appearance of a crab apple, but contains only a single seed. It grows on a spiny tree, long and bare of trunk, with its foliage cropping out at the very top like a royal palm of the tropics. The jujube itself has been used for years to flavor candies and other confections. But the essence is very expensive and comparatively rare, despite the profusion with which the fruit grows in its native habitat.

"Dr. Fairchild, however, imported several specimens for the Department's gardens in California, where they are bearing prolifically. The arid sands of the southwest, where nothing but cactus and sage-brush formerly would grow, have been found to be excellent soil for the jujube, and it is the hope of Uncle Sam's food experts to see the entire Arizona and New Mexico deserts dotted with jujube orchards, with income to their owners. The jujube is delicious eaten raw, but it may be cooked in any manner in which apples are prepared, used as a sauce or for pie, preserved or dried. Finally, its juice may be used as a delicious and highly nutritive fruit broth."

Petsai, or, as the Chinese have it, Pe-tsai, is a substitute for the cabbage. In appearance it is as different from cabbage as can be imagined. It is tall and cylindrical and its leaves are narrow, delicately curled, with frilled edges. The petsai can, however, be grown on any soil where the ordinary cabbage could be cultivated and in many sections where the native vegetable would languish. We are told it is no uncommon thing for a petsai to reach sixty pounds in weight. Department of Agriculture officials, however, advise that it be plucked when about eight pounds in weight, its flavor being then the most delicate and appealing.

This new importation, Uncle Sam's experts hope, will cause a drop in the price of dinners. Cabbage long ago ceased to be a cheap dish. But petsai requires none of the care which has to be lavished on cabbage and will thrive in almost any climate and any soil.

The soy bean, once started, grows wild and yields several crops a season. It can be prepared in a multitude of ways, from baking to a delicious salad. According to Doctor Yamei Kin, the head of the Women's Medical School near Pekin, milk can be made from it to cost about six cents a quart and equal to cows' milk. It would be a blessing if we could get rid of the sacred but unclean cow. One of the state dairy inspectors told me, "We consider milk a filthy product."

It may be remembered that, only twenty years ago, almost all the dates consumed here came from the oases of Arabia and the valley of the Euphrates. To-day there are more than a hundred varieties successfully produced in California and Arizona. The wonders of today are the commonplaces of to-morrow, and there is no telling to what apparently impossible lengths science will go to relieve people of the burden they now bear in the price of food. It has scoured the ends of the earth for new delicacies and now experts will do their best to teach the people to use them.

Have you ever heard of *"Whitloof"* or *"Belgian Chicory"* or have you ever dined in one of the better restaurants of large city where they have served during the winter months a salad composed of golden blanched oblong leaves about 2 inches wide and 5 inches long, only the outer edges showing a faint green? It is as delicate as the perfume of roses, as crisp as young lettuce, as delicious as asparagus, and as ornamental upon the table as the freshest fruit.

In former years this salad had to be imported and you had to pay dear for a portion of it, a good reason why so few people know it. A Belgian farmer located near New York has grown many thousands of these plants this past summer.

How would you like to grow this dainty salad right in your living room and cut several crops from a single planting lasting nearly three months? Secure an 8-inch pot and plant in it 12 roots packed in light sandy soil or pure sand. Invert another but empty 8-inch pot over this to keep out the light, place in a heated room, water daily, and in from three to four weeks you will find full-grown crowns, beautifully blanched ready for cutting. Six of such crowns make a large portion, sufficient for an entire family.

In cutting, do not cut too close to the root, for another growth is made directly after the cutting, which matures in from three to four weeks, and still two other crops can be grown in this way, so that from a single planting four full crops can be had. Considering, then, that eight such treats can be had for the cost of a single dozen roots, we can all now enjoy what was formerly a luxury. This method is most interesting, for you can watch the daily progress of the growth of the roots, fascinating to young and old, and with three weekly plantings of a pot each this treat can be enjoyed twice a week from the 1st of February until May.

For those who wish to enjoy it more often or in larger quantities, we suggest the following:

Prepare a bed of soil 12 inches deep in your cellar in a dark place where the temperature is always above freezing. Plant the roots as close as their size will permit and cover the crowns with at least 3 inches of soil. On top of this put straw so that when the crowns come through the soil they will not strike the light. When ready to cut, remove the soil as far back as the original root so that you can intelligently cut the growth to produce the crops to follow.

As a substitute for the potato of commerce the "Dasheen" long ago passed the experimental stage. It has been served at a number of banquets in Washington, Philadelphia, and New York.

While the tops of potatoes are useless as food, the tops of the dasheen make delicious greens, and tests indicate that good growers can depend on a crop of from four hundred to four hundred and fifty bushels per acre.

The Udo is the plant intended by the Department of Agriculture as a substitute for asparagus, a delicacy which it closely resembles. It is more prolific than asparagus, grows in the same soil, and requires less attention.

Not only plants but animals are experimented with by Uncle Sam's experts. Officials of the Bureau of Animal Industry claim that before long we will partake of antelope steak. For the antelope has been found to be particularly adapted to the more arid western sections of the country. And beyond that the gastronomist of the future will have to reckon with loin of hippopotamus!

The lower valley of the Mississippi is admirably suited to these huge beasts, the flesh of one of which equals a score of cattle. African traveled epicures maintain that hippopotamus steak is as tender and inviting as the choicest beef. "For those who like that sort of thing, it is just the sort of thing they would like."

It seems a bit remote to urge hippopotamus on us who do not yet know enough to eat sharks, tortoises, painted turtles, or even English sparrows. Anyhow the small gardener is more likely to succeed raising pheasants than to muss with a hippopotamus, at least in the suburbs. Pigs are more practical and make prettier pets.

Our population bids fair to approximate two hundred million within the next fifty years, and, because of the exigencies of business, an increasing number of people will be engaged in non-food-producing vocations. These people, however, are all consumers and must be fed and clothed, and even now America offers the greatest market for the produce of the farm that any farmer in any country has ever had in all history.

One of the coming ways of feeding them is the discovery and use of new foods. As in other things, after the war, whether we live in a better world or not, we shall live in an entirely different world, new ways, strange thoughts, and other foods. For the most of the following, **Business America** and **Current Opinion** are responsible.

For the creation of new crop varieties or the improvement of those now in use we must depend upon the practical scientists who are engaged in plant breeding. The work of one of these, Professor Buffum, has been accomplished in a region that is apparently sterile and where plants grow only by coaxing through artificial moisture.

His plant-breeding farms near Worland in the Big Horn Basin of Northern Wyoming lie at an elevation of 4000 feet, in a region of almost total natural aridity.

After twenty years' work in Western agricultural colleges and Government Experiment Stations, Professor Buffum chose his present location because nowhere in the United States could he find conditions of soil and climate that induce to such a remarkable degree the breaking up of species, and mutation or "sporting" of plants.

When the modern plant breeder seeks to produce something new by cross-fertilization a problem is encountered. For many years we were ignorant of the principle upon which nature operated in these hybrids or crosses. Finally a Bohemian priest named Mendel discovered the law. The central principle is that when the seed produced from a cross between two different species is planted, the progeny breaks up into well-defined groups. A certain percentage of the plants resemble one of the parents, a smaller percentage are like the other parent, and the rest seem to be a blend of both parents. These intermediates will not breed true to themselves, however; if seed from them is planted the progeny will split up into groups, showing the same percentages as the first generation to which they belonged. This has been generally accepted by scientists.

In many of his productions Professor Buffum apparently has set the Mendelian law at defiance, for, by cross-fertilization, he has evolved plants which breed true to themselves, and their progeny does not break up into groups, according to the accepted theory. They show specimens resembling each parent, with the third composed of seemingly, but not really, blended specimens.

These results are particularly vital in the development of plants adapted by selection for semi-arid agriculture. The Professor believes that the great areas of high plain country to be found from Canada to Mexico can be made more productive through planting crop varieties that have been bred to withstand the existing conditions which produce meagre returns from the vast expanse of territory under the present methods.

In place of corn, which is difficult to mature even at moderate elevations, Professor Buffum has introduced improved emmers and the various hybrids resulting from crosses with other grains.

Emmer itself is not a new grain, having been grown for centuries in Russia and southern Europe, and it is believed to have been the corn of Pliny, which he said was used by the Latins for several centuries before they knew how to make bread.

Several years ago emmer began receiving attention as a stock food. The first planting of the grain at Worland resulted in some exceptional "sports," seemingly of a different type, with coarse straw and very large heads. With this as a basis, the seed was replanted and subjected to many experiments to increase its drouth and winter resisting qualities. Continued selections have shown, a yield of from a third more to twice as much as corn, that it is thirty per cent more valuable than oats for feeding horses, and that for stock fattening it is equal to corn, pound for pound. It is the most drouth-resistant and prolific of small grains, has been successfully raised from Montana to Mexico, and is being planted in Louisiana to replace oats because it is not affected by rust.

Some of the yields recorded are enormous, varying from 40 to 104 bushels per acre under dry farming, and as high as 152 bushels under irrigation.

One stalk of Turkey red wheat was noticed as differing in many ways from all varieties, principally that the head was over eight inches in length, whereas the ordinary Turkey red wheat commonly used in the West has a head of only four or five inches.

From this one stalk has been developed the Buffum No. 17 Winter wheat. The heavy beards were eliminated and the grains or kernels in each spikelet increased from the normal number of three to five, seven, and even nine. The hardiness of the new variety, together with its remarkably large head, means that when it is placed on the market the farmers who sow it need not fear winter killing and will have a splendid flouring grain, which will produce nearly double the average crop per acre.

It is said that if a single kernel could be added to each head of wheat, the increase in annual production of this country would amount to over fifteen million bushels.

If fodder crops can be substituted for a part of the corn now used for stock, it will be a great gain.

In his alfalfa-breeding garden, Professor Buffum is raising over seventy different kinds, gathered from all parts of the world, showing that the plant is capable of wide variations. One hybrid has been obtained by crossing sweet clover with alfalfa; the clover grows wild in every state in the Union.

There seems to be no limit to man's ingenuity and skill in plant improvement. Perhaps sometime we will try it with our children.

In thirty years an exceptional ear of dent corn, through continued planting and careful selection each succeeding season, resulted in a few days' shortening of the growing period and an increased resistance to the cool nights of the higher elevation where it was under improvement; to-day, this corn matures about the middle of August at an altitude of 4000 feet, and has been yielding forty to sixty bushels per acre.

CHAPTER XXV
DRIED TRUCK

As a war measure the surplus vegetables in many city markets have been forced by the governments into large municipal drying plants. Community driers have been established in the trucking regions and even itinerant drying machines have been sent from farm to farm drying the vegetables which otherwise would have gone to waste.

The drying of vegetables may seem strange to the present generation, but we are very young; to our grandmothers it was no novelty. Many housewives even to-day prefer dried sweet corn to the canned, and find also that dried pumpkin and squash are excellent for pie making. Snap beans often are strung on threads and dried above the stove. Cherries and raspberries still are dried on bits of bark for use instead of raisins.

This country is producing large quantities of perishable foods every year, which should be saved for storage, canned, or properly dried. Drying is not a panacea for the waste evil, nor should it take the place of storing or canning to any considerable extent where proper storage facilities are available or tin cans or glass jars can be obtained cheap.

For the farmer's wife the new methods of canning are probably better than sun drying, which requires a somewhat longer time. But dried material can be stored in receptacles which cannot be used for canning. Then, too, canned fruit and vegetables freeze and cannot be shipped as conveniently--in winter. Dried vegetables can be compacted and shipped or stored with a minimum of risk. String them up to the ceiling of the storeroom or attic.

A few apples or sweet potatoes or peas or even a single turnip can be dried and saved. Even when very small quantities are dried at a time, a quantity sufficient for a meal will soon be secured. Small lots of dried vegetables, such as cabbage, carrots, turnips, potatoes, and onions, can be combined to advantage for soups and stews.

In general, most fruits or vegetables, to be dried quickly, must first be shredded or cut into slices, because many are too large to dry quickly, or have skins the purpose of which is to prevent drying out. If the air applied at first is too hot, the cut surfaces of the sliced fruits or vegetables become hard, or scorched, covering the juicy interior so that it will not dry. Generally it is not desirable that the temperature in drying should go above 140 deg to 150 deg F., and it is better to keep it well below this point. Insects and insect eggs are killed by the heat.

It is important to know the degree of heat in the drier, and this cannot be determined accurately except by a thermometer. Inexpensive oven thermometers can be found on the market, or an ordinary chemical thermometer can be suspended in the drier.

Drying of certain products can be completed in some driers within two or three hours. When sufficiently done they should be so dry that water cannot be pressed out of the freshly cut pieces, they should not show any of the natural grain of the fruit on being broken, and yet not be so dry as to snap or crackle. They should be leathery and pliable.

When freshly cut fruits or vegetables are spread out they immediately begin to evaporate moisture into the air, and if in a closed box will very soon saturate the air with moisture. This will slow down the rate of drying and lead to the formation of molds. If a current of dry air is blown over them continually, the water in them will evaporate steadily until they are dry and crisp. Certain products, especially raspberries, should not be dried hard, because if too much moisture is removed from them they will not resume their original form when soaked in water.

The rotary hand slicer is adapted for use on a very wide range of material. Don't slice your hand with it.

From an eighth to a quarter of an inch is a fair thickness for most of the common vegetables to be sliced. To secure fine quality, much depends upon having the vegetables absolutely fresh, young, tender, and perfectly clean; one decayed root may flavor several kettles of soup if the slices from it are scattered through a batch of material. High-grade "root" vegetables can only be made from peeled roots.

Blanching consists of plunging the vegetables into boiling water for a short time. Use a wire basket or cheesecloth bag for this. After blanching as many minutes as is needed, drain well and remove the surface moisture from vegetables by placing them between two towels or by exposing them to the sun and air for a short time.

A mosquito net is thrown over the product to protect the slices from flies and other insects. Fruits and vegetables, when dried in the sun, generally are spread on large trays of uniform size which can be stacked one on top of the other and protected from rain by covers made of oilcloth, canvas, or roofing paper.

A very cheap tray can be made of lath three fourths of an inch thick and 2 inches wide, which form the sides and ends of a box, and smoothed lath which is nailed on to form the bottom. As builders' laths are 4 feet long, these lath trays are most economical of material when made 4 feet in length.

A cheap and very satisfactory drier for use over the kitchen stove can be made by any handy man of small-mesh galvanized-wire netting and laths or strips of wood about 1/2 inch thick and 2 inches wide. By using two laths nailed together the framework can be stiffened and larger trays made if desirable. This form can be suspended from the ceiling over the kitchen range or over a clear burning oil, gasoline, or gas stove, and it will utilize the hot air which rises during the cooking hour. It can be raised out of the way or swung to one side by a pulley or by a crane made of lath. When the stove is required for cooking, the frame is lowered or swung back to utilize the heat which otherwise would be wasted. Still another home drier is the cookstove oven. Bits of food, left overs, especially sweet corn, can be dried on plates in a very slow oven or on the back of the cookstove and saved for winter use.

Where the electric "juice" is not monopolized, an electric fan in drying is economical, especially for those who already have a fan.

Many sliced fruits placed in long trays 3 by 1 foot and stacked in two tiers, end to end, before an electric fan can be dried within twenty-four hours. Some require much less time. For instance, sliced string beans and shredded sweet potatoes will dry before a fan running at a moderate speed within a few hours.

The dried fruit or vegetables must be protected from insects and rodents, also from the outside moisture, and will keep best in a cool, dry, well-ventilated place. In the more humid regions, moisture-tight containers should be used. If a small amount of dried product is put in each receptacle, just enough for one or two meals, it will not be necessary to open a large container.

Your American ingenuity and the American practice of reading will show you a lot of ways of saving waste: for example, frozen potatoes are not necessarily spoiled, we are told by Mr. de Ronsic, a writer in the ***Reveil Agricole***. They may be dried and then cooked as usual. The ***Revue Scientifique*** (Paris), abstracting the article in question, says:

"The potatoes must be dried to prevent decomposition, which takes place very rapidly after they have thawed out. . . . "The oven should be heated as for baking bread. Then, when it has reached the necessary temperature, which is easily recognized, the potatoes are put in, cutting up the largest. They are spread out in a layer so that evaporation may easily take place, the door of the oven being left open. From time to time the mass is stirred up with a poker to facilitate the evaporation. When the drying has gone far enough, the potatoes having become hard as bits of wood, they are withdrawn to make room for others.

"Potatoes thus dried may be boiled with enough water to make a paste similar to that which they would have furnished if mashed in the ordinary manner, and which will answer very well, at least to feed stock. The potatoes will be found to have lost none of their nutritive value."

Even if you haven't any acres--yet, there isn't any law against drying in the city. Either in sales or in saving it will help to pay for the country place later and the country place can be made to pay it back again.

Call your product say "Landers' Desiccated Beans" or "Glory's Dehydrated Corn." They will sell better, they may even taste better, trying to live up to the description. There's dollars in a name.

As a preservative ice must not be neglected. The ***Country Gentleman*** says:

While the temperature is below the freezing point we should take advantage of even short frosts to lay up ice for next summer. The man without an ice pond need not be, without ice--he can freeze it in pans outdoors. An ice plant of this sort will cost from fifteen to twenty dollars.

A double tank should be made of galvanized iron. The inner compartment of this tank should be ten feet long, two feet wide, and twelve inches deep. The top of the tank should be slightly wider than the bottom. The inner tank should be divided into six compartments by means of galvanized iron strips. The double tank should be placed near the outdoor pump, or stream, where it can easily be filled.

Being exposed on all sides, the water will freeze in from one hour to three hours. A bucket of hot water poured into the space between the tanks will loosen the cakes of ice, each weighing 200 pounds. Four tons of ice will last the average family a year. The cakes may be packed away in the icehouse as they are frozen.

CHAPTER XXVI
HOME COLD-PACK CANNING

To save vegetables and fruits by canning is a patriotic duty. The war makes the need for food conservation more imperative than at any time in history. America is mainly responsible for the food supply of the world. In this way the abundance of the summer may be made to supply the needs of the winter.

By the modern cold-pack method it is as easy to can vegetables as to can fruits. Some authorities say it is easier. At any rate, it is more useful.

In the cold-pack method of canning, sterilization does away with the danger of spoilage by fermentation or "working." Sterilization consists in raising the temperature of the filled jar or can to a germ-killing point and holding it there until bacterial life is destroyed.

The word "container" is used to designate either the tin can or the glass jar.

Single-period cold-pack canning, as distinguished from old-fashioned preserving, offers a saving in time, labor, and expense, and satisfactory results. As the food-stuffs are placed in the containers before sterilization, they are cold and may be handled quickly and easily. Then the sterilization period is frequently short. This is time-saving. Finally, no rich preservatives, such as thick syrups or heavily spiced solutions, are required. Fruits may be put up in thin syrups. Vegetables require only salt for flavoring and water to fill the container.

Another advantage of this method is that it is practicable to put up food in small quantities. It pays to put up even a single container. Thus, when there is a small surplus of some garden crop, or something left over from the order from the grocer's, one can take the short time necessary to place this food in a container and store it for future use. This is true household efficiency--the kind which, if practiced on a national scale, will conserve our war food supply and will, after the war, cut heavily into the high cost of living.

There are five principal methods of canning: (1) the cold-pack, single-period method; (2) the intermittent, or fractional sterilization method; (3) the cold-water method; (4) the open kettle or hot-pack method; and (5) the vacuum-seal method. Of these the one worked out on scientific lines by leading experts and used by many commercial canners is so much the best method for home canning, because of its simplicity and effectiveness, that it is recommended by the National Emergency Food Commission and the details are explained in their manual.

The cold-water method can be used effectively in putting up rhubarb, green gooseberries, and a few other sour berry fruits. The process is simple. The fruit is first prepared and washed and then blanched, and finally packed practically raw in containers, which are next filled with cold water and then sealed. Some sour fruits packed in this way will keep indefinitely.

A serviceable outfit may be made of materials found in any household. All that is necessary is a vessel to hold the jars or cans--such as a wash boiler or a large tin pail. This should have a tight-fitting cover. Provide a false bottom of wood or a wire rack to allow for free circulation of water under the containers.

While suburban gardeners with large surplus of vegetables find it desirable to use tin cans, being more easily handled for commercial purposes, most of us find glass jars the more satisfactory and economical containers for canned vegetables and fruits. This is especially true when there is a shortage of tin cans. All types of jars that seal perfectly may be used. Use may be made of those to which one is accustomed or which may be already on hand. The rubbers must be sound but the glass jars may be used indefinitely. Glass jars are adapted for use in any of the cold-pack canning outfits. Be sure that no jar is defective.

For use in the storing of products which are already sterilized, such as jellies, jams, and preserves, and the bottling of fruit juices, housewives may practice effective thrift by saving all jars in which they receive dried beef, bacon, peanut butter, and other products and bottles that have contained olives, catsup, and kindred goods.

Blanching is important with most vegetables and many fruits. It consists of plunging them into boiling water for a short time. Spinach and other greens should be blanched in steam. To do this, place them in an ordinary steamer or suspend them in a tightly closed vessel above an inch or two of boiling water.

Blanching should be followed by the cold dip, plunging into cold water after removal from the hot water. Cold dipping hardens the pulp and preserves the original color, enhancing the appearance. Blanching cleanses the articles and removes excess acids and strong flavors and odors. It also causes shrinkage, so that a larger quantity may be packed in a container. After blanching and cold dipping, surface moisture should be removed by placing the vegetables or fruits between two towels or by exposure to the sun.

All this is so simple and the directions so easily followed that the average 12-year-old may successfully can vegetables or fruits. The steps and the precautions are:

1. Select sound vegetables and fruits. (If possible can them the same day they are picked.) Wash, clean, and prepare them.

2. Have ready, on the stove, a can or pail of boiling water.

3. Place the vegetables or fruits in cheesecloth, or in some other porous receptacle--a wire basket is excellent--for dipping and blanching them in the boiling water.

4. Put them whole into the boiling water. The Commission gives a time-table for blanching. After the water begins to boil, begin to count the blanching time; this varies from one to twenty minutes, according to the vegetable or fruit.

5. When the blanching is complete, remove the vegetables or fruits from the boiling water and plunge them a number of times into cold water, to harden the pulp and check the flow of coloring matter. Do not leave them in cold water.

6. The containers must be thoroughly clean. It is not necessary to sterilize them in steam or boiling water before filling them, as in the cold-pack process both the insides of containers and the contents are sterilized. The jars should be heated before being filled, in order to avoid breakage.

7. Pack the product into the containers, leaving about a quarter of an inch of space at the top.

8. With vegetables add one level teaspoonful of salt to each quart container and fill with boiling water. With fruits use syrups.

9. With glass jars always use a good rubber. Test the rubber by stretching or

turning inside out. Fit on the rubber and put the lid in place. If the container has a screw top do not screw up as hard as possible, but use only the thumb and little finger in tightening it. This makes it possible for the steam to escape and prevents breakage. If a glass top jar is used, snap the top bail only, leaving the lower bail loose during sterilization. Tin cans should be completely sealed.

10. Place the filled and capped containers on the rack in the sterilizer. If the homemade or commercial hot-water bath outfit is used, enough water should be in the boiler to come at least one inch above the tops of the containers, and the water, in boiling out, should never be allowed to drop to the level of these tops. Begin to count processing time when the water begins to boil.

At the end of the sterilizing period remove the containers from the sterilizer. Fasten covers on tightly at once, turn the containers upside down to test for leakage, leave in this position until cold, and then store in a cool, dry place. Be sure that no draft is allowed to blow on glass jars, as it may cause breakage.

11. If jars are to be stored where there is strong light, wrap them in paper, preferably brown, as light will fade the color of products canned in glass jars, and sometimes deteriorate the food value.

That's the whole trick.

CHAPTER XXVII
RETAIL COOPERATION

COOPERATION in buying supplies at wholesale, in standardizing and shipping crops, in keeping grain in elevators, and fruit and some meats and poultry in cold storage has reached a high development among the farmers largely in the Northwest, much ahead of us "city folks."

There are more than five thousand active Farmers' Cooperation Associations in the United States. Minnesota alone has over six hundred cooperative creameries, some of which have a laundry annex. The associations have six hundred and sixty thousand members and do a business of nearly a thousand dollars a year for each member. These are the people that we call "hayseeds"; if we could plant some more such "seeds," it would be a good job. But in cooperative retail domestic supply we are far behind England and other countries, even behind Russia. That is partly because our better retail business methods leave less room for the savings.

A simple and easy but important beginning of cooperation was where each one took turns in delivering the milk and fetching supplies. One farmer might do it all every day for a small charge.

The new South is developing a great business in this line. When you go to New Orleans look up the stores whose letter head reads:

NELSON CO-OPERATIVE ASSOCIATION, INC. *Food Suppliers* OFFICE, 506 So. PETERS STREET. CREAMERY, ERATO ST. WAREHOUSE, 511 SO. PETERS ST. BAKERY, ELYSIAN FIELDS AVE. 61 RETAIL STORES 4 MEAT MARKETS

In August, 1917, N. O. Nelson of the above concern writes in answer to my request:

"It does not take 2500 words to tell all I know about Cooperation. I trust the inclosed may be serviceable for your book, and shall feel proud if it is.

"I am doing my job here for two very practical reasons; first, the immediate service of reducing the cost of living to say 15,000 families, mostly poor; second, to introduce economy in retailing.

"The readers of such a book as yours are well aware of the wasteful ways of retailing goods. In every town and city there is a multiplication of stores, advertising clerks, teams, and other incidentals.

"Likewise there is a lot of middle men and drummers, the buyers at the producer's end, the wholesalers or middle men at the consumer's end, with speculator and landowner at both ends. All of these have to be supported by the system, and the dear consumer pays for it.

" The Cooperative store system, which was started in England 73 years ago, eliminates most of these waste expenses. The system has kept spreading at an astonishing rate; in Great Britain there are now 3 1/2 million members, and more than a billion of sales a year. Other European countries are full of these stores. Many of the retail stores have from twelve thousand to fifty thousand members; their sales run into the millions. They are federated in a wholesale agency which buys for them and manufactures on an extensive scale.

"By the economies thus introduced they are able to save regularly about 15%, besides paying interest on the capital employed, and accumulating a liberal surplus. It is simply a question of people getting together (all civilization is), contributing their own money and their trade, and thus avoiding all the waste expenses.

"It is a very democratic plan; anybody is welcome to join it; every member has one vote and no more, they elect their directors, the directors elect the managers, and the managers employ the clerks. They sell at the market prices and every three or six months take account of stock and rebate the profits in proportion to each member's purchases, with half rate to non-members.

"It appeals to the economical sense of the ordinary housekeeper, and to the ethical sense of those who want no advantage of their neighbor. It prevents some from getting unduly rich and it helps to keep many from being unduly poor.

"The same principle has spread into farmer's work, especially Creameries. In Cooperative Creameries and Stores Russia has grown faster in the last 15 years than any other country, having at last reports over thirteen million members. This orderly getting together for common social needs has much to do with the orderliness of the Russian Revolution.

"The United States has made large progress in producers' cooperative associations, but not much in stores.

"I have in New Orleans a system of 65 stores on a modified system; it is a cooperative association but we sell at as low prices as can be afforded, for cash in hand. The sales amount to about 2 1/2 millions, the most of it in the winter. The Association owns a Bakery, a Creamery, Condiment Factory; and Coffee Factory, and a 1550-acre plantation. We are able to undersell the market about 20 %

"People anywhere can make a cooperative store if they take it seriously. There should be about 200 members and $2000 in cash to start with: then get an honest and intelligent manager; start with a grocery, buy and sell for cash, either on the Rochdale plan of selling at full market prices and dividing the profits periodically, or on my plan of selling as cheaply as can be afforded. In either plan it works out into producing a large part of the goods sold, thus eliminating entirely the superfluous middleman.

"Three acres and Liberty is the correct way of producing a living; with the adjunct of a cooperative store to do the selling of the surplus produced and the buying of goods needed, the small farmer is free from all the waste and trammels of trade."

Now what's the matter with your helping your county and country and humanity by organizing those two hundred waiting buyers in your own town? You can be the "honest and intelligent manager" at a decent salary. If, later, the cooperators want another manager, why you can easily organize another store. The best information on this subject is the Cooperative News, Manchester, England; subscription two dollars.

Evidence is daily accumulating that the food and farm problem is not so easy as many thought it to be a few months ago. This is made clear when economists say: "The really important question in the food problem is not distribution, it is production." It is unfortunate that this statement should gain belief at this time, when those who prey upon the producer are watching for any support from whatever direction.

Passing by the obvious fact that production must precede distribution, notice that, with all the energy that has been devoted to production of farm products by the government experts, it is clear that not only is there a shortage, but that it has required all kinds of inducements, from the President down, to get the farmers to increase their output, the most potent of all being the cry of patriotism.

Some explain this by showing how land monopoly prevents men going back to the farms. While this is perfectly true, it does not answer the question why farmers now in possession of farms are not working them near their capacity.

The answer of the ordinary man to this is inefficiency on the part of the farmer, and up to the present this idea has passed as sufficient to account for the situation. The publicity given the whole farm question during the past six months, however, has to a large extent dispelled the inefficiency answer, as the farmer has responded so completely to the call, and the amateurs are beginning to realize that there is something in farming besides tickling the earth with a feather. All the facts so far brought out show the farmer abundantly able to produce all the foodstuffs needed, provided he has a reasonable certainty that he will be able to dispose of his produce at a price that will give him a fair return for his labor. This being the case, it is easy to see that putting more men back on farms would not remedy the condition we are now in; but would rather increase the difficulty.

The fact is, the two blades of grass theory has been exploded, the increased production cry has been tried out, carried to its logical conclusion, and found wanting, and the inefficiency explanation has been proved a falsehood on its face. It is, therefore, obvious that with a proper system of distribution, the entire question of production will take care of itself; but just so long as the producers find it unprofitable to produce food, just so long will they have to figure carefully not to grow too much, or it would be better for them had they grown nothing at all.

The reason why we have such divergent ideas on this subject is that so many people write about it who have had no experience in farming, while on the other hand there are few farmers who can state the case so the public can grasp the most obvious facts.

Finally, it is a question of the government doing what it ought not to have done and leaving undone those things it ought to have done. It has granted to a few monopolies transportation and terminal facilities which enable them to hold up deliveries and thus control prices. The remedy lies in seeing that the government attend to its own business, which is securing equality of opportunity for all, and special privileges to none.

It follows that cooperation should not stop either at production or at distribution. It must embrace the source of both, nor even stop at governmental plans of small holdings.

As a business enterprise, combining philanthropy and percentage, capital has an opportunity.

Accordingly an option should be secured upon a large piece of land not over forty miles from a large city, near a railroad station. The transportation at first is not important, as the new commuters will make a demand for it, and cheap autos will largely fill the gap; it will improve rapidly.

If possible it should have a lake or a fair stream on it for irrigation and small water power; the soil should be examined by experts, to see that it is suitable for trucking and market gardening.

The object should be to make a sort of vacant lot gardening plan on a grand scale. Heretofore the trouble has been that we have been unable to get land where there was any assurance that we could have it again the second year, and that the limited amount of land makes it impossible to give the men as much as they ought to have. They do not need much land, because a man working at intensive culture with only the rough plowing done for him cannot take good care of much more than one acre of land. He will probably make as much money out of one acre of land as he will out of two. Those who are willing to work should be given one acre of land, with the assurance that they can have it as long as they work it faithfully and comply with the simple rules which we have found so effective in the Vacant Lot Gardening work,--which are practically, that a man should attend to business and not annoy his neighbors. No contract or lease should be given the men, or indeed the women, for both work such gardens, as they have been doing for the past twenty years in several large cities, making at least a living upon the land and often a very large return.

There must be a competent superintendent, for everything depends upon him, who would show the men what land they should use, what they should put in, instruct them how to do it, and market their products cooperatively. Experience in Philadelphia, and in some score of other cities where they have established Vacant

Lot Gardens, shows that about ten per cent annually of the people prefer to work for others, and consequently take places in the country after they have learned to do market gardening. Some others, being dissatisfied with so little land, and wanting to own their own place, go off and buy land or lease it for themselves. This makes a constant drain from the gardens, leaving openings for others who will learn in time their trade; it is possible to make in this way a steady drain out of the cities to the country, and what is better still, an automatic drain.

The land must be so near to a center of population that it may be possible to take a gang of men down there in the morning, show them what it is, and send back those who do not seem likely to make good, or who are dissatisfied; and that when men get their gardens successfully running, they may be able to bring their friends there to see what they have done, and say to them, "Go thou and do likewise."

I have been at Trudeau, Saranac Lake, and at Stony Wold, the consumptive sanitariums, and found there both by observation and by testimony that to send back the convalescents to the bench or the workshop from which they came is practically to repronounce upon them the sentence of death from which the sanitarium has offered them a reprieve. The only practical thing to do with such convalescents, and with such persons who are not capable of their ordinary avocations, is to get them in some way upon the land. There is a large demand for persons who understand the new intensive gardening, and places can be found for more than we can hope to educate in that line.

There should be buildings upon the land sufficient to bunk one hundred to one hundred and fifty men; accommodations could be made with the small timber for a considerable number. Many of these men would need some help, but most of them would shift for themselves if only they could get the opportunity to build upon the land and to have a secure tenure of it. A mere tenant knows that it is bunkum when he says "Our Country."

It is perfectly practicable to sell about one half of the land in a year or two, and have a thousand acres or more left free and clear, which will cost the promoters nothing. Renting this out or selling it will repay the whole cost, and probably bring a large profit besides.

This is no experiment, it is only to do the thing that we have been doing under various conditions with various sorts of men in different localities for the past twenty years in the Vacant Lot Gardens: namely, to give men the opportunity of living upon and cultivating land, putting up their own tents, shacks, or bungalows, and giving them such instruction and such help as does not cost anything more than the salary of the superintendent. There are abundant men who can make good and shift for themselves under those circumstances; the men who are available are single men, such men as those for whom Mr. Hallimond, a clergyman working in the Bowery, has been finding rural employment in the past ten years. Also many families will come to us through the Vacant Lot Gardens and the Little Land agitation. People such as these will increase the land value, for every decent man carries around with him at least five hundred dollars' worth of increase in land values which his presence adds to somebody's holdings of land. The struggle to pocket this increase accounts for much of the human drift from the field to the factory.

God made the country; man made the city--and the devil made the suburbs, by the aid of the speculator.

Alpha of the Plough says in the London *Star:* "I was walking with a friend along the Spaniards-road the other evening talking on the inexhaustible theme of these days, when he asked, 'What is the biggest thing that has happened to this country as the outcome of the war?'

"'It is within two or three hundred yards from here,' I replied. 'Come this way and I'll show it to you.'

"He seemed a little surprised, but accompanied me cheerfully enough as I turned from the road and plunged through the gorse and the trees towards Parliament Fields, until we came upon a large expanse of allotments, carved out of the great playground, and alive with figures, men, women, and children, some earthing up potatoes, some weeding onion beds, some thinning out carrots, some merely walking along the patches, and looking at the fruits of their labor springing from the soil. 'There,' I said, 'is the most important result of the war.'

"He laughed, but not contemptuously. He knew what I meant, and I think he more than half agreed.

"And I think you will agree, too, if you will think what that stretch of allotments means. It is the symptom of the most important revival, the greatest spiritual awakening this country has seen for generations. Wherever you go, that symptom meets you. Here in Hampstead allotments are as plentiful as blackberries in autumn. A friend of mine who lives in Beckenham tells me there are fifteen hundred in his parish. In the neighborhood of London there must be many thousands. In the country as a whole there must be hundreds of thousands. If dear old Joseph Fels could revisit the glimpses of the moon and see what is happening, see the vacant lots and waste spaces bursting into onion beds and potato patches, what joy would be his! He was the forerunner of the revival, the passionate pilgrim of the Vacant Lot: but his hot gospel fell on deaf ears, and he died just before the trumpet of war awakened the sleeper.

"Do not suppose that the greatness of this thing that is happening can be measured in terms of food. That is important, no doubt, but it is not the most important thing. I am confident that it will add more than anything else to the spiritual resources of the nation. It is the beginning of a war on the disease that is blighting our people. What is wrong with us? What is the root of our social and spiritual ailment? Is it not the divorce of the people from the soil? For generations the wholesome red blood of the country has been sucked into the great towns, and we have built up a vast machine of industry that has made slaves of us, shut out the light of the fields from our lives, left our children to grow like weeds in the slums, rootless and waterless, poisoned the healthy instincts of nature implanted in us, and put in their place the rank growths of the streets. Can you walk through a working-class district or a Lancashire cotton town, with their huddle of airless streets, without a feeling of despair coming over you at the sense of this enormous perversion of life into the arid channels of death? Can you take pride in an Empire on which the sun never sets when you think of the courts in which, as Will Crooks says, the sun never rises?

"And now the sun is going to rise. We have started a revolution that will not end until the breath of the earth has come back to the soul of the people. The tyranny of the machine is going to be broken. The tyranny of the land monopoly is going to be lifted. Yes, you say, but these people that I see working on the allotments are not the people from the courts and the slums; but professional men, the superior artisan, and so on. That is true. But the movement must get hold of the *intelligenzia* first. The important thing is that the breach in the prison is made; the fresh air is filtering in; the idea is born--not still-born, mind you, but born a living thing. It is a way of salvation that will not be lost, and that all will travel.

"We have found the land, and we are going back to possess it. Take a man out of the street and put him in a garden, and you have made a new creature of him. I have seen the miracle again and again. I know a bus conductor, for example, outwardly the most ordinary of his kind. But one night I mentioned allotments, touched the key of his soul, and discovered that this man was going about his daily work irradiated by the thought of his garden triumphs. He had got a new purpose in life. He had got the spirit of the earth in his bones. It is not only the humanizing influence of the garden, it is its democratizing influence too.

"When Adam delved and Eve span Where was then the gentleman?' You can get on terms with the lowliest if you will discuss gardens."

CHAPTER XXVIII
SUMMER COLONIES FOR CITY PEOPLE

(Condensed from the Annual Report of the U. S. Department of the Interior
of the Commissioner of Education. Vol. 2, now out of print.)

BERLIN has not been boastful of a new sociological feature which it has developed within the last fifteen years, a feature so revolutionary in its bearing upon education and upon the general health of future generations, that it should be made known to the world. As yet little has been said about this new agency. It may be because it is not a governmental institution, but the result of self-help and of the recognition of a plain necessity. It may be assumed that if the summer colonies had been instituted by the government for the great majority who are poor it would not have succeeded so well as it has.

The teachers, seeing that the horizon of their pupils was limited by brick and mortar (for open park spaces are rare in Berlin), came to the conclusion that only by giving their pupils opportunity to live in the open air could they lay a sound foundation of knowledge of natural objects and processes as a basis for school studies. The teachers of themselves, however, could apply only palliative remedies, such as having sent to them, from the botanical gardens, thousands of specimens of plants, twigs, flowers, fruit, etc., for nature study in the schoolroom; planting flower beds around the schoolhouses; also, brief excursions into parks, and hanging up before the class colored pictures of landscapes and rural scenery.

While in many cases, especially in large cities, the necessity was recognized of getting the children out of the great desert of brick and mortar into the open air and into companionship with life in the field, the garden, the brooks, and the woods, it had nowhere resulted in a systematic effort to aid the children of an entire city in that way until it was tried in Berlin. Of course it is well understood, not only abroad, but in New York and in other large cities of this country, that something must be done to alleviate the want of space and fresh air, and so recreation piers and roof gardens are provided, excursions of schools into parks are undertaken, open-air playgrounds are instituted, and similar efforts are made tending to mitigate the evil effects of city life; but all these efforts are merely sporadic or temporary; they do not attack the evil at the roots; moreover they are only drops in the bucket when compared with that which is necessary.

This tendency to cooperative and collective action has resulted in this particular case in thousands of the children's *"Arbor Gardens"* round about the city. It is an experience "en gros," one of such dimensions that cavil ceases and admiration rises supreme.

The German poor are very poor indeed, but parents were induced to rent, at a price of 4 marks ($1) or about 20 cents a month from May to October for the summer season, a patch of land in the suburbs of Berlin unfit for farmland because cut up by railroad tracks and newly laid-out streets. On one of these patches a family might erect an arbor, or a small structure of boards with a wide veranda and a corrugated iron roof, for housing themselves and children during the summer months. The dwellings are of the most primitive kind and rather flimsy; no permanent structure can be allowed, for at any time the owner of the land may give notice to vacate for the purpose of erecting a row of houses, railroad buildings, or other permanent structures. The tenants themselves build fences of wire or plant hedges to keep the different plots apart. On these patches the children, under the guidance of teachers, parents, and appointed guardians, began to sow flower seeds, plant shrubs, vines, and trees, or raise kitchen vegetables, each group or family according to its own desires and needs. Since the "arbors" are small they do not decrease the arable land of the allotments much, and there is still room left for swings, gymnastic apparatus, and similar contrivances, as well as bare sandy spots for little tots to play in. The various allotments are mostly uniform in size and are reached by narrow three- or four-foot lanes, on which occasionally are seen probationary officers or guardians who keep the peace and settle cases of disturbance.

The "arbor gardens" are established on every square rod of unused land round about the city, on vacant lots, far out to the borders of the well-trained woods and royal forests. Small tradesmen, laboring men, civil officials of low degrees, etc., have found it profitable to forsake their tenements in the city and move kith and kin into those "arbor colonies." The tenements in Berlin are as bad as in our own big cities, only better policed.

Not all of these arbor gardens are occupied by families during the night. Thousands return to their city homes evenings. Some parents, unable to free themselves from toil in town, send their children under guidance of servants, and spend only occasional Sundays and holidays with them.

The people, especially the children, getting some information concerning the treatment of the crops from competent advisers in school and out in the arbor colonies, derive great good from their horticultural and floricultural work. Families who are aesthetically inclined devote their space to flowers and trailing vines exclusively; others, utilitarians from necessity, plant potatoes, carrots, turnips, beets, beans, strawberries, and the like. The feeling of ownership being strongly developed in the children in seeing the results of their own labor, the crops are respected by the neighbors and pilfering rarely occurs, except perhaps in a case of great hunger.

Several hundred or a thousand of such patches of land, or gardens, situated in close proximity to each other, form an arbor colony, which has a governor, or mayor, who is an unpaid city official. He arranges the leasing of the land, collects the rents, and hands them over to the gratified landowners who don't even have to collect them. There is always a retired merchant or civil officer to fill the office, to which is attached neither title, emolument, nor special honor. He is assisted by a "colonial committee" of trustees selected from the colonists, who act as justices of the peace, in case disturbances should arise. If colonists prove frequent disturbers of the peace or are found incapable of living quietly, their leases are not renewed. Of course there are such cases, but they are rare.

Since the size of an "arbor garden" is from about two sixteenths to three sixteenths of an acre, say two or three New York City Lots, those forming a colony make a considerable community, in which the authority of the committee, or board of trustees, is absolute, and the few cases they have had to adjudicate have generally been caused by nagging women. It is claimed in the press that these colonists are literally without scandals, and that the life led by young and old is a most peaceful and happy one. People who are hard at work are not likely to be quarrelsome: good wholesome food, much exercise in play and labor, and an abundance of fresh air and sunshine are conducive to happiness, especially as the clothing may be of a primitive kind, or need not conform to the dictates of fashion.

A teacher remarked: "It is noticeable that since these school children are engaged in lucrative work which does not go beyond their strength, and since they see with their own eyes the results of their labor, a sense of responsibility is engendered which has a beneficial influence upon school work also. Respect for all kinds of labor and a decrease in the destructiveness so often found among boys are unmistakable effects of the arbor gardens. It is not easy work which the children perform, for spade and rake require muscular effort; but it is ennobling work, for it leads to self-respect, self-dependence, and respect for others, as well as willingness to aid others. The most beautiful sight is afforded when, on a certain date agreed on by the members of a colony, a harvest festival is held. Then flag raisings and illuminations and singing and music make the day a memorable one."

Most of the families had not the means to buy the lumber and hardware to erect an "arbor," and yet they were the very ones to whom the life in the open would be of the greatest benefit. Hence philanthropy erected the structures. The Patriotic Woman's League of the Red Cross built half of all the "arbors" of the colony found on the "Jungfernheide." Many colonies reach into the woods, and naturally are of a different character from those in the open, for there tents are used instead of wooden structures. For protection during the night watchmen pace up and down the lanes; this before the war entailed a cost of 7 1/2 cents a month to each family. The season lasts from May 1 to October 1.

The school-going population meanwhile attend their schools, which used to be reached by means of the elevated cars or surface tramways for 2 1/2 cents and much cheaper if they have commuters' tickets. Many schools are near enough to be reached on foot. The children do not loiter on the way, but when school is out they hurry "home" to begin work in the garden, or to sit down to a meal on the veranda, which is relished far more than a meal in a city tenement house filled with fetid air and wanting in light. Nearly every one of these gardens has a flagpole, and at night a Japanese paper lantern with a tallow dip in it illuminates the veranda. These, with flags by day, make a festive appearance. The teachers find that city children who spend the five months in the open air are well equipped with elementary ideas in physical geography and astronomy. Their mental equipment is better, indeed, in all fields of thought, their physical health is improved, as well as their ethical motives and conduct.

To realize the full extent of these wholesale efforts (for put children into close contact with nature and they will improve in all directions), it is well to take a ride on the North belt line (elevated steam railroad), the trains of which start from the Friedrich's street depot and bring one back after a ride of an hour and a half. Then one may do the same on the South belt line. On these two trips one will see, not hundreds, but tens of thousands of such "arbor gardens" full of happy women and children at work or play. The men come out on the belt line when their work in town is done. The writer was riding through the city on an open cab, and seeing hardly any children on the streets and in the parks, he asked, "How is it that we see no children out?" "Ah, sir," was the reply, "if you will see the children of Berlin you must go out to the arbor colonies outside of the city. There is where our children are." Subsequent visits to these colony gardens showed that Berlin is by no means a childless city. To judge from the multitudinous arbors to be seen from the windows of the belt line cars there must be 50,000 to 75,000 of them. As far as the eye reaches the flagpoles, the orderly fences, and the little structures can be seen; and since the city has 2,000,000 inhabitants, it is very likely that an estimate made by a city official of several hundred thousands of children thus living in the open air, is not excessive. The most beautiful and best-arranged gardens are not found in the vicinity of railroads, but several miles out toward the north and the south of the city. Here, where the soil is better, fine crops are raised.

If we turn our eyes homeward and contemplate the many thousands of small efforts made in this country toward the alleviation of city children's misery, we can say truthfully that we in America are perhaps fully alive to the necessity which has prompted the people of Berlin to action; we only need to be reminded of Mayor Pingree's potato patches on empty city lots, our children's outing camps, our occasional children's excursions, and the like. Still, there is nothing in this country to compare with the thousands of Berlin "arbor gardens" and their singularly convincing force. Like a circus, all this is supposed to be for the children, though it usually seems to need about two grown people to escort each child. The elders enjoy the gardens even more than the circus.

The arbor gardens of Berlin should not be mistaken for the numerous "forest schools" (Waldschulen) in Germany. These schools "in the woods" are for sickly children, both physically crippled and mentally weak. The pupils have their lessons in the open, and the teachers live, play, and work with them; long recesses separate the various lessons and a two-hour nap in the middle of the day out in the open is on the time-table of every one of these schools. These special open-air schools for weaklings and defectives are now found in many parts of Germany, notably in Charlottenburg, Strassburg, and the industrial regions of the Rhineland.

The example of Berlin has been followed in other German cities, such as Munich, notably in Dusseldorf on the Rhine, where the arbor gardens are called "Schreber gardens" in honor of the man who promoted their establishment. There is a large colony of such gardens along the Hans-Sachs street, where Lima beans, peas, lettuce, cucumbers, potatoes, and many other garden vegetables are raised; even strawberries, raspberries, and fruit trees are found here. But the city being more lavishly provided with parks and open spaces than others of its size, the necessity for open-air life has not made itself felt as forcibly as in Berlin.

And think of the cleansing influence of all this. Light and air and labor--these are the medicines not of the body only, but of the soul. It is not ponderable things alone that are found in gardens, but the great wonder of life, the peace of nature, the influences of sunsets and seasons and of all the intangible things to which we can give no name, not because they are small, but because they are outside the compass of our speech. The God that dwells in gardens is sufficient for all our needs--let the theologians say what they will.

"'Not God! in gardens? When the eve is cool? Nay, but I have a sign-- 'Tis very sure--God walks in mine.'"

The Codes Of Hammurabi And Moses
W. W. Davies

QTY

The discovery of the Hammurabi Code is one of the greatest achievements of archaeology, and is of paramount interest, not only to the student of the Bible, but also to all those interested in ancient history...

Religion   **ISBN:** *1-59462-338-4*   **Pages:132**

MSRP $12.95

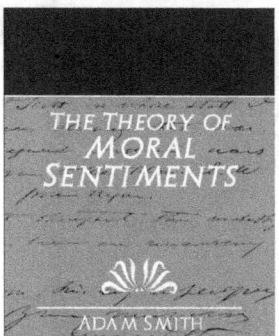

The Theory of Moral Sentiments
Adam Smith

QTY

This work from 1749. contains original theories of conscience amd moral judgment and it is the foundation for systemof morals.

Philosophy ISBN: *1-59462-777-0*   **Pages:536**

MSRP $19.95

Jessica's First Prayer
Hesba Stretton

QTY

In a screened and secluded corner of one of the many railway-bridges which span the streets of London there could be seen a few years ago, from five o'clock every morning until half past eight, a tidily set-out coffee-stall, consisting of a trestle and board, upon which stood two large tin cans, with a small fire of charcoal burning under each so as to keep the coffee boiling during the early hours of the morning when the work-people were thronging into the city on their way to their daily toil...

Childrens   ISBN: *1-59462-373-2*

Pages:84

MSRP $9.95

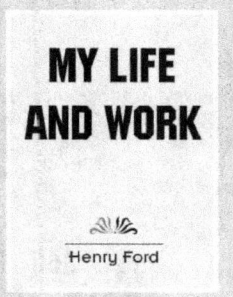

My Life and Work
Henry Ford

QTY

Henry Ford revolutionized the world with his implementation of mass production for the Model T automobile. Gain valuable business insight into his life and work with his own auto-biography... "We have only started on our development of our country we have not as yet, with all our talk of wonderful progress, done more than scratch the surface. The progress has been wonderful enough but..."

Pages:300

Biographies/   **ISBN:** *1-59462-198-5*   *MSRP $21.95*

www.bookjungle.com *email: sales@bookjungle.com fax: 630-214-0564 mail: Book Jungle PO Box 2226 Champaign, IL 61825*

The Art of Cross-Examination
Francis Wellman

QTY

I presume it is the experience of every author, after his first book is published upon an important subject, to be almost overwhelmed with a wealth of ideas and illustrations which could readily have been included in his book, and which to his own mind, at least, seem to make a second edition inevitable. Such certainly was the case with me; and when the first edition had reached its sixth impression in five months, I rejoiced to learn that it seemed to my publishers that the book had met with a sufficiently favorable reception to justify a second and considerably enlarged edition. ..

Pages:412

Reference   **ISBN:** *1-59462-647-2*   *MSRP $19.95*

On the Duty of Civil Disobedience
Henry David Thoreau

QTY

Thoreau wrote his famous essay, On the Duty of Civil Disobedience, as a protest against an unjust but popular war and the immoral but popular institution of slave-owning. He did more than write—he declined to pay his taxes, and was hauled off to gaol in consequence. Who can say how much this refusal of his hastened the end of the war and of slavery ?

Law   **ISBN:** *1-59462-747-9*   **Pages:48**

MSRP $7.45

Dream Psychology Psychoanalysis for Beginners
Sigmund Freud

QTY

Sigmund Freud, born Sigismund Schlomo Freud (May 6, 1856 - September 23, 1939), was a Jewish-Austrian neurologist and psychiatrist who co-founded the psychoanalytic school of psychology. Freud is best known for his theories of the unconscious mind, especially involving the mechanism of repression; his redefinition of sexual desire as mobile and directed towards a wide variety of objects; and his therapeutic techniques, especially his understanding of transference in the therapeutic relationship and the presumed value of dreams as sources of insight into unconscious desires.

Pages:196

Psychology   **ISBN:** *1-59462-905-6*   *MSRP $15.45*

The Miracle of Right Thought
Orison Swett Marden

QTY

Believe with all of your heart that you will do what you were made to do. When the mind has once formed the habit of holding cheerful, happy, prosperous pictures, it will not be easy to form the opposite habit. It does not matter how improbable or how far away this realization may see, or how dark the prospects may be, if we visualize them as best we can, as vividly as possible, hold tenaciously to them and vigorously struggle to attain them, they will gradually become actualized, realized in the life. But a desire, a longing without endeavor, a yearning abandoned or held indifferently will vanish without realization.

Pages:360

Self Help   **ISBN:** *1-59462-644-8*   *MSRP $25.45*

www.bookjungle.com *email: sales@bookjungle.com fax: 630-214-0564 mail: Book Jungle PO Box 2226 Champaign, IL 61825*

QTY

The Rosicrucian Cosmo-Conception Mystic Christianity *by Max Heindel*   ISBN: *1-59462-188-8*   **$38.95**
The Rosicrucian Cosmo-conception is not dogmatic, neither does it appeal to any other authority than the reason of the student. It is: not controversial, but is: sent forth in the, hope that it may help to clear...   New Age/Religion Pages 646

Abandonment To Divine Providence *by Jean-Pierre de Caussade*   ISBN: *1-59462-228-0*   **$25.95**
"The Rev. Jean Pierre de Caussade was one of the most remarkable spiritual writers of the Society of Jesus in France in the 18th Century. His death took place at Toulouse in 1751. His works have gone through many editions and have been republished...   Inspirational/Religion Pages 400

Mental Chemistry *by Charles Haanel*   ISBN: *1-59462-192-6*   **$23.95**
Mental Chemistry allows the change of material conditions by combining and appropriately utilizing the power of the mind. Much like applied chemistry creates something new and unique out of careful combinations of chemicals the mastery of mental chemistry...   New Age/Business Pages 354

The Letters of Robert Browning and Elizabeth Barret Barrett 1845-1846 vol II   ISBN: *1-59462-193-4*   **$35.95**
by Robert Browning and Elizabeth Barrett   Biographies Pages 596

Gleanings In Genesis (volume I) *by Arthur W. Pink*   ISBN: *1-59462-130-6*   **$27.45**
Appropriately has Genesis been termed "the seed plot of the Bible" for in it we have, in germ form, almost all of the great doctrines which are afterwards fully developed in the books of Scripture which follow...   Religion/Inspirational Pages 420

The Master Key *by L. W. de Laurence*   ISBN: *1-59462-001-6*   **$30.95**
In no branch of human knowledge has there been a more lively increase of the spirit of research during the past few years than in the study of Psychology, Concentration and Mental Discipline. The requests for authentic lessons in Thought Control, Mental Discipline and...   New Age/Business Pages 422

The Lesser Key Of Solomon Goetia *by L. W. de Laurence*   ISBN: *1-59462-092-X*   **$9.95**
This translation of the first book of the "Lernegton" which is now for the first time made accessible to students of Talismanic Magic was done, after careful collation and edition, from numerous Ancient Manuscripts in Hebrew, Latin, and French...   New Age/Occult Pages 92

Rubaiyat Of Omar Khayyam *by Edward Fitzgerald*   ISBN:*1-59462-193-4*   **$13.95**
Edward Fitzgerald, whom the world has already learned, in spite of his own efforts to remain within the shadow of anonymity, to look upon as one of the rarest poets of the century, was born at Bredfield, in Suffolk, on the 31st of March, 1809. He was the third son of John Purcell...   Music Pages 172

Ancient Law *by Henry Maine*   ISBN: *1-59462-128-4*   **$29.95**
The chief object of the following pages is to indicate some of the earliest ideas of mankind, as they are reflected in Ancient Law, and to point out the relation of those ideas to modern thought.   Religion/History Pages 452

Far-Away Stories *by William J. Locke*   ISBN: *1-59462-129-2*   **$19.45**
"Good wine needs no bush, but a collection of mixed vintages does. And this book is just such a collection. Some of the stories I do not want to remain buried for ever in the museum files of dead magazine-numbers an author's not unpardonable vanity..."   Fiction Pages 272

Life of David Crockett *by David Crockett*   ISBN: *1-59462-250-7*   **$27.45**
"Colonel David Crockett was one of the most remarkable men of the times in which he lived. Born in humble life, but gifted with a strong will, an indomitable courage, and unremitting perseverance...   Biographies/New Age Pages 424

Lip-Reading *by Edward Nitchie*   ISBN: *1-59462-206-X*   **$25.95**
Edward B. Nitchie, founder of the New York School for the Hard of Hearing, now the Nitchie School of Lip-Reading, Inc, wrote "LIP-READING Principles and Practice". The development and perfecting of this meritorious work on lip-reading was an undertaking...   How-to Pages 400

A Handbook of Suggestive Therapeutics, Applied Hypnotism, Psychic Science   ISBN: *1-59462-214-0*   **$24.95**
by Henry Munro   Health/New Age/Health/Self-help Pages 376

A Doll's House: and Two Other Plays *by Henrik Ibsen*   ISBN: *1-59462-112-8*   **$19.95**
Henrik Ibsen created this classic when in revolutionary 1848 Rome. Introducing some striking concepts in playwriting for the realist genre, this play has been studied the world over.   Fiction/Classics/Plays 308

The Light of Asia *by sir Edwin Arnold*   ISBN: *1-59462-204-3*   **$13.95**
In this poetic masterpiece, Edwin Arnold describes the life and teachings of Buddha. The man who was to become known as Buddha to the world was born as Prince Gautama of India but he rejected the worldly riches and abandoned the reigns of power when...   Religion/History/Biographies Pages 170

The Complete Works of Guy de Maupassant *by Guy de Maupassant*   ISBN: *1-59462-157-8*   **$16.95**
"For days and days, nights and nights, I had dreamed of that first kiss which was to consecrate our engagement, and I knew not on what spot I should put my lips..."   Fiction/Classics Pages 240

The Art of Cross-Examination *by Francis L. Wellman*   ISBN: *1-59462-309-0*   **$26.95**
Written by a renowned trial lawyer, Wellman imparts his experience and uses case studies to explain how to use psychology to extract desired information through questioning.   How-to/Science/Reference Pages 408

Answered or Unanswered? *by Louisa Vaughan*   ISBN: *1-59462-248-5*   **$10.95**
Miracles of Faith in China   Religion Pages 112

The Edinburgh Lectures on Mental Science (1909) *by Thomas*   ISBN: *1-59462-008-3*   **$11.95**
This book contains the substance of a course of lectures recently given by the writer in the Queen Street Hall, Edinburgh. Its purpose is to indicate the Natural Principles governing the relation between Mental Action and Material Conditions...   New Age/Psychology Pages 148

Ayesha *by H. Rider Haggard*   ISBN: *1-59462-301-5*   **$24.95**
Verily and indeed it is the unexpected that happens! Probably if there was one person upon the earth from whom the Editor of this, and of a certain previous history, did not expect to hear again...   Classics Pages 380

Ayala's Angel *by Anthony Trollope*   ISBN: *1-59462-352-X*   **$29.95**
The two girls were both pretty, but Lucy who was twenty-one who supposed to be simple and comparatively unattractive, whereas Ayala was credited, as her Bombwhat romantic name might show, with poetic charm and a taste for romance. Ayala when her father died was nineteen...   Fiction Pages 484

The American Commonwealth *by James Bryce*   ISBN: *1-59462-286-8*   **$34.45**
An interpretation of American democratic political theory. It examines political mechanics and society from the perspective of Scotsman James Bryce   Politics Pages 572

Stories of the Pilgrims *by Margaret P. Pumphrey*   ISBN: *1-59462-116-0*   **$17.95**
This book explores pilgrims religious oppression in England as well as their escape to Holland and eventual crossing to America on the Mayflower, and their early days in New England...   History Pages 268

QTY

The Fasting Cure *by Sinclair Upton*   ISBN: *1-59462-222-1*   **$13.95**
In the Cosmopolitan Magazine for May, 1910, and in the Contemporary Review (London) for April, 1910, I published an article dealing with my experiences in fasting. I have written a great many magazine articles, but never one which attracted so much attention... New Age/Self Help/Health Pages 164

Hebrew Astrology *by Sepharial*   ISBN: *1-59462-308-2*   **$13.45**
In these days of advanced thinking it is a matter of common observation that we have left many of the old landmarks behind and that we are now pressing forward to greater heights and to a wider horizon than that which represented the mind-content of our progenitors... Astrology Pages 144

Thought Vibration or The Law of Attraction in the Thought World   ISBN: *1-59462-127-6*   **$12.95**

by William Walker Atkinson   *Psychology/Religion Pages 144*

Optimism *by Helen Keller*   ISBN: *1-59462-108-X*   **$15.95**
Helen Keller was blind, deaf, and mute since 19 months old, yet famously learned how to overcome these handicaps, communicate with the world, and spread her lectures promoting optimism. An inspiring read for everyone... Biographies/Inspirational Pages 84

Sara Crewe *by Frances Burnett*   ISBN: *1-59462-360-0*   **$9.45**
In the first place, Miss Minchin lived in London. Her home was a large, dull, tall one, in a large, dull square, where all the houses were alike, and all the sparrows were alike, and where all the door-knockers made the same heavy sound... Childrens/Classic Pages 88

The Autobiography of Benjamin Franklin *by Benjamin Franklin*   ISBN: *1-59462-135-7*   **$24.95**
The Autobiography of Benjamin Franklin has probably been more extensively read than any other American historical work, and no other book of its kind has had such ups and downs of fortune. Franklin lived for many years in England, where he was agent... Biographies/History Pages 332

Name	
Email	
Telephone	
Address	
City, State ZIP	

☐ **Credit Card**   ☐ **Check / Money Order**

Credit Card Number	
Expiration Date	
Signature	

Please Mail to: Book Jungle
PO Box 2226
Champaign, IL 61825
or Fax to: 630-214-0564

ORDERING INFORMATION

web*: www.bookjungle.com*
email*: sales@bookjungle.com*
fax*: 630-214-0564*
mail*: Book Jungle PO Box 2226 Champaign, IL 61825*
or PayPal *to sales@bookjungle.com*

Please contact us for bulk discounts

DIRECT-ORDER TERMS

**20% Discount if You Order
Two or More Books**
Free Domestic Shipping!
Accepted: Master Card, Visa,
Discover, American Express